D0629959

> *"A few evenings after we sailed, I was suddenly startled, by a most tremendous crash upon deck. . . ."*

—from *Journal of a Whaling Voyage 1864–1868*
by Augusta Penniman

There was a scraping, scuffling sound on the roof. Something big and brown flew past the pilothouse window and landed with a thud on the deck below. Pete felt the tremor of it through his feet. For half a moment Pete and Emmett looked at each other. Then Emmett reached down and flicked a switch from a position marked "hand" to one marked "auto." They bolted out the door and down the ladder. Jackson Beers lay on the deck. His head was thrown back, eyes and mouth open wide. His back was arched at an awkward angle, one leg bent under him, arms askew. Pete reached him first. He gripped Jackson by the shirt, intending to roll him off his leg, but it wasn't the leg that had contorted Jackson's torso. About a foot of Emmett Grey's iron harpoon protruded from Jackson's back. Emmett straightened Jackson's neck, pinched his nose, and pressed his mouth over Jackson's. It seemed to last forever. Pete checked the carotid pulse periodically, shaking his head each time. After an eternity Emmett sat back on his heels and said it. "Dead." Pete dropped his weary arms. His eyes met Connie's. Then he looked across the dead body of Jackson Beers, and saw his sister. . . .

Books by Sally Gunning

Hot Water
Under Water
Ice Water
Troubled Water
Rough Water

Published by POCKET BOOKS

ROUGH WATER

SALLY GUNNING

MYST
GUNNI

POCKET BOOKS

New York   London   Toronto   Sydney   Tokyo   Singapore

This book is a work of fiction. Names, characters, places and
incidents are products of the author's imagination or are used
fictitiously. Any resemblance to actual events or locales or persons,
living or dead, is entirely coincidental.

An *Original* Publication of POCKET BOOKS

POCKET BOOKS, a division of Simon & Schuster Inc.
1230 Avenue of the Americas, New York, NY 10020

Copyright © 1994 by Sally Gunning

ISBN: 0-671-87137-4

First Pocket Books printing December 1994

10 9 8 7 6 5 4 3 2 1

POCKET and colophon are registered trademarks of
Simon & Schuster Inc.

Cover art by Jeffrey Adams

Printed in the U.S.A.

For Tom, for all the usual reasons, but also for taking to sea with me on behalf of my book and leaving the marine disaster out

Acknowledgments

My old friend Lorrie Beachen Brown contributed much to this book with her recollections of our days as stewardesses aboard a cruise ship that was nothing like *The Pequot Princess* and contained none of the more colorful aspects of its passengers and crew. My apologies for those instances where I've chosen to ignore her kinder and I'm sure more accurate observations in favor of my nausea-induced, jaundiced view. I'm also most grateful to my nephews, Alex and Brent Carlson. Between them they got *The Pequot* started and stopped as needed, Alex did some excellent nautical editing, and Brent even threw in the murder weapon to boot. Many thanks to Dennis Waite, captain of the *Dolphin V* whalewatch vessel, for a most hospitable and fascinating session aboard his ship. I'd also like to extend my heartfelt gratitude to "Commander Zarak" for his insights into the world surrounding the study and preservation of marine mammals. Five books' worth of thanks to my editor, Jane Chelius, for all the talent and care she has poured into them, to editorial assistant Brigid Mellon for sweating with me over every word, and to my agent, Andrea Cirillo, for always being on the other end of the phone with her common sense and encouragement.

Foreword

The quotations that preface each chapter of this book were excerpted from *Journal of a Whaling Voyage 1864–1868*, written by Augusta Penniman, the wife of whaling captain Edward Penniman of Eastham on Cape Cod, Massachusetts. Augusta Penniman kept this journal while traveling with her husband aboard the bark *Minerva* on a four-year whaling voyage to the Arctic Ocean. She was twenty-six years old at the start of this voyage, the first of three such voyages she made with her husband.

Augusta Penniman's original journal is on display in the National Seashore Visitor's Center in Eastham, on Cape Cod. The excerpts and historical facts used here were taken from a transcript and foreword compiled by Dorinda Partsch, former museum curator, but any creative spelling and punctuation is Augusta's own. The journal was initially purchased and published through the assistance of the Eastern National Park and Monument Association for Cape Cod National Seashore.

ROUGH WATER

Chapter
1

Arose at 9 A.M. Breakfast on cherry pie.

Peter Bartholomew stood on his stoop, looked down at the small blond head in front of him, and said, "What?"

Tweetie Cunningham, source of nickname unknown, repeated her request as patiently as any eight-year-old faced with a retarded adult. "I said how much to blow up these here balloons? That's your job, right? Factotum? Person employed to do all kinds of work?" Tweetie pointed a scabby forefinger at the sign Pete had hung off the front of his house fifteen years ago when this odd-job company of his had seemed like such a hot idea.

It didn't seem like such a hot idea now. Pete's partner, Rita Peck, was in traffic court with her daughter,

1

Maxine. Pete's most recent employee, his ex-wife, Connie, was painting shutters with his only other employee, Andy Oatley, and here was Tweetie Cunningham, holding out a bag with enough balloons in it to close the Republican Convention.

"I'll give ya a quarter," she said.

It was an offer he couldn't refuse. Pete sat down on the stoop, routed around in the bag for a small balloon to warm up with, stretched it out a couple of times, and began to blow.

Tweetie watched him.

"You don't smoke, do you?"

"No." Pete tied off the balloon and reached for another one, a little bigger this time. He gave it a good blast.

"You sure you don't smoke?"

Inside the house, the phone began to ring.

"I'll get it," said Tweetie.

"No," said Pete. Whoever it was, it had to be better than balloons.

Pete caught it on the fourth ring. "Factotum."

"Pete? It's me! Polly!"

Pete grinned. His sister always began like that, as if he were constantly mistaking her for someone else.

"Hi, Pol. How's everything?"

"How's everything? How's everything? Everything is what I would call glorious. Everything is what I would call gloriferous."

Gloriferous? Even for Polly this was a bit excessive in the vocabulary department. Pete tried to remember if she'd sounded like this the last time he'd talked to her, only he couldn't remember when he'd last talked to her. Pete lived on the island of Nashtoba and Polly lived in Southport, about 150 miles down the New England coast by car, 90 or so miles south-southwest

2

by sea. It wasn't much of a distance, but it was enough to result in separate lives, and, of late it seemed, a dwindling number of phone calls.

But Pete still possessed a certain radar when it came to Polly, and now the radar told him something was up.

"Gloriferous, huh?"

"Better than gloriferous. Guess what?"

Why did Pete suddenly smell trouble? "What?"

"I'm getting married."

Big trouble. He sat down. "Anybody I know?"

"Not yet. But that's why I'm calling. I have this plan and if I can talk you into it you'll know him just great by the end."

Pete had given up on Polly's taste in men two or three boyfriends ago, and took this last remark of hers as something like a threat. "What plan?"

"A cruise."

"A what?"

"A cruise! All the way up to Nova Scotia! To watch the whales! Well, not a real cruise, I mean no chandeliers or anything. The ship's small, only thirty passengers have signed on. It's part of that No Frills Cruising here in Southport, you've heard of them, haven't you? They're leaving here on the first, for a week. Jackson and I are going. Most of us are paying passengers, but they'll also have some research scientists on board. It's going to be a real-life scientific expedition, not just a pleasure cruise—we never dock, we stay off the coast the whole way and chase around after whales. But they're stopping in Close Harbor, Pete."

Close Harbor. Nashtoba's own Close Harbor. Suddenly Close Harbor seemed *too* close.

"So when do you land here? I could meet the boat, take you guys to Lupo's for—"

3

"*Meet* the boat! You're getting *on* the boat. Come on, Pete. It's just for a week."

Tweetie Cunningham appeared in the doorway, with Rita Peck behind her. Pete could see them out of the corner of his eye, Rita's gleaming black bob, Tweetie's white-blond tufts. They hovered in the doorway, watching Pete.

And listening.

"Just a week. You want me to sail off on a cruise to Nova Scotia, on the first, for a week? To meet some guy you're—"

"Not some guy. The guy I'm marrying. On September twenty-fourth. This'll be your last chance to do your favorite thing—talk me out of it."

"I've never talked you out of marrying anybody," said Pete, injured. He'd never talked Polly out of anything at all, at least not that he could remember.

In the doorway, Rita's downy eyebrows buckled, not a good sign.

On the phone, Polly laughed, also not a good sign. That little whiff of trouble Pete had detected earlier picked up steam.

"I know, Pete. Hey, forget it. No big deal. I just thought you might want to meet him."

"Of course I want to meet him, Polly. But you don't give me much leeway if you're marrying him on September twenty-fourth and calling me on—"

Pete looked at the calendar.

"August twentieth," said Rita from the door.

"August twentieth," repeated Pete.

"Busy, huh?"

Pete looked at the bag of balloons in Tweetie's fist. "Yes, very busy."

Rita coughed.

4

"Hey," said Pete. "Maybe you and—what's his name?"

"Jackson."

"Maybe you and Jackson could stay over on the way back."

This time Tweetie coughed, an eight-year-old's fake cough.

"No," said Polly. "We won't have any time on the way back. Forget it, Pete."

"Or you could come to Nashtoba ahead of the boat and pick it up here on the—"

"Jackson can't leave till the first. Never mind, Pete."

"Hey, Polly. I'm sorry. It's just—"

"I said it's okay."

Tweetie had worked herself into a world-class coughing fit by now. Rita, an old hand at eight-year-old attention-getting devices, ignored her, but Pete knew Rita hadn't missed a word of his conversation. Her eyebrows hadn't smoothed out any, either.

"What's that noise?" asked Polly.

Pete looked at Tweetie, her face beet red now from coughing. "An impatient customer."

"Oh. Okay. Good-bye, Pete."

"Polly—"

But Polly was gone.

Pete hung up the phone.

Tweetie stopped coughing.

"Well?" said Rita. Nobody said "well" like Rita, unless it was June Cleaver. It always made Pete start acting like The Beaver.

"I'm not going. It's nuts. She wants me to take off on some cruise for a week. It's the week before Labor Day. The busiest—"

5

"What does she want you to go for?"

"To meet this guy she's marrying. On September twenty-fourth. What's the big rush, that's what I want to know. That week I'll be closing up the Gilbersons' cottages, and taking Kenny Street camping, and dropping Jennifer Stroughton off at—"

"Did you ask Polly?"

"Ask Polly what?"

"What's the big rush? Apparently there is one. And apparently she feels she needs you there."

"She doesn't need me there. She just thinks it would be nice to have me there, to meet this guy before the wedding. Which would be no big deal if she hadn't decided on August twentieth to get married September twenty-fourth. And then to take some dumb trip to Nova Scotia in between."

Tweetie started coughing again.

"Just because she called you today doesn't mean she decided to get married today."

"Right," said Pete. "She called me today. August twentieth. And I'm not going. What does she think I do around here, twiddle my thumbs?"

"Up to you," said Rita. She said that like June Cleaver, too. Pete seemed to recall that every time June Cleaver said it, and Beaver decided to believe it, he ended up breaking an arm or something.

Rita left.

Tweetie stayed.

"Here," said Pete. "Give me those balloons."

Tweetie held out the bag of balloons, coughed one more time, gagged, and threw up on the floor.

Pete decided it was safe to assume this was not going to be a good day.

Chapter 2

Afternoon—went a visiting

Connie Bartholomew rested the tube of oozing black goo in the crevice behind the chimney, braced her back against the bricks and her sneakers against the shingles, and looked down.

It was August, and at six o'clock on the island of Nashtoba, already fall-cool. The beach in the distance was deserted, and one lone sail spiked the horizon, a triangular marker separating the blue-gold of the sky from the silver-blue of the sea.

It was like a map of her life down there—in the foreground the tiny island that she had run away from, in the distance, the mainland she had run away *to*. She strained her eyes at the distant lump of land, looking for something of import. She found no hidden secrets now, just as she had found nothing then. The mainland had not held whatever answers Connie had expected it to hold, but then again, neither had the man she had run away *with*.

Connie dropped her gaze closer to home. Coming up the path from the beach was the man she had run away *from*.

And back to.

Connie started to slide down the roof, but when she reached the top of the ladder she stopped and looked again. Maybe from this height she could finally become a dispassionate observer of the man who continued to cause her such a mixture of joy and pain.

Peter Bartholomew picked his way along the fringe of battered scrub as if he were walking among hybrid roses. He snapped off a piece of bayberry, crushed it, and gave the pungent leaf a good sniff. Connie sneezed. He picked a beach plum, a fruit so sour it was practically rancid, and popped it in his mouth. Connie's salivary glands puckered up. He stopped dead in his tracks and stared out to sea at the sinking sun. Connie went half-blind following his gaze. Finally, finally, he reached the top of the path, came into the clearing, and looked up.

From up here he could be anybody, thought Connie, any six-foot-tall guy with dark hair and a body kept lean from hard work. Six feet if you counted the cowlick, that was.

Pete saw her and smiled. That was no big deal either. Not from here anyway, not when you couldn't see how even the teeth were, or how the crow's feet winked around the eyes. And maybe it was just as well that she couldn't see what was in those eyes, eyes that were just starting to warm up after years of anger and hurt.

8

Did Connie's own wounds still show? Hers had laid her lower, all the way down into the black pit of depression, but it was Pete who had dug her out. And kicked her out. And hired her.

And now?

Once Pete got close Connie could see that his eyes held a mix of things. They usually did. Today it was mostly fatigue, not unusual for a man who had probably just chopped a cord of wood; and worry, also not unusual, not for a guy who was still chewing over some wrong answer he gave his math teacher back in grade six.

"Want to climb up and see the roof?" she hollered.

"Sure. Sure." But Pete continued to look out to sea.

"Hey," she called.

Pete whipped around. "Oh! Yeah." He pulled himself up the ladder, clambered onto the roof, and glanced at the flashing. "Looks good." Then he turned and gazed out to sea.

Again.

But two years of divorce had taught Connie something her nine years of marriage hadn't. If you want to know what someone's thinking, ask. "Hey," she said. "What's up?"

Pete sat down and sighed. "Polly called."

"Oh?" Polly calling used to be good news. Connie tried to wait patiently for Pete to tell her why this time it wasn't, but Pete was back to sea-gazing, and waiting patiently wasn't one of Connie's particular skills. "And?"

"She's getting married."

"Oh." Now Connie understood. The odds of this being good news was slim. Connie had always suspected Polly's parents of prereading their daughter's true nature when they named her Pollyanna. If there

9

ever was a woman more positive that every cloud, or every jerk, had a silver lining, Connie had yet to meet her. Polly attached herself to, and tried to resurrect, everyone from the plain old boring to the criminally insane. No wonder Pete was worried. If Polly wanted to marry somebody boring, that was one thing, but if she wanted to marry an ax-murderer, that was something else.

"So who's the guy?"

"Jackson somebody," said Pete. Then he looked at Connie in a way that made her want to check behind her for low-flying planes. "Want to meet him?"

"Sure. When?"

"September first. Through eighth."

"They're coming here? For a week?"

"They're coming to Close Harbor, for about an hour. On a cruise to Nova Scotia. She wants me to go. She wants me to meet him. They're getting married the twenty-fourth. We'd be gone a week."

A week-long cruise? The two of them? Pete kept his eyes on the horizon, and Connie could see why. This was pretty heavy-duty for two people who had only just mastered the two-minute ride to the dump.

"I think Rita and Andy could handle Factotum for a week, don't you? If Maxine helps out?"

Connie didn't. The teenage Maxine was prone to hindering more than helping, and the resultant near-death experiences from a long day working beside Andy were still fresh in Connie's mind. Add to that the prospect of being confined in a small space for a week with an ex-husband, an ex-sister-in-law, and an ax-murderer, and this cruise had to be right up there on the top ten list of Things Not To Do On Your Vacation.

Then Pete withdrew his eyes from the sea and

looked at her. Suddenly another scenario began to take shape, a scenario Polly might have thought up—a secluded deck, moonlight on still water, soft salt air . . .

The kind of air that healed old wounds.

So why not? thought Connie. After all, she'd given less thought to dumber decisions than this.

Chapter
3

Monday Morning we bade good bye . . .
[and] went aboard of the ship. . . .

Pete stood on the dock and peered at the spot on the horizon as it became larger.

And rustier.

"That's it?" asked Connie.

Pete hadn't expected the QE2, exactly, but this wide white bucket with the rusty anchor chain looked like the stopper to the QE2's pool.

"If this is how Polly picks boats I'm getting real worried about this fiancé." Connie tossed a baggy gray pullover over her shoulders and yanked the sleeves into a knot. Pete had always suspected she chose her muted hues in an attempt to subdue the rest of her, but it never seemed to work. Connie was a person you looked at. Her green eyes snapped too much, her body was too kinetic, her figure took up too much space to be ignored. And there was always something a little odd going on—today, for example, she was in the throes of a self-inflicted haircut that made her head look like a gone-to-seed dandelion.

Pete flipped through the brochure Polly had sent him, looking for some tidbits of comfort. "It says it's constructed for maximum stability."

"Right," said Connie. "I'm sure it'll be very stable, resting on the ocean floor."

Pete looked around, hoping none of the other prospective passengers had heard her. The trouble was, he couldn't find any other prospective passengers —all he could find was the entire population of the island of Nashtoba, here to see them off.

Or to laugh them off.

Sarah Abrew, ancient and half-blind, stood with the top of her short white hair just even with Pete's shoulder, her gnarled fingers gripping his arm. "Damn-fool idea, sailing all over God-knows-where just to look at a couple of whales."

"She's right, Pete, if you want to see whales just stay here and look at Ed!" Bert Barker, one of the retired loungers who had strolled to the wharf from the bench in front of Beston's Store, jabbed Ed Healey's obese frame with an elbow and guffawed.

"Is it licensed?" asked Rita.

"Licensed to kill, maybe," said Bert.

"You ask to see their license," said Rita. "And the captain's license, too."

"You ask to see the food," said Ed.

The boat chugged closer.

Connie wrinkled her nose. "What's that smell?"

"Trouble," said Pete. But the very minute Pete's

13

trepidation crept in, Connie's seemed to leave her. "Oh, come on," she said, shouldering her bag. "We're gonna get off this island for a whole week. We're going to hang out with Polly, meet her boyfriend, see some whales. We're gonna cruise."

Which was all well and good, except that Pete had never particularly liked leaving the island, let alone for a whole week. And he liked his sister all right, liked her a whole lot as a matter of fact, when it was just the two of them, but something happened to her when she was around her boyfriends that he didn't particularly like. And whales? Whales lived out in deep water. They were going to cruise out in deep water.

In this boat.

Up close the white bucket turned out to be yellowed and rust-streaked, but at least its name, *The Pequot Princess,* was freshly painted under the bow.

"Pequot?" asked Evan Spender. "Isn't that the ship that went down in *Moby Dick?"*

"The Pequod, Evan," said Rita. "Honestly. The Pequots are the Indians."

The Pequot Princess slammed into the piling and sent a shudder through the dock.

"Oh Lord," said Sarah.

The boat creaked. A deckhand in mismatched khakis jumped onto the dock, looped a huge line over the piling in front, then raced to the back of the boat and wound another line around the rusted cleat. The line looked frayed. From the deck to the dock they laid out a gangplank that looked like Captain Hook's original.

Sarah gave Pete's arm one final squeeze, and abandoned it for Andy Oatley's.

"Good-bye." Rita kissed his cheek.

Suddenly Pete remembered a few million things

he'd forgotten to tell her. "Wait a minute. Maxine's going to read Sarah the paper, isn't she?"

"She is. Those rails don't look very high. Don't lean over them."

"And Kenny Street's camping trip?"

"Andy's taking him. Did you remember my package for Polly?"

"I've got the package. And Tweetie Cunningham. She's been over every day with these inner tubes and beach balls and—"

"I'll take care of Tweetie if I've a breath left in my body. Did you pack the Dramamine I gave you?"

"Yes. And don't—"

"I won't," said Rita. "Good-bye. Good luck!"

Rita backed away. The next thing Pete knew he was on board, actually standing on the gently rocking steel deck.

Steel?

"Is this thing steel? How do they expect it to stay afloat if it takes on water? No wonder it's—"

"Jesus, Pete," said Connie, but the rest of her sentence was lost.

"Pete! Connie!" Polly was racing toward them down the deck, her feet, knees, arms, elbows, and dark curls dancing every which way. She launched herself into the air when she got within range, and her lips landed on Pete's left eyebrow. "This is great! Isn't this great? Look at this boat! Isn't it great?"

"Great, Pol. It's great."

Out of the corner of his eye Pete could see Connie grinning.

"So I guess you're used to your sister's method of attack by now," said a deep voice behind them.

They turned around.

He wasn't tall, not as tall as his voice, anyway, but he was plenty wide. Weight-lifting-wide. Polly stopped bouncing and moved to his side. "This is Jackson Beers. Jackson, this is Pete. And Connie."

Pete held out his hand. Jackson Beers cracked a few bones in it, then dipped a dark head to Connie.

"I remind Polly she's no longer a child, but it doesn't seem to sink in any," said Jackson. "She insists on running everywhere."

"I don't—" began Pete, but he was interrupted. Someone, somewhere was calling his name.

"Pete!" It was a tiny voice, a voice from on shore someplace.

Pete looked longingly backward.

"Pete!" Bobbing down the hill was Tweetie Cunningham, a canvas bag as big as she was banging her in the knees. Behind her, in heels more suited to the QE2 than *The Pequot Princess,* tottered her mother, Madeline.

The Cunninghams clattered on board.

The mismatched deckhand pulled in the gangplank and cast off the line.

They were at sea.

Chapter
4

*Spent forenoon in unpacking and arrangeing
my bureau drawers. Just dark felt kind of
seasick. retired early.*

Connie wasn't sure how the procession got started,
and neither was she sure how she ended up in the
front of it, directly behind the cruise director, Aura
Caine. Aura Caine wore a pseudo-nautical, polyester
navy blue suit and a couple of coats of makeup that
made her look about fifty, although she was probably
a few years from it. She scooped up the party where
they stood at the rail, and led the newcomers to their
cabins.

Madeline Cunningham appeared at Connie's side.
In fashionable heels and cream linen suit she didn't
look like the whale type. She didn't act like it, either.
She seemed in a hurry to get in out of the breeze,
holding onto her precisely combed hair with both

hands. Madeline's hair was the same white-blond as Tweetie's, which should have made it believable.

It didn't.

They filed down a wide set of stairs covered in mold green indoor-outdoor carpeting. The steel staircase seemed to divide the ship. Forward of the staircase was a lounge with more of the same carpeting on the floor, and lawn-chair-plaid cushioned benches lining the perimeter. Above the benches were banks of foggy Plexiglas. "The Seaview Lounge," chirped Aura. She waved behind her. "The dining room is that way."

Connie peeked into the dining room. Four dented but gleaming wood tables reached out from the walls like fingers. Each table was bolted to the floor and had an electrified hurricane lamp screwed into its center. There was a lip to keep dishes from sliding off; the minute Connie saw the bolts and the lips she felt queasy. But three cruise attendants in white pants, white sneakers, and navy blue polo shirts were putting forks, knives, and spoons in place as if they expected them to stay there.

"How quaint," said Connie.

"How tacky," said Madeline.

"Ladies, please!" called Aura Caine.

What was this, camp? Connie and Madeline hurried after the cruise director, and were whisked down more stairs into the bowels of the ship.

They entered a corridor as small and dark as a tunnel. "I'd like to know what I'm doing here," said Madeline Cunningham. "We were supposed to leave the island for New York this week, but Tweetie heard about this trip, and she wanted to see the whales. She begged me and begged me. Of course she's never even mentioned the word *whale* till this trip came up, but all of a sudden nothing would ever mean anything again in her entire life if she couldn't see the whales. I called her father. He's on a business trip in Japan. He thought I was crazy to go back to work a week late, I've got a brand-new trust officer waiting for me this minute, but finally I said to him it's not like you're the one stuck here alone with her night after night, listening to nothing but whales, whales, whales! But what are you going to do? When she gets like this it's easier to go."

Ahead of them, Aura Caine stopped. She consulted a clipboard she held in the crook of one arm, and a collection of keys that dangled from the other.

"Ah! Here we are! Mr. Bartholomew, this cabin is yours. And Ms. Bartholomew, you're right next door." She paused. Why, to see if Connie would contradict her? Connie didn't.

"And the Cunninghams, your two cabins are right here, across the way. Now don't forget, we meet in the Seaview Lounge at five for the safety lecture, and right after the lecture, there's the cocktail party."

Connie perked up. If this was camp, at least it was geared toward older campers. She fitted her key to the lock and the door swung open, smack into the narrowest bunk she'd ever seen.

And that was the biggest thing in there.

Connie looked at the two-foot-square metal shower stall, the six-inch sink, the foldaway toilet bowl, and the porthole the size of a large cabbage.

She dumped her bag, backed out of the room, and gulped air. Then she coughed.

Pete poked his head out of his cabin.

"What *is* that smell?"

"Diesel fuel," said Pete.

"Is your cabin—"

Pete waved Connie in. When the two of them were

19

inside they could barely shut the door. "These are the cheap cabins," he said. " 'Moderate space,' it said in the brochure. So what do you think?"

"If they're going to call this moderate they're—"

"Not this. Him."

"Him? Jackson Beers?" Connie opened her mouth, all set to let fly with her doubtful first impressions, but she surprised herself by closing her mouth and thinking for a minute first. She had a feeling Pete wasn't going to need any help in *not* liking old Jackson. "I think we don't even know the guy yet."

"I'd like to know what's wrong with her running."

"He didn't say anything was wrong with it, he just said she did it. And she does run everywhere, you have to admit that."

"So what?"

"So maybe he didn't know what else to say. Maybe he was nervous. He opened his mouth and out it came. He probably secretly gets a kick out of her running everywhere, and that's what made him think of it."

To Connie's surprise, Pete's forehead smoothed out. "You think so?"

"Sure," said Connie. "Now what do you say we—" She was going to suggest that they go for a tour around the boat. It was never too early to start looking for that secluded spot on the deck, but a small voice interrupted them.

"Pete!"

Pete turned, knocking into Connie. Connie backed up, and knocked down the towel rack.

Tweetie Cunningham stood in the door. "Wanna go spit in the wake?"

Pete looked at Connie. "What do you say? It could be the highlight of the trip."

Tweetie eyed Connie skeptically. "The lady, too?"

"That's no lady," said Pete, "that's my ex-wife."

Tweetie and Connie leaned over the stern rail sucking in diesel fumes and hurling gobs of spit into *The Pequot*'s wake. Pete stared out to sea, watching his tiny island of Nashtoba slip out of sight. "There it goes," he said finally.

"Hey," said Tweetie. "Come on, spit."

Nobody spat. Pete was too busy staring at the spot on the horizon where Nashtoba had once been, and Connie was too busy trying to ignore the spot where her stomach had just been. She took a deep breath, all diesel.

"I think I'll go below," she said.

She made it just in time.

Pete stood in the middle of the Seaview Lounge, feet planted a good eighteen inches apart to steady him. Two hours outside port and the corrugated cardboard sea had begun to buckle under them. It was a good idea to have the safety lecture before the cocktail party, thought Pete—if it looked like *The Pequot* were going down, he wouldn't work too hard at getting to know anybody later.

Connie had told him she'd meet him in the lounge. Pete looked around. At least two-thirds of the passenger list seemed to be retirees. There was a smaller number of younger people in their early thirties to forties who had already grouped together in the corner of the lounge, but no Connie.

The captain, Emmett Grey, welcomed them aboard. He *looked* like he had a license—about forty-five, close-cropped hair, neat beard, tanned face, clear blue weather-eye. Not only did his khakis match, they were pressed. He introduced the crew, and then reeled off the basic amenities and a few general rules: breakfast was served from seven to nine, lunch from noon to two, one dinner sitting at seven P.M., sharp. The bar was open, manned by rotating members of the crew, from five to six-thirty. The cruise attendants were responsible for meal service. The deckhands, first mate, and captain were responsible for the running of the ship. The cruise director was responsible for passenger comfort, and would be available afterward in the lounge to answer any questions. Captain Grey thanked them all for climbing aboard, and handed the show over to Sam Lederman, the deckhand who had not appeared on the dock. His khakis matched, too.

Sam's job was the safety lecture. He rambled on about life vests in cabins and lounge, fire axes and hose on every deck, two lifeboats on the upper deck, boxes of flares and emergency provisions in each lifeboat as well as in the wheelhouse. By the time he got that far, half the retirees were thumbing through guidebooks, and most of the younger crowd were whispering.

Pete caught every word.

Drinks were served, and still no Connie. Pete stood alone, a gin and tonic in a plastic glass clutched to his shirt, scanning the crowd. The cruise director circled the passengers once, like a sheepdog working, and then disappeared. Pete edged away from the pack, sipping his drink. The gin was rotgut, but that didn't bother him. The lousy tonic did.

And where the hell was Connie? Then Pete saw Polly, heading his way with a slightly built, sparsely bearded man in tow.

"I want you to tell Pete what you just told me,

Brady," said Polly. "Pete, this is Brady Pearson, our resident marine biologist. You're not going to believe this."

"I only commented to Polly that I believe whales are left- and right-handed the same way people are," said Brady.

"But tell him why you think it! You won't believe this, Pete."

Brady Pearson sounded a lot less excited than Polly, but then again, he didn't look like the excitable type. There was a quiet sense of assurance about him, as if he knew beforehand what he had to say would be found interesting, and that if by some strange chance it wasn't, it wouldn't be his fault. "It's the scarring," said Brady. "Humpbacks feed on sand lance, a fish that burrows into the ocean floor. As the whales rub along the sand they scar the side of their jaw, but generally only one side. I've concluded they use the same side each time. Most humpbacks have the scars on the right. A few, maybe twenty percent, have the scars on the left. I'm beginning to conclude the same is true with their flippers. A humpback who breeches with a right twist—"

"And the use of this information?" asked Jackson Beers behind them.

Brady Pearson turned, and blinked. "I beg your pardon?"

"What use is this information to someone like me, for example, the ordinary taxpayer?"

Pete looked at Polly.

Polly looked carefully from Brady to Jackson, skipping over Pete.

"The taxpayer?" Pete had to admit Brady Pearson sounded like he'd never heard the word.

"Taxpayer," said Jackson. "I take it you do receive

some sort of federal or state funding? That money doesn't come from thin air. I take it the whales don't spew it out their blowholes."

"Jackson." Polly laughed.

Jackson glanced at her.

Polly stopped laughing.

"But even if we discount the plight of the taxpayer, what about the plight of the whale? Isn't that the bottom line here? Isn't that your *raison d'être,* to improve the plight of the whale? But aren't you in actual fact doing more persecuting than improving? Do the whales themselves benefit by knowing which among them breeches with a twist to the right or the left? I think not. I surmise further that they'd prefer to be left alone. To live or die. To sink or swim. So to speak."

Polly laughed again.

Brady Pearson's mouth had gone slack.

Pete looked around for Aura Caine. This was a time when the cruise director could have been some use, maybe cutting Jackson out of the herd and chasing Connie in, but she seemed to have mysteriously vanished. Pete kept looking, and finally he spied Connie, a blue-jeaned oasis on the far side of the room. "Excuse me," he said.

He walked over to her, tossing down his drink as he went. Pete didn't usually toss off drinks, even good ones.

"I take it Jackson's still a little nervous," said Connie.

"A little, yes. Can I get you a drink?"

"Yes. No. I don't know." Her face under the blowsy dandelion looked pale.

"Or one of Rita's Dramamine?"

"We keep a large jar of Dramamine at the bar."

24

Pete turned around. The captain stood in front of him with his hand held out. "Emmett Grey."

Pete shook his hand. "Peter Bartholomew."

"I know. Factotum. All kinds of work. Including a little crime solving, I hear."

Pete grimaced. "You've been talking to my sister. This is Connie Bartholomew, Captain—"

"Emmett. I'm Emmett to Polly, and I'd just as soon be Emmett to both of you." He nodded to Connie as if he'd heard a few things about her, too. "I hail from Southport, I know Polly well. All the crew knows Polly."

All the crew? It must have been the nautical surroundings, but Pete envisioned a dingy room above a bar with red velvet drapes, sailors lining up, money changing hands at the door.

But right now Emmett Grey was attending to Connie. "About that Dramamine. I'd be happy to get you some. It might make your evening more . . . pleasant."

"Yes," said Connie. "Please."

Captain Grey left them for the bar.

"He looks like he knows what he's doing," said Pete hopefully. Then he remembered something. "Hey. If he's down here, who's driving this thing?"

Connie didn't answer him. She was leaning against the window with her eyes closed.

Emmett returned with a glass of water and a bottle of pills. Since Connie's eyes were still closed, Pete took them from him. Emmett wandered away, and Pete examined the bottle. An enlarged warning label was taped to its side. Never one to ignore a warning, Pete began to read this one out loud.

"Do you have glaucoma or acute asthma?"

"No."

"Arrhythmias, GI or urinary tract obstruction, chronic respiratory disease or phenylketonuria?"

"No. What the—"

"Are you nursing or pregnant?"

Connie didn't answer him.

Pete looked over. The dandelion was stem green. He handed her the water and hurriedly untwisted the top, reading faster. "Have you had any sedatives, tranquilizers, antidepressants, or alcohol? It may cause drowsiness, sedation, impaired mental and physical—"

Connie got up and ran.

Chapter
5

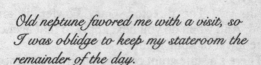

*Old neptune favored me with a visit, so
I was oblidge to keep my stateroom the
remainder of the day.*

Pete decided not to follow Connie. He'd witnessed her throwing up before, and had learned it was best not to remain in the same room. Or the same house. He figured the best he could do in this case would be to keep to a different deck. He looked around.

Jackson Beers had collected enough of a crowd around him so that the marine biologist couldn't have left the group if he wanted to.

He looked like he wanted to. His assured manner had fled. His voice was high and tight. "Yes, I draw a salary. I'm a paid scientist. This is what I do."

"And your money comes from where?"

"We receive a considerable amount of private, charitable funds that—"

"Yes, but what government agencies support you?"

Brady Pearson cleared his throat. "The National Marine Fisheries Service, the State Department—"

"The U.S. State Department?"

"Yes, the U.S. State Department."

"And locally? From the state? I should imagine the bulk of your funds would come from the state."

"Yes, they do. From the State Environmental Agency."

"Ah, yes. The director, Gary Fowler, is an old friend. And when do you next apply to that agency for the renewal of your grant?"

"There's a state grant coming up in several months. But I don't see—"

"Gary and I should be lunching soon, that's why I ask," said Jackson Beers. "And frankly, I think the political climate, the economic climate, makes this the ideal time to do a little rethinking about some of this, don't you?"

Pete looked at Polly. Her smile was fixed and stiff, her eyes darting between Jackson and Brady. Then she saw Pete. She moved closer to Jackson and placed a hand on his arm.

Pete looked away from Jackson. A few feet to the left he found a face he liked better. She appeared to be in her late-fifties, gray and neat and alone.

Pete stepped nearer. "Peter Bartholomew," he said.

She held out her hand, cool and firm. "Libby Smith. Was that your wife who left? I hope she's all right, she looked quite ill."

"Not exactly," said Pete. "I mean yes, she's ill, she's just not exactly my wife." *Hell,* thought Pete. *Now for the long, sordid tale.* But Libby Smith gazed at him a

28

moment with hazel eyes as cool as her hands, and left it alone.

"Are you interested in whales, Mr. Bartholomew?"

"Pete," said Pete. "No, not really. My sister wanted me to come, so I came. Are you?"

"I'm interested in whales, yes. I didn't expect to be. But you may find what I found on my first trip out—there seems to be . . . something about them."

"So you came for the whales."

"This time, yes. The first time, not really." She smiled.

"Are you from Southport?"

"Yes, but I'm afraid I don't know many people on board. I'm a bit of a recluse. We . . ." she stopped, as if recalling an unfamiliar word, and started again. "I live somewhat off the beaten path. In the woods. On a pond." Then she looked beyond Pete.

"I believe you're a Mrs. Smith," said the voice Pete was beginning to know well.

Libby Smith inclined her head.

"Jackson Beers," he said. "I understand you came on this trip alone?"

The question seemed to startle her. "Yes, I came alone."

Jackson shook his head. "It always amazes me when I find elderly women traveling alone."

Libby Smith's smile froze.

"Could I get you a drink, Mrs. Smith?" Pete interjected, fast.

"Libby," said Libby Smith. "Thank you, no."

"An older woman such as yourself is the ideal prey for every penny-ante pickpocket, con artist, and rapist around," said Jackson.

"Does anyone know when dinner is?" asked Pete.

"And muggers," said Jackson. "Muggers in particular are on a constant lookout for handicapped people, elderly people, those whose reflexes are liable to be—"

"Seven," said Pete. "I think they said dinner's at seven."

Jackson turned to Pete. "So tell me about this Factotum. Is it making money?"

"I do all right."

"Oh, really? Of course we each have our own definition of all right. Polly's described your business to me—running errands, washing windows, feeding chickens, painting barns? Oh, and an occasional spot of crime detection. I'm sure *that* pays well."

Pete said nothing.

"I'm opening a jet ski dealership in Southport," Jackson went on. "You ought to think about it for Nashtoba."

Pete thought about it. Jet skis. The lawn mowers of the waves. The gasoline fumes, the incessant whine, the hot-rodders from hell, buzzing his beach.

Libby Smith must have been thinking the same thing. Pete could see her spine stiffen beside him, as if with real pain. She turned to Pete. "You know, I think you're right, I think dinner *is* at seven. And I have a few things to take care of before then, if you'll excuse me, please." Dulled reflexes or not, her retreat was neatly executed.

Pete's wasn't. "I have to go, too," he said to Jackson. He turned around and tripped over Tweetie Cunningham.

"Where the heck are you going? I just got here."

"Connie's sick. I'm taking her a pill."

Tweetie's expression indicated this was not her idea

of a good time, but it seemed to beat whatever else was being offered. "So come on then," she said.

Tweetie led the way out of the lounge. From Pete's position in the rear he could see she had dressed up, or had been dressed, in clean white shorts and jersey for the occasion, but at some point between her cabin and the party she seemed to have sat on something pink. And gooey.

They descended into the lower reaches of the ship. No sounds of Connie so far. Pete walked down the hallway, leaned close to her door, and still heard nothing. He knocked. "Connie?"

"What."

Pete pushed open the door. Connie sat on her bunk. She looked less green, but more pale. "Want a Dramamine?"

She reached for the pill.

"Think you can manage dinner?" asked Pete.

Connie pitched toward the head.

"I'll bring you some crackers," called Pete, retreating.

"I'll eat with you," said Tweetie. At least that's what Pete thought she said. It was hard to tell with Connie drowning out her voice.

But once they hit the top of the stairs Tweetie didn't turn right to the dining room. She kept climbing instead.

"Where are we going?"

Tweetie pointed up.

The wide staircase led to the main deck and rows of larger cabins, with real windows. "We're in the crummy cabins," said Tweetie.

She turned right along the rail toward an expanse of open deck, complete with plastic lounge chairs, in the rear. This was where they had spent the afternoon,

31

spitting into the wake. Tweetie kept going, along the opposite rail this time, to the bow and a second deck area with more plastic chairs. Above them was the wheelhouse, accessible only by a steel ladder welded to the wall. Before Pete realized where she was going, Tweetie had scrambled up, opened the door to the wheelhouse, and disappeared inside.

"Hey!" Pete climbed after her.

"See?" said Tweetie. "Isn't this great?"

At least Pete was pleased to see that someone was indeed driving the ship. "I'm sorry," Pete said to their driver. "I didn't know she was heading up here. Tweetie, come on."

"It's okay," said Tweetie.

"'S okay," said the fellow behind the wheel, but he said it half into his chin. He didn't look old enough to be running a ship, but Pete hoped that was only an illusion, created by some leftover baby fat and an inexpert shave.

"Peter Bartholomew." Pete held out a hand. To his surprise the fellow behind the wheel blushed.

"Totum. 'Ployed all kinsa work."

He was so shy he seemed to swallow every other syllable, but Pete got the idea.

"So you know Polly?"

The driver nodded, still a little pink around the edges. "Sowpot. Larimer Ant. Fur State."

"Excuse me?"

It took a while, but finally Pete got it. Southport. Larry Morant. First Mate.

"He lets me steer," said Tweetie.

"Swell," said Pete.

"But not right now," said Larry distinctly.

Pete's confidence in the baby driver went up a notch.

"I don't have to steer," said Tweetie. "Sometimes I can just sit."

And that's what she did. There was a cushioned bench behind Larry. Tweetie wiggled onto it and sat there quietly, looking out.

Larry didn't say anything either. Pete cleared his throat once or twice to strike up a conversation but there was something about the small, Spartan room with its bank of silently winking electronics, or maybe it was Larry's intense shyness hot on the heels of the overflow chatter in the lounge that made conversation seem superfluous and unwelcome.

Or maybe it was the view.

Earlier, spitting into the wake with Tweetie and Connie, smelling diesel fumes over the back rail as his little island of Nashtoba got smaller and smaller, all Pete had noticed about *The Pequot* was the scratched paint, the dirty plastic, and the fact that it was heading out to sea.

But now he was facing forward, not back. Nashtoba was nowhere in sight. The evening shadows erased the dirt from the plastic and the last gold wash of light polished the deck. The diesel fumes might still trail behind them somewhere, but through the open windows of the wheelhouse all Pete could smell was clean salt air.

For the first time since his sister's phone call, the oppressive sense of doom that had hovered over Pete seemed to lift. For the first time since he'd boarded *The Pequot,* Pete's jaws unclenched, his shoulders settled, his mind went blank.

Tweetie's stomach rumbled, and Pete came to.

It was time to go. They were missing dinner. Pete waved Tweetie ahead of him out the door. "Thanks for letting me up here, Larry. It's . . . nice."

Larry seemed to take the compliment personally. He smiled proudly, shyly. "Upanytime."

Pete figured he meant it, or he wouldn't have struggled through two whole words to say it. Pete left the wheelhouse feeling almost cheerful. If things got too rough down below, at least he'd found a port in the storm.

Chapter
6

We dined upon Boiled ham, Boiled meat, Turnip, potatoes, pudding, warm bread, cheese, pear perserves. Felt little bit homesick this day.

The dining room on *The Pequot Princess* didn't feature place cards, or a captain's table. Seating was random, but as Pete looked around for a spot, he hesitated. It seemed to him that at each table there was either a comfortable silence of old friends, or the frantic babble of people trying too hard to become new ones. One of the more raucous tables of young people seemed to be running a singles club. Pete gave it a wide berth. One man at a table full of retirees pontificated about mutual funds. Pete passed on that table, too. Then there was Madeline Cunningham, who had reserved a spot for Tweetie and was waving them invitingly to her side. The captain sat at that table, and he waved to Pete, too, but Pete reluctantly

35

went the other way. He had just spied Polly and Jackson. Pete's early warning system screamed alert as he moved in their direction, but his conscience screamed louder. The reason he had come on this trip in the first place was because Polly wanted him there, wanted him to get to know Jackson, and it would be hard to do so from across the room. Or would it? Jackson's voice seemed to carry into every corner.

Behind Polly's table, in the corner, was a smaller, cozier table, apparently reserved for crew. Sam Lederman, the deckhand who had given the lecture in the lounge, was just leaving. He handed a beat-up handbook of some sort to the mismatched deckhand from the dock—Ned Tate, according to his name patch. The cruise director, Aura Caine, sat beside Ned Tate and peered over his shoulder as he thumbed through the book. *Knot Tying for Beginners?* wondered Pete. There was no one else at the crew table. Larry Morant was doing wheelhouse duty while the captain wined and dined his guests, the three cruise attendants were milling around preparing to wait on tables, and the chef, Pete assumed, was in the galley.

Pete took a seat at Polly's table between a stick-thin, black-haired young passenger named Jenny Sears, and a sinewy, sandy-haired woman who turned out to be the ship's resident naturalist, Stephanie Schrock.

The group at this table did not appear to be one of the more homogenous ones. An elderly couple at one end could certainly have belonged to one of the retiree tables, and the women on either side of Pete could have fit in well with the singles crowd. There was a middle-aged man with a perpetually sour expression, sitting alone, gazing into space. Pete nodded to him. No response. Pete attempted to address himself to the elderly couple, but they appeared to prefer conversation with each other. They even looked like one another, with pinched faces, noses like beaks, and small, birdlike eyes. What was this, the table for the social misfits? Pete turned to the naturalist instead, but before he could say anything, Polly interrupted him.

"Where's Connie?"

"She's kind of sick," said Pete. "I'm going to bring her some stuff in a little while."

"Seasickness is nothing more than tension," said Jackson.

"Really?" asked Polly. Her dark curls were freshly tamed, she wore a plain but striking lemon-yellow dress, and her amber eyes sparkled at Jackson, waiting for him to say more.

"She does appear remarkably tense, doesn't she?" asked Jackson.

"No," said Pete. "She doesn't."

"Yes, she does," said Polly. "But I think she's doing very well, considering the situation." The look that passed between Polly and Jackson hinted of confidences shared. *Pete's* confidences shared.

"The situation," said Jackson. "Yes. Of course you can't really blame yourselves. Many divorced people fall into the very same trap, deluding themselves that one or the other of them has changed, that whatever objectionable behavior caused the problem in the first place is miraculously gone. In actual fact, of course, no one ever really changes."

The cruise attendant for their table was a petite redhead whose name tag read Janine Moss. She appeared with the salads, and Jackson addressed her by name. Sort of. "Janine, love, see if you can hustle

37

me up some fresh ground pepper, will you? And some lemon. *Fresh* lemon. There's a doll.''

Pete turned away from Jackson, toward Jenny Sears.

"Are you from Southport, too?"

Deep-set eyes darted toward Pete, then quickly averted. She shook her head, and her long hair rippled like black water. "Penfield, Connecticut."

"And how did you end up on this boat?"

This time her eyes lifted longer. "I've taken them all. Every cruise. I'll follow them south again soon."

"Follow who?"

"The whales," interceded Stephanie Shrock. "They'll migrate south to the West Indies for the winter. But right now they're here, and that's why we are, to identify as many of them as we can, and to gather some data on entanglements."

"Entanglements?"

Jenny Sears came to life. She gripped Pete's arm with long, yellowing nails that curled at the ends. "We're killing them. We discard our fishing gear willy-nilly. We saturate the ocean with waves of wandering nets. The whales are trapped, starved, strangled, drowned. Whales have to breathe. Whales drown. *We* drown them. You have no idea what agonies they go through! But *I* know. They tell me. They cry out to me."

"Oh," said Pete. He looked at Stephanie Schrock. He wasn't sure but he thought she winked.

"You see this quite often," Jackson said to Polly from across the table in a whisper that probably carried all the way back to land. "Especially among people who are uncomfortable with human interaction. They attribute human traits to nonhuman species in order to feel that they can relate to something. Anything at all."

"So," said Pete to Stephanie. "How do you go about collecting data on entanglements?"

"We document their scars. Scars from lines and nets are very distinctive."

"As my friend Gary Fowler from the State Environmental Agency was saying just the other day," began Jackson, "it's been well documented that marine mammals will live longer in captivity."

Stephanie Schrock looked up sharply.

"So that's how you identify whales?" Pete asked. "By the scars from the nets and things?"

The naturalist shook her head. "We don't need scars to identify humpbacks. Every humpback carries his own natural fingerprint, or tailprint, I should say. They each have a unique set of black and white markings on the underside of the tail, and often they have a uniquely shaped or marked dorsal fin. We're documenting entanglement scars not to identify the whales, but to give us some accurate statistics on the number of whales who are injured this way."

"Even one is too much!" Jenny Sears burst out. "We have to do something! We have to stop it, now!"

Jackson Beers's salad fork clattered onto the table. "Miss Sears. Give me one concrete contribution a whale makes to Man, would you do that for me, please? Other than getting in the way of our efforts to feed off the more delectable fruits of the sea?"

Jenny Sears looked up, trembling slightly, her face dead-white against the black of her hair. "The whales are the gods," she whispered. "It is *you,* an ugly mortal, who must justify your existence to *them.*"

Jackson chuckled. "Mortal, I grant. But ugly?" He

looked at Polly, but Polly's salad appeared to intrigue her just then.

Their dinners arrived and served to excuse what Pete was beginning to feel was a much needed period of silence. Jackson Beers ran Janine Moss back and forth between table and galley three or four more times. Her smile got tighter and tighter, but it never went away.

"So!" said Polly, finally. "Can you tell us when we might begin to see the whales, Stephanie?"

"We should have seen some by now. The herring are here, and that's what the whales come for, the herring. That's why the Pilgrims settled here. There were so many whales romping around the *Mayflower* the Pilgrims knew there would be good fishing. But I guarantee you we'll see whales tomorrow, when we hit Johnson's Ledge. Last year we saw seventy-three humpbacks there. Get your cameras ready."

Polly's hand went to her mouth. "Oh no!"

"You forgot your camera," said Jackson. "I'm not surprised. You do have trouble retaining more than one thought in your head at a time."

Pete pushed back his chair and stood up. "Excuse me," he said. "I promised I'd try to scrounge up some crackers for Connie."

Janine Moss heard him. "Wait here." She disappeared around the corner into the galley, and came back with a deep tray on which she had arranged an assortment of crackers, two cans of ginger ale with a tall glass of ice, and what looked like pudding of some sort. "Here, take this. And if you need anything else, just ask me, or the chef, Drew. He acts like a bear, but really he's very nice." She smiled, a real smile this time. Drew probably was a bear, Pete decided. It was Janine who was nice. He thanked her profusely.

On his way through the dining room, he collected his caboose, Tweetie.

"Hey, how come you didn't sit with us?"

"I promised my sister I'd sit with her."

"Are you going to sit with her for breakfast?"

If Pete sat with Jackson Beers again he was liable to punch him in the nose. "Maybe I could sit with you," he said.

Tweetie beamed. "So where are you going now?"

"To see Connie."

"Again?"

"I promised to take her some food."

"You do a lot of promising, don't you?"

"I guess I do."

"Why?"

Pete thought that over. "I guess it's one of those things that goes with being an adult."

"Don't you ever just play?"

"Hardly ever."

"Why not?"

"The Puritans," said Pete. "It's all because of the Puritans."

That lasted her till they reached Connie's cabin. Pete didn't think it would be a good idea to bring Tweetie inside, considering what he'd learned about her gag reflex. "You'd better go back to dinner now," said Pete. "I have to see Connie alone."

Connie was out like a light. But when Pete came in, she sat up groggily, still white as a sheet. "Did you eat?"

"Sort of. If you're up for real food, you could still catch some, I think."

Connie put her head back down. "No way. These pills are knocking me out."

"Do you think you'll make breakfast?" Pete didn't

think Connie could have heard the note of desperation in his voice, but she gave him a longish look just the same.

"Sure, I'll make breakfast." She took a cracker.

Pete took one, too. He was starting to feel a little sick himself, but for different reasons.

Chapter
7

*Nice fair wind and we are bounding merrily
in our journey.*

Pete woke up the next morning to the sound of Connie, banging on his door. He knew it was Connie right away—nobody else ever banged on a door like that.

"Come in," he said, before she came *through.*

She came in. She looked better, but she glanced nervously out the porthole at the chop. "I'm starved. Aren't you going to breakfast?"

"Sure." Pete hesitated. He was unclear on the etiquette for a nine-years-married, two-years-divorced nude man getting out of bed with his ex-wife in the room. He wasn't sure there was enough space for him to get out of bed with his ex-wife in the room.

Connie must have sensed his dilemma. She snorted. "Meet me down there, then."

It was still early when Pete reached the dining room. Only about half the retirees were up, and four from the singles set—one good-looking young man, apparently playing the role of gigolo, obsequiously attentive to three women who dramatically out-aged him.

Connie sat at a table with the captain, the sourpuss, the birdlike couple, and Libby Smith.

"Now wait a minute," she was saying as Pete sat down. "You're trying to tell me we don't *stop?*"

"Not till we hit Southport on Sunday."

"I thought we were going to Nova Scotia. I thought—"

"We're going to Nova Scotia. To the waters of Nova Scotia, at any rate. Some of our best whale sightings have occurred at the mouth of the Bay of Fundy. We go that far, turn around, and don't dock again until we land back in Southport."

"On Sunday. We just keep going until Sunday."

"If we're lucky." The captain grinned at Connie, but Pete knew it was going to take more than a few white teeth in a tanned face to cheer her up. He watched her gulp her coffee too fast and struggle with the ill effects before she was able to respond.

"Is this a joke? Do you mean I'm going to have to throw up for five more days or spend them drugged like a zombie?" She glared at Pete.

"I thought you knew that," said Pete. "I thought you understood. The purpose of the trip is to see the whales, not the scenery. We go out to sea. We travel quite a distance from the coast the whole way."

"Don't worry," said a voice behind Pete that was fast becoming synonymous with the word *worry*. Jackson Beers slid into the chair across from Connie. "We shouldn't hit rough water until later this afternoon."

Connie waved out the window at the fine rickracks of foam. "What do you call that, a lake?"

"Where's Polly?" asked Pete.

Jackson raised his eyebrows over the menu. "Polly? I assume she's in our cabin where I left her, but I couldn't really say."

"Oh, really," said Pete. "Maybe you could say whether she—"

Janine circled within range, and Jackson cut him off.

"Item number one, Janine, love. Watch my coffee cup, and don't let it get any less than half-full. Understand? And I'd like orange juice, please, and two eggs sunny-side, home fries, and steak, very rare." Jackson glanced at Connie. "And when I say rare I do assure you I mean rare. Let the blood run, along with the yolks."

Connie pushed back her chair and ran.

Pete brought Connie another Dramamine. This time he left her the box. Connie barely spoke.

Pete climbed to the main deck and knocked on Polly's door.

Tweetie was right. They were in the crumby cabins. Jackson and Polly had a wood-framed double bed, a large, built-in bank of drawers, a whole closet, an enclosed bathroom, and a picture window, of sorts. True, it wasn't being shown off to its best advantage—the bed was unmade, two drawers were trailing

45

clothes, the closet door was draped with wet towels, and Polly was crying.

"What's the matter?"

Polly turned away. "Nothing. Nothing's the matter."

"Right. I can see that. Is it him?"

Polly whipped around. "Him? Him? Of course, that's what you think, isn't it? You think it's him! It doesn't take you long, does it, Pete? No, it isn't *him!* It's me. Me and my big mouth. I just said something stupid, that's all. He was upset, that's all. And that makes me upset. All right?"

Pete pictured Jackson as he had just seen him downstairs, ordering runny eggs and raw steak. *Upset, my ass.* He sat down on the edge of the bed, hard. "Listen, Polly—"

Polly stayed standing, hands planted aggressively on hips. "You don't like him. Just say it, will you, and get it out of your system."

"Whether I like him or not doesn't matter. It's whether you like him that—"

"Oh, right. Like I'm deciding to marry somebody I don't even like. Thanks, Pete. Thanks a lot. You really know how to boost me up. What do you think I am, a dolt?"

"No, I don't think you're a dolt. I just wonder how long you've known him, that's all. I just wonder if you really do know him. It sometimes takes a lot of time, being with a person in all kinds of situations, before you can make an adult decision about—"

"Adult! And this from the big adult himself, the big expert on relationships. You and Connie are a real pair of *adults,* I can sure see that."

Pete stood up. That hurt. That hurt big time, and

Polly knew it. She was right behind him by the time he reached the door.

"Oh, come on, Pete. I'm sorry. It's just that I knew this was going to happen. I knew you weren't going to like him. You never like anybody."

"What do you mean? Who have I never liked?"

"Donald. You *hated* Donald."

"Donald?" Pete couldn't remember any Donald.

"And Matthew. Don't try to tell me you liked Matthew."

"I never even *met* Matthew."

"See? You never met him and you hated him. That's why I knew you'd hate Jackson."

"Well, if you knew that, why'd you ask me to come on this trip? I told you, what I think isn't the issue, here. It's you who has to live with the guy."

Polly sat down on the bed. The tears welled up in her eyes. "You don't know him. He's nothing like you think. We're happy."

"Well, if that's true, I'm delighted to hear it. Excuse me if I have a little trouble believing it when I walk in here and find you in tears."

Polly hastily wiped her eyes. "It's me, I tell you. This has nothing to do with him. Things were fine until we came on this trip. It's just me being a jerk, that's all."

"You're not a jerk, Polly. And you're really going to tick me off if you start thinking you are."

Or if you marry one, Pete wanted to add.

"Even you'll think I'm a jerk when I tell you what I said to him, Pete. I told him about Sam."

"Sam who?"

"Sam Lederman. Didn't you even know I used to go out with Sam?"

Pete looked at Polly, surprised. "The deckhand?"

"Yeah. The cute one. But it didn't work out. We sort of agreed we'd better split. We wanted . . . different things. We broke up about three months ago. Then I met Jackson."

Swell, thought Pete. *Three whole months ago, and now you're going to marry him.* "I still don't see why you're a jerk for telling him about Sam Lederman. It seems an aboveboard kind of thing to do."

"It did to me, too. I didn't do it to throw it in his face, or anything. I didn't know Sam was going to be on this particular boat. I even tried to explain how it hadn't worked out between Sam and me. But Jackson said it was extremely 'tacky' of me. He said it was a 'brainless' thing to do. He seems to think I've put him in this mortifying position, trapping him on a boat with one of my old boyfriends." Polly shrugged. "Sam and I aren't anything to each other anymore. I thought Jackson would rather know, you know? In case it came up." Polly laughed. "I guess I am brainless."

Pete started to seethe. "You're not brainless. You just assumed the person you were planning to marry was an adult, that's all."

It was a poor choice of words. Polly seemed to take it as more evidence of her brainlessness.

"I'm sorry, Pete. I didn't mean what I said about you and Connie. It's just that I get so out of patience with you two. Like this trip. When I heard she was coming I thought, great, things are finally getting somewhere. Then you come on board and what do I find? Separate cabins. What is it, Pete? What's going on with you two?"

"So," said Pete, fast. "What about breakfast?"

48

Polly gave Pete a funny look, almost as if he'd hurt her somehow, but he couldn't think why. Then she jumped up. "I'm dying for breakfast." She rummaged around for her shoes and bounced out the door ahead of him. She kept bouncing, too, right up to the minute they entered the dining room and she saw Jackson, talking with Madeline Cunningham.

Chapter
8

This morning, the cry of there she blows greeted our ears.

Stephanie Schrock had predicted whales by the afternoon. *The Pequot* buzzed with anticipation all morning, and increased chop didn't seem to deaden it any. By noon most everyone was lined up at the bow rail, peering into the distance for whales. It wasn't easy. The sky was sharp blue and clear, but every peaked wave looked like a fin. Pete looked ahead and behind and sideways as far as his eye could see and saw . . . nothing. But he wasn't looking for whales, he was looking for land.

"Odd, isn't it?" said a voice beside him, and Pete turned to see Libby Smith. "Odd to get so stirred up in anticipation of a fish. Excuse me, they aren't fish, are they? Mammals then. Large mammals."

"Yes, it is odd," said another voice behind Pete, and even if he hadn't recognized the voice, Pete would have known who it was by the look of quickly masked dismay in Libby Smith's eyes.

"That's what I've been trying to tell these people," said Jackson. "These creatures are mere mammals, the same as we are, and inferior mammals at that."

"But they *are* near to extinction," said Libby Smith. "I suppose if we were near to extinction we'd generate some excitement ourselves."

"And so what if the whale becomes extinct? What would we have lost? A large, useless animal. If Man were in danger of extinction, however, think what the world would lose."

"Wars," said Libby Smith. "Famine. Drugs. Murder. Yes, I see your point, Mr. Beers."

Jackson Beers peered at Libby Smith. There was something hard and black in his eyes. "You do know, of course," he said, "that the best place to watch for whales is not here, on the bow, but up there, on top of the wheelhouse?"

"Sorry," said Sam Lederman from behind him. "That area's off-limits to everyone but scientists and crew. You'll see just fine from down here."

Jackson's eyes got blacker. "Excuse me," he said to Libby Smith.

"And excuse *me,*" said Libby Smith.

First Jackson, and then Libby left him, but Pete was by no means alone. He looked around. Everyone but Connie and Polly seemed to be on the bow. Pete once again evaded the singles club that looked like it wanted to include him, and the investments group that looked like it didn't, and moved up to join Sam Lederman, curious about the fellow now that his sister had revealed their history to him. But before Pete could strike up a conversation, Tweetie wedged herself between the two men and draped herself over the rail. "Are there whales yet?"

"Not yet," said Pete. "Be careful, there."

Tweetie grabbed onto the rail and jumped up and down.

"Stand still, Tweetie, will you?"

"I want to see the whales."

"You can see them just as well standing still." Pete decided he'd been hanging around her too long. He was starting to sound like a parent. He looked around for her real parent, and found Madeline leaning against the ladder to the wheelhouse, talking to Jackson Beers. She actually looked interested in what he was saying.

Pete looked again.

Too interested.

Pete returned to Tweetie. "So. Your dad's in Japan, I hear?"

"He's on a business trip."

"And when does he come home?"

"He *never* comes home."

Swell.

Connie appeared at the back of the crowd. Pete waved, and she worked her way unsteadily over the deck until she was beside him.

"How are you doing?"

Connie rolled her eyes.

Tweetie lunged at the rail again. Pete clamped his hand around her wrist. Tweetie didn't seem to mind, so he held on, and it was a good thing he did; suddenly she lunged forward, shrieking, "I see one! I see one!"

The passengers behind Pete surged toward the rail

in a press of flesh. It was the closest Pete had gotten to most of them since the trip began. Sounds of "Where? What? Where?" echoed around the deck. Even Sam Lederman bent down behind Tweetie and squinted. "Where?"

Pete studied Sam. Cute, Polly had called him, but Pete couldn't tell. All he could tell was that Sam had the look of a human being around the eyes, something Jackson Beers did not.

"It's seaweed," said Sam.

Tweetie slumped.

"Hey," said Sam. "I thought it was a whale, too."

Polly suddenly appeared beside them with Jackson. "Any whales?" she asked.

"I thought I saw one, but it was seaweed," said Tweetie.

"I thought it was a dead body," said Pete.

"Dead body?" said Jackson. "Talking about your sister's old boyfriend again?"

Sam Lederman turned around.

"They're talking about me," said Connie. Her skin was cadaverish. Her hair whipped around like dead grass in the breeze. The boat hit a swell and the deck fell away under their feet. "Christ," she said.

The boat surged again and salt spray smacked them in the face. One by one the passengers retreated. Finally Madeline Cunningham snatched a furious Tweetie away from the edge, and Pete and Connie were alone, hanging onto the rail.

"So what's eating you?" asked Connie.

Pete sighed. "Polly. I tried to talk to her about Jackson and I really messed it up. She's never going to admit she's made a mistake, not while I'm around, anyway. She's going to prove some big point and marry this guy just because I can't remember some guy I supposedly hated, some guy named Donald."

"Donald Eisling. The guy in the cult."

Pete groaned. "And there was some guy named Matthew I never even met. She says I hated him, too."

"She's right, you did. Something about the way she talked about him made you think it was all sex."

"I didn't hate him, I just didn't trust him."

"You hated him. And when you hate somebody you really hate them, Pete. You can hear it right over the phone." More spray smacked Connie in the face, but instead of discouraging her it seemed to revive her. "So she figures you were going to hate Jackson right off the bat. So she's not going to listen to you if you try to tell her what a turkey he is."

"I didn't try to tell her what a turkey he is. What do you think I am, a dolt?"

"No," said Connie. "But you're a lousy liar. And you do think he's a turkey."

"Don't you?"

Connie was silent for so long that Pete thought maybe he was wrong, maybe he hadn't given Jackson Beers a fair shake. What did he know, anyway? Had he hated Donald and Matthew and God knows who else? What was he doing, refusing to let Polly grow up, to make her own decisions?

A burst of laughter behind them made Pete and Connie turn. Jackson Beers and Madeline Cunningham had reappeared. Jackson nodded to Pete and Connie. Then he curled a hand around Madeline's neck and pulled her ear close to his mouth.

"Yeah," said Connie, facing front again. "He's a turkey all right."

For one brief, shining moment Pete was filled with a

sense of relief, of vindication. Then he felt sick. His sister, Polly, was going to *marry* this turkey.

For a while neither of them spoke.

"Hey," said Connie finally. "Cheer up. They can always get a divorce. See how well it worked for us?"

Pete didn't laugh.

But then again, neither did Connie.

Chapter
9

*Ordered my water to be heat to do my
washing with, washed to-day for the first
time, got through about noon. Had but
little skin left on my fingers.*

The *Pequot* rose and fell and Connie took another
shot of spray in the face. She shivered.

"Want to go in?" asked Pete.

"No." It was wet, all right, and Connie was getting
cold, but the sun was snapping along the crests of the
waves and the wind was whipping some life back into her. Besides, her stomach seemed to have settled
down and she was half-afraid to move. "Wasn't there
a coffee machine in the lounge? Let's get some and
come back out."

They staggered side by side into the corridor,
heading for the stairs, but outside Polly and Jackson's
door, the sound of raised voices made them stop.

"I'm sorry."

That was Polly.

"And being sorry is the extent of your effort?"

That was Jackson. "No forethought, no common sense, just these insipid apologies after the fact. And tears. Do you know how annoying your tears are, Polly?"

Tears? Annoying? The hairs on the back of Connie's neck stood up. She started to move away, but Pete grabbed her.

Inside the cabin, she heard the sound of drawers opening. "I see only white socks in here. I assumed when you washed my socks you washed all my socks, but I see only white socks in here."

There was no answer from Polly. Apparently nobody expected one. The door opened so suddenly that Pete and Connie were caught gaping at it. Pete took one look at his sister and headed for the stairs. Polly headed for the bow. Connie started to follow Pete, but then she hesitated, changed direction and followed Polly.

They stood side by side and silent at the bow rail, letting the deck pound at the bottoms of their feet and the spray pound at their faces.

"So Pete doesn't like him," said Polly finally. "Do you?"

The question caught Connie off-guard. She considered saying all that stuff about how she hadn't known Jackson Beers long enough yet, but the truth of the matter was that Connie didn't like him. The hell with it. If Polly was dumb enough to ask the question, Connie was plenty dumb enough to answer it. "No, I don't," she said.

But Polly surprised her. She laughed. "Well, at least we've got that little item out of the way. You will, of course, defend my right to my own opinion?"

"Defend your own rights," snapped Connie.

Polly pulled back from the rail, stung. "I see."

"I don't think you do, Polly. And you have a lot more rights than just the right to your own opinion."

Polly's eyes filled with tears.

"Ladies!" Jackson called from behind them.

Polly scrambled to wipe her eyes.

"You have a right to your goddamned tears," Connie shouted, but it didn't do any good. By the time Jackson reached them the tears had been erased, and Polly followed him back to their cabin.

Pete arrived on the bow with two coffees, looking for Connie, but the only other human being in sight was the deckhand, Ned Tate. He was doing something to a line with a long steel spike.

"Hi," said Pete.

Ned nodded at him. Was he going to be as comatose as Larry Morant?

"Want a coffee?"

Ned shook his head. "Just had one, thanks. You're Polly's brother, right?"

"Right," said Pete. He held out his hand and Ned shook it.

"I've heard a lot about you from Polly. A lot of laughs, Polly."

That's easy for you to say, thought Pete. "So how does this work, anyway? You ship out on *The Pequot* every Monday all year long?"

"Out on Monday, in on Sunday. One night off. We get laid off in December, and start up again in March."

"So what do you do all winter?"

"Me and Sam go south, working a boat out of the

Keys. The captain goes to the Caribbean. He runs a charter boat down there. Larry, a couple of the C.A.'s and the chef, Drew Baker, hang around Southport collecting unemployment."

"And the cruise director?"

Something undefinable left, or entered, Ned's eyes. "I don't know. Hibernates, I guess." He recoiled the line, slipping the spike into his back pocket. "Gotta go. Nice to meet you."

"You, too," said Pete.

Ned Tate left.

Pete moved into the lee of the ship, sipping his coffee and worrying about Polly until Brady Pearson's voice carried his way on the wind.

The scientist was talking to Stephanie Schrock at the opposite end of the rail, his voice raised angrily. The grant. He was talking about the grant, about possibly losing it, and at the risk of giving Jackson Beers any credit, Pete had to admit that he was staggered by the sum of money mentioned. Stephanie Schrock snapped back with something about a book. Something about money for a book. Jackson's name was mentioned, and then Gary Fowler, Jackson's friend, the director of the agency in charge of the grant. Could they be serious? Could this connection of Jackson's cost them their grant?

But now the subject changed. The scientists still appeared to be arguing, but not about Jackson. Stephanie Schrock said something about Brady ignoring her application. Brady Pearson said it had nothing to do with him. Stephanie Schrock snapped something about team players. Finally Brady moved off, but Stephanie stayed. There was something so stiff and straight about her back that Pete felt kind of sorry for her. She *had* been an obliging and informative companion the night before at dinner. She'd even winked. He moved closer.

"Hello," he said. "Could I interest you in a luke-warm cup of coffee? I can't seem to find its owner."

Stephanie Schrock shook her head. Pete thought her lips moved, but he wasn't sure. She didn't seem quite as obliging as she had been the evening before.

"So have you been doing this long? Taking to sea on *The Pequot?*"

"Long enough."

"It's helpful to have you scientists around. I've lived on Nashtoba all my life, and I've seen plenty of whales, out at sea and washed ashore. I never knew that about the entanglements, and the Pilgrims. And Brady's thing about the left- and right-handedness of whales—"

Stephanie snorted. "If *I'd* come up with that idea they'd have laughed me out of the Institute."

"Oh," said Pete. He thought maybe he'd better be moving along after all.

"It's funny how they can always manage to find air time for *that,* and then when I need a small plug for my book—"

"Your book?" asked Pete politely. It had been his experience that you could always cheer up an author by talking about his book.

And yes, she did appear to perk up. "Did you know that some whales can communicate across the entire Atlantic Ocean?"

"No," said Pete. "I—"

"Hey!" said a small, gleeful voice from the vicinity of Pete's pocket. "Here you are!"

Pete looked down. "Hi, Tweetie." He turned around to introduce Stephanie to Tweetie.

Stephanie was gone.

"What are you doing out here, Tweetie?"

"Looking for my twenty dollars."

"What? You lost some money?"

"Yeah," said Tweetie. "Wanna help?"

"If you dropped it out here, it's long gone."

"I didn't drop it. Somebody stole it. Out of here." Tweetie unzipped a tiny leather pouch decorated with Indian beads. "See?"

"Oh for heaven's sake." Madeline Cunningham staggered up to them across the bouncing deck. "Really, Tweetie—"

"Leave us alone," said Tweetie. "We're looking for my twenty dollars."

"Out here? Don't be silly. And what an eight-year-old child is doing running around with twenty dollars in a—"

"Dad gave it to me," said Tweetie. "It was a present. For no reason."

By the look on Madeline's face, Pete figured it had been some time since anyone had given her a present for no reason. Madeline yanked at Tweetie's arm. Tweetie yanked back. Pete decided it would be best to leave mother and daughter alone. He swung himself up the ladder to the wheelhouse, where Larry Morant had just arrived to relieve Emmett at the wheel.

"Pete," said Emmett. "Come on in."

Pete went in, pleased that the captain himself didn't seem to mind Pete being in the wheelhouse.

"We've decided to head farther out," said Emmett. "Got a report of a couple of right whales, two hundred fifty miles out. Right whales are rare, only three hundred or so in the whole world. It's worth the trip, don't you think?"

"Two *hundred* and fifty miles?"

"Sure. That's what we're here for, to find whales. Since we haven't seen any around here, we head farther out. We've got a week."

"Oh," said Pete. He must not have sounded enthusiastic. Emmett changed the subject.

To a worse one.

"So Polly and Jackson Beers are getting married, I hear."

"Yes," said Pete. "He's from Southport. Do you know him?"

"I don't move in the same circles as Jackson," said Emmett carefully. Too carefully. "I must say I didn't know Polly did, either. I was . . . surprised when I heard they were getting married. I didn't know she'd known him that long."

"Three months."

They were interrupted by Sam Lederman, swinging through the wheelhouse door like a sea squall.

"I've been looking for you," he said to Pete. "I tried to talk to your sister but she was scared to death old Jackson would see us or something. I want to know what she's doing."

"If you mean in regard to the remark Jackson made on the deck, I don't think Polly—"

Sam waved a hand impatiently. "Polly never said that. She's not nasty. I just didn't think she was so—"

Sam Lederman and Emmett Grey exchanged a look.

"Gullible?" Pete finished for him. "Blind? Deaf?"

"Can't you talk to her?" asked Sam. "You have no idea what a man like that will do to a woman like Polly. It's already begun. She's becoming afraid to . . ." Sam stopped.

"Run," Pete finished for him. "Cry. Breathe."

"Yes. *Yes*. Talk to her, will you?"

Pete shook his head. "I did. I made things worse. She's got this thing about me thinking all her boy-friends are jerks, and this time she's going to ruin her whole life just to prove me wrong." Too late Pete remembered he was talking to one of Polly's boy-friends. "I don't mean you, I never even met you. I didn't know anything about you."

Sam laughed. "Then go down to the lounge and listen to Jackson. You'll find out plenty. All about the intellectually inferior who can't compensate in the sack."

"And you're laughing it off. If it were me I'd be ready to kill him."

Suddenly Sam stopped laughing. "Oh, I'm ready to kill him," he said. "Make no mistake about that."

Chapter
10

Just dark felt kind of seasick. retired early.

Sam Lederman exited the wheelhouse, but Pete was reluctant to move. His way was clear, Tweetie and Madeline had left the deck, but slowly, steadily, the wheelhouse had begun to work its magic once again.

It was peaceful there. Even Emmett Grey, relieved of his shift, seemed reluctant to leave this quiet place. He lingered, saying nothing. The three men sat in silence and watched the bow of *The Pequot Princess* slice through the chop, but finally Pete decided it was time to leave the man at the wheel undistracted. He said good-bye and hit the door. He was surprised to find that Emmett Grey came with him.

"Got a minute?"

"Sure," said Pete.

Emmett led Pete to his cabin, a room even more commodious than Polly and Jackson's, tucked in below the wheelhouse. Everything in here was dark wood—bed frame, bank of drawers, even a file cabinet. The walls were painted off-white, and centered on the one over Emmett's bunk was a two-foot-long wrought-iron harpoon.

Emmett followed Pete's gaze. "Nice, huh? A real antique. From the real whalers." He reached up and removed the harpoon from the wall. "Single flue, see? Barbed only on one side. Here." He handed it to Pete.

Pete hefted it. It was obviously very old, but neither time nor countless whale hides had destroyed its lethal edge.

Pete handed it back.

"That Sears woman came in here last night to get after me about some foolish petition and took one look at that thing and nearly had a stroke. She wanted to know what I thought I was doing carrying around a symbol of 'the very murderers who drove the whales to near extinction.' I told her those who don't remember the past are condemned to repeat it. She wasn't impressed." Emmett hung the harpoon on its hooks and turned around. "Now, Pete, I can see that you've got problems of your own right now, but I've got one, too, and some of the things Polly has told me make me think you can help."

"Me? How?"

"I'm afraid there's been a theft."

"Tweetie's twenty?"

Emmett looked blank. "What?"

"Tweetie Cunningham lost twenty dollars. She thinks it was stolen."

Emmett looked thoughtful. "I see. Actually, it's another theft I'm hoping to put you to work on."

Pete groaned. "Listen, Emmett. This sleuthing business is being blown way out of proportion. I don't solve crimes, I don't solve thefts, I don't solve murders. I *tripped* over a couple of bodies. That's all."

"But you do have eyes?"

Pete sighed. "What was stolen?"

"Libby Smith's gold watch."

Libby Smith. Pete wished it had been some one else.

"She came to me reluctantly. She has no desire to broadcast this news, and I was grateful for her discretion. But she expects me to do something about it, and frankly, I'd prefer to do something as inconspicuously as possible. That's why I thought of you. If I start poking around asking questions it will be only too clear to the rest of the passengers that something's up. The same goes for Sam or Ned or Larry."

The idea of Larry asking questions was amusing, to say the least, and Pete could see that neither Sam nor Ned were particularly well suited to the job either. "What about Aura Caine?"

Emmett said nothing.

"I don't see what you think I can do, Emmett, short of searching cabins and frisking people. A watch is a pretty small—"

"Just keep your eyes open. Libby says it was taken early this morning. She leaves the watch on her dresser every night, and this morning she walked out on deck early to check the temperature. She didn't lock her cabin. She stayed on deck longer than she had planned, the sunrise left quite an afterglow today. When she returned and went to put on her watch, it was gone."

"She's sure? I mean you're sure she's sure it was stolen, and not just stashed someplace else?"

"You've talked to Libby Smith. You tell me if you'd

believe her if she came to you and said her watch was stolen."

Pete smiled ruefully. Emmett was right.

"All I want you to do is to keep alert. See if you can find out who was roaming the corridor topside around sunrise time. See if anyone on board strikes you as 'off.' See if anyone's suddenly flashing a gold watch. And while you're at it, talk to Madeline Cunningham about her daughter's twenty, and if it appears that there's anything to it, let me know."

"And if I come up with nothing?"

"I know." Emmett sighed. "Frankly, Pete, I'm not expecting you to come up with much, but I would like to be able to tell Libby Smith that I've got someone with some police experience working on the problem."

"You don't."

"Police connections, then. Polly tells me you've been indirectly involved with the police in several investigations, and that the police chief is a good friend."

"So's the butcher, but you wouldn't want me hacking up your roast."

Emmett laughed, dropping a hand on Pete's shoulder. "My roast, no. Libby Smith's watch, why not? What have we got to lose? The watch is gone. The worst that can happen is it stays gone."

Pete had to admit he had a point.

As he left the cabin he gave one more look at Emmett's harpoon. "So what do your scientists think about that thing?"

Emmett shrugged. "I have no idea. No one's said anything. And knowing Brady and Stephanie, they'd be saying plenty."

"I gather they don't get along?"

Emmett studied Pete a minute before he spoke. "One's doing one thing, one's doing another, each one thinks the other is somehow interfering or not being supportive enough, but I've thought of it as a personal problem. If it's getting so it shows, I guess it's time we all have a little talk."

"I wouldn't say it shows," said Pete. "I just happened to overhear a few things, being in the wrong place at the wrong time."

"Wrong place, wrong time," said Emmett. "You'd be surprised how often those come up on a boat the size of this one."

No, thought Pete, his mind on Jackson, he wouldn't be surprised at all.

Connie's cabin rolled to starboard as she stepped inside and with that one short step any stability her stomach had achieved left her. She took a Dramamine and a shower, in that order, and by the time she was out of the shower and toweled and robed she was ready for bed.

She slept through dinner.

Again.

The Dramamine wore off around nine, just about the time Pete came knocking on the door with the usual crackers and ginger ale from Janine.

"Have you noticed this isn't working out real well?" asked Connie.

"You're not alone," said Pete. "We were down a few at dinner. But I was talking to Emmett and he says the best thing to do is to get out in the middle of the bow and ride it."

Connie threw back her covers and picked up her jeans from the floor. "What have I got to lose? I've had it with pills. At least it's dark. If I throw up, who's going to know?"

"I'll stay upwind."

Connie glared at him. She pulled her jeans on under her robe. She supposed a real lady would have asked Pete to leave, but what was the point? He'd seen it all before. She turned her back, dropped her robe, and pulled a jersey over her head. When Pete spoke from behind her she could tell he wasn't exactly looking at the ceiling.

"Connie."

"What?" She buttoned her buttons with her back still to him. He was so close she could feel him breathing.

"I don't *know* what, dammit. I keep wanting to talk to you and I don't know what to say." His hands closed on her arms.

Connie had a line all ready. "I have to throw up." For a mood-wrecker, it was pretty good.

Connie finally struggled out of her room and headed topside, intent on taking Emmett Grey's advice. She was not going to take any more Dramamine. She was going to try this fresh air method of his.

It was late. *The Pequot* was quiet. Pete must have been right—Connie wasn't the only one laid low by the storm. As she passed the Seaview Lounge there were only two people in it, Pete and Polly, sitting at the deserted bar with their backs to the door. Their hands punctuated the air. Their dark heads bobbed back and forth, alike in color and intensity. Connie watched them for a minute, trying to tell by the occasional snaps and jerks if things were amiable. But how bad could it be since nobody was throwing up?

She went straight to the bow. The deck was deserted, the sky navy blue, the water black with white riffs of foam, touched by the moon. She planted her feet, leaned into the wind, and clutched the rail. Was this how you rode with it? Her short hair bristled like fur, the salt spray stung her eyes and soaked her clothes, but Connie could tell almost at once that Emmett Grey was right.

This *was* better.

Connie wanted to stay on the bow rail forever, but soon she was shivering with wet and cold. She turned to go below just as Pete and Polly's heads topped the stairs in the passage. They were deep in conversation, still, and Connie drew back, not wanting to interrupt. Pete walked Polly toward her stateroom door. It appeared to be locked. Polly rattled the handle and called Jackson's name. Connie retreated across the bow to the corridor along the far rail, and stopped in her tracks.

The back end of someone was slithering out of a stateroom window, three rooms down.

The back end was followed by the front end.

Madeline Cunningham.

Connie ducked out of sight and peered into the central passage. The door was just closing behind Polly, three rooms down.

Chapter
11

. . . came very near of going overboard . . .

Connie jumped out of bed at daybreak the next morning. She could tell by the tug at her feet that the sea hadn't quite subsided, but outside the porthole she could see the sky was still bright blue, with a peach-colored wash of sunrise along the horizon. She reached into her knapsack for her camera. She'd head straight for the deck and play tourist, catch a few shots of the day's first glimpse of sun. She groped in the bag. She picked it up and peered in.

The camera was gone.

Connie climbed to the deck thoughtfully, trying to remember if she'd left her camera anywhere else, but she was sure she hadn't taken it out yet at all. She hadn't exactly been in the mood to take pictures so far on this trip, and she was feeling less and less like it now.

She hit the deck expecting to be the first, to be alone, but not only had Pete beaten her to her spot, Libby Smith was beside him. As Connie made her way toward them, she caught snatches of their conversation.

"It was a gift," said Libby. "From my husband. He's . . . dead. If they'd stolen anything else I wouldn't mind a bit, but that watch means a great deal to me."

"I'm sorry," said Pete. "I think I understand what you feel. But I don't want you to expect anything. The odds of—"

"Try," said Libby Smith. "Just . . . please . . . try." She touched Pete's arm and left.

Connie joined Pete at the rail. "Hi."

Pete's face, cloudy before, got sunnier. "Hi!" He gave her a long look. "You look better."

"A lot better. The air helps. What was all that with Libby Smith? Her watch was stolen?"

Pete nodded. "Just about this time yesterday. She came out to watch the sunrise, left her cabin unlocked, went back and it was gone. Emmett Grey spoke to me about it and asked me to keep an eye out. Sort of on the sly. And Tweetie thinks someone stole twenty dollars."

"I left my cabin unlocked, too. My camera's gone. But that's not the worst news of the day." Connie figured bad news only smelled worse the longer it was left around, so she didn't stall. She told Pete about Madeline Cunningham crawling out of Jackson Beers's window the night before. She watched his face cloud over. He looked out to sea, turning his knuckles white on the rail, and then the storm broke.

"God*damn* him," said Pete. "That's it. That is *it*. No more Mister Nice Guy. I spent half the night talking to Polly, trying to figure out where the sister I knew had gone. We talked about everything. Mom. Dad. Factotum. Southport. The island. Being kids. Being adults. We talked about everything, everything except that turkey. I decided it was none of my business to throw stones. I decided she must know something about him that we don't, she must have some good reasons for wanting to spend the rest of her life with him. I figured the more I said about Jackson the more she'd dig in her heels. I laid off. But this does it. This is it. She's going to hear about this. And if she marries him after this she deserves to be miserable."

"This might not be the best time to discuss—"

"There is not going to be any discussion." Pete stormed away.

"Hey!" Connie scrambled after him. "Pete. It's six-thirty. Wait a minute, will you?" She tugged Pete into the lee of the wheelhouse. There was no one else around. "Let's think about this for a minute."

"I can't think, I'm so stinking—"

"So don't act until you can think."

Pete looked at her in surprise. As a matter of fact, Connie was a little surprised, too. *Don't act until you can think.* It was good. Damned good. Maybe she should listen to herself more often. Maybe she should have listened to herself a long time ago.

Pete inhaled and exhaled in one loud gust. "Okay. But what's wrong with that woman?"

"Oh, I don't know," said Connie. "I've been thinking about it. Maybe Polly's just—"

Pete shook his head. "Not Polly. I'm talking about that Cunningham woman."

Connie looked out to sea. "Oh, I bet there's no big

73

puzzle there. She's feeling lonely, shut out, disconnected from her husband, she tries to connect someplace else."

Now Pete looked out to sea, too. "Maybe her husband doesn't know how she feels," he said finally. "Or maybe he knows, but he just can't admit something's wrong. If she talked to him—"

"Yeah," said Connie. "Talking. The hard part."

Pete cleared his throat. "Is that Emmett up there in the wheelhouse? Maybe we should tell him about your camera."

It was as good an out as any. They climbed the ladder to the wheelhouse.

Both Emmett and Larry were in the wheelhouse, and Connie could see why. It was nice up there. *The Pequot* looked fresher from up there, the deck bigger, the few people stumbling onto it more congenial. Even the vast ocean beyond *The Pequot* seemed more picturesque, the sun softening the hard, gray water into a gentle silver-blue.

Connie told Emmett about her camera.

"That does it," said Emmett. "I'll speak to Aura, have her remind people to lock their doors."

"Without specifically mentioning any thefts?"

"I see no need for setting everyone off at this point. If the thief is frustrated by locked doors, that may be the end of it. What do you think, Pete?"

Pete shrugged, silent and dismal.

"Hey," said Emmett. "Don't worry about it. I told you before I don't expect you to come up with much."

"I'm not worried," said Pete. "At least not about that."

Emmett shot a look at Connie. "Tell me to butt out if you want to, Pete, but Polly's talked so much about you I feel I know you pretty well. You wouldn't be worrying about our friend Jackson Beers?"

Pete slumped against the wheelhouse door. "I'm that obvious?"

"You aren't, he is. He's hanging all over that Cunningham woman. Sam thinks it's because of him. He thinks Jackson's out to prove he's still got the right stuff, now that he knows an old boyfriend of Polly's is on board."

"I don't care why he's doing it. I don't even care *what* he's doing. If I trusted Polly to think straight I'd even thank him for showing her his true colors before they got married so she could dump him flat. But Polly's not going to dump him. She's going to marry this creep just to prove a point. Worse yet, she'll stick with him. She's that type. She'll blame herself for everything that goes wrong. And plenty will."

The pilothouse fell silent.

Connie squirmed. She knew Pete somehow felt responsible for Polly's attitude. So what to do? If Pete told Polly about Madeline Cunningham the odds were that Polly wouldn't believe him; even if she did believe him, she might decide to blame the messenger who brought the bad news. "I'm the one who saw Madeline coming out of Jackson's cabin," she said.

Emmett's eyebrows shot up.

"I think I should be the one to tell Polly about it," said Connie. She almost laughed. It sounded like she was fighting for the chance to drop the bomb on Polly. "I'll give her time to wake up. Then I'll talk to her. Not that it'll do any good. But let me give it one more try."

Pete and Emmett looked at Connie as if they both wanted to say something, but only Emmett did.

"Good luck," he said. "I wish you luck. We all love Polly."

Gradually the sea calmed, and it remained sunny. By ten o'clock the deck was crowded with passengers straining their eyes for whales, but they strained in vain. By eleven Tweetie Cunningham was just about beside herself between false alarms and a distracted Pete, Jenny Sears had reached a fevered pitch about the captain's disgusting penchant for implements of whale-murder, The Gigolo had given up on whales and was now training his eyes on two of the most faded flowers of the singles set, The Sourpuss was just as sour, The Bird Couple had sat down with *The Whalewatchers Handbook,* and Jackson Beers was talking refund. Since Madeline Cunningham appeared to hang on Jackson's every word, it wasn't too hard for Connie to cut Polly from the herd and steer her toward the cabin.

They sat on either end of the bed and Connie came straight out with it. Polly didn't seem too surprised at Connie's news, but then again, neither did she seem too angry, and that was what puzzled Connie.

"Polly, I'm getting the idea that you think by marrying Jackson you can change him."

"So what's wrong with that? I can help him. I can help him achieve his goals in life. Once he's more settled—"

Connie groaned. Pollyanna was at it again. "And what about *your* goals in life, Polly? What's going to happen to those? It's supposed to be a two-way street. Do you think Jackson's going to help you achieve your goals?"

"I don't have any goals," said Polly. "Other than getting married."

Getting married?

Connie bolted off the bed. She walked to the dresser and studied it until she could trust herself to turn around. "Getting married. Since when is getting married a goal? Getting married isn't something you aim at, getting married is something that happens after all the other conditions are in place. It's like . . . like catching chicken pox, or something."

Okay, so that didn't come out just right.

Polly snorted. "An apt analogy in your case."

"I mean it, dammit, Polly! What's the matter with you? You used to want to be things! What about that plan to become a reporter? What about that? Have you talked to Jackson about that?"

"So what are your big goals?" snapped Polly. "Painting shutters? Mowing lawns? I don't see you making any quantum leaps here. What's so important to you?"

It was a good question. A fair question. And, Connie was happy to realize, not a very hard one anymore. "Being me," she said. "And feeling okay about that. That's important to me."

Polly eyes widened. "That's it. Being you. That's all that's important to you?"

"There are other things."

"Like what? Taking people's garbage to the dump?"

"Okay, yes, Factotum is important to me. And your brother. Your brother is important to me."

"Hah! You've got a funny way of showing it, don't you? And what if you can't have both things together, did you ever think of that? What if you can't be okay as you and have my brother, too?"

"So maybe I can't," said Connie. "But the second one won't amount to much if I don't do the first one first."

Polly stared at Connie for a long time. "Okay, okay. Great speech. Now let's see you put your money where your mouth is. Tell Pete what you just told me. Tell him how important he is to you."

Connie stood up. "Point taken. And you? What are you going to tell Jackson?"

"Who knows. But I do know we can't do any worse than the two of you."

I was wrong before, thought Connie. Polly's plenty angry, she just isn't angry at the right person.

Yet.

Chapter
12

*Raised whales . . . the first of the season . . .
very fine and pleasant weather.*

Pete didn't see Polly until dinner. At the table he
watched her. Something was different, but what? He
wanted to talk to her, but not there. He also didn't
want to talk to Madeline Cunningham, who was
seated on his other side. But Tweetie and Connie,
across the table from him, were engaged in a long
discourse with Stephanie Schrock about the absence
of whales on the trip, and Jenny Sears was carrying on
about Emmett's harpoon again. Even Pete's conversational standby, Janine Moss, had been replaced by a
cruise attendant named Heather Seasons. Heather
was young, surely less than twenty, even though her
short, blunt hair was solid silver, and Heather was a
little too defiant with things like hot coffee and sharp

knives for Pete to feel safe in prolonging conversation. That left only Jackson Beers nearby. After a half-second of indecision, Pete opted for Madeline. "Did Tweetie find her money?"

"No. Of course I had no idea she even had twenty dollars. Her father doesn't feel obligated to share these little details with me. If I'd known, I'd have made sure it was kept in a safer place. I'm sure she just dropped it somewhere, but she continues to insist it was stolen. As if anyone on this boat would take money from an eight-year-old child. Although there are a few people I've noticed who don't seem to be quite all there, if you know what I mean." Madeline jerked her head in the direction of The Sourpuss.

Pete decided that for now this was sufficient investigating of Tweetie's missing twenty. Besides, he'd just picked up on something Polly was saying on the other side of him.

"Yes, I've decided to go back to school. I'm going to become a journalist."

Pete, Connie, and Jackson all looked up in surprise. Pete and Connie held their tongues.

Jackson didn't. "And whose bright idea was this?"

Polly speared three carrots and chewed them. "We talked about this a month ago, if you recall. We discussed my going back to school."

"And I told you I thought very little of the idea, I believe?"

"You may have told me you thought very little of the idea, but that doesn't automatically eradicate the idea, now does it, Jackson?"

Connie and Pete looked at each other across the table.

"I'd say that if you're expecting me to foot the bill it pretty much eradicates the idea, my sweet. What do you have in the bank right now, thirty-eight dollars and seventy-two cents? Of course you could hock your engagement ring. That would pay for a semester or two." Jackson smiled, but not at his fiancée. Pete followed Jackson's gaze and concluded that it landed in the general vicinity of Madeline Cunningham.

Polly must have concluded the same thing. She stood up, wiped her mouth with her napkin, yanked off her engagement ring, and handed it to Pete. "Here," she said. "Your aim's pretty good. *You* throw it in his face." She strolled out of the room.

It took Pete a second. Then he pushed the ring across the table at Jackson, kicked back his chair, and followed Polly out.

Connie was right behind him.

"What the hell did you say to her?" he asked over his shoulder.

"Nothing. At least I didn't think it did anything. I asked her what her goals were. I asked her if she thought Jackson would help her meet them, stuff like that."

"Well, whatever you said, it appears to have been enough. God, I'm almost afraid to believe it. Now we just want to make sure she doesn't pitch herself over the side."

They charged down the passageway to Polly's cabin. Pete rattled the door.

"Go away, Pete."

Pete looked at Connie.

"Polly?" Connie called.

"Go away, Connie. Jeeze, you're as bad as he is!"

"Polly," said Pete.

"Pete," said Polly. She sounded like she was laughing. She opened the door. She was laughing. Sort of. "I'm all right, okay? I know you won't believe me until you see me, so here I am. Okay? Boy, that felt good. Now if you don't mind, I'd like to lock myself away and revel in my own glory for an hour or two."

"But what about—" Pete looked behind Polly at the bed.

"What's the matter, don't you think he can find accommodations elsewhere?"

Pete was only afraid he wouldn't *have* to find accommodations elsewhere.

Polly looked at Pete and laughed. "Trust me, all right? Now good night." She shut the door.

"She's all right," said Connie.

"I think so," said Pete.

Instinctively they turned together for the solitude of the bow.

"Thank you," said Pete. "For whatever you did."

"I'm not so sure I did anything," said Connie. "Actually, she did something for me, I think."

"What do you mean?"

They had reached the bow. Connie turned around and faced Pete squarely. "She told me I should tell you something and she was right. I . . . give me a minute, here."

Pete waited.

Too long.

Emmett Grey appeared behind them. "Is Polly all right?"

"I think so," said Pete. "Thank you." He said nothing more.

Emmett didn't take the hint. "Sam's just about throwing a party up there in the wheelhouse. He heard what happened and raced up to spill the beans."

"Great," said Pete. But right now Polly and Jackson and Sam and the rest of the world were of no interest to him. *The Pequot Princess* loped through the gentle waves and Connie's gone-to-seed-dandelion head was flame-tipped from the last of the sun. Her sea green eyes turned toward him full of torment and . . . and . . .

"Emmett," said Pete. "Do me a favor and—"

"Look," said Emmett softly. "Whales."

It figured.

Whales.

Pete peered out over the gilded water and saw a rubbery-looking island rise, a black triangular fin appear, a huge tail flip into the air and disappear.

"Wow," said Connie softly.

"That's a humpback," said Brady Pearson, materializing beside them. "See the dorsal fin? And look over there. Two more."

"That's how you tell a humpback?" asked Connie. "They have that fin in the middle of their back?"

"The dorsal fin is not unique to the humpback," said Brady. "But see how it appears to sit on a hump? They arch their backs and raise those long white flippers when they dive. And its blow is short and bushy. Look, over there."

In the distance, what looked like a cloud of steam shot into the air. Pete supposed he would call it a short and bushy cloud of steam, but then again, he didn't have much to compare it to.

Pete turned to see if Connie had spotted the blow, but all of a sudden it was as if there had been a newscast. Every inch of deck around him was swarming with whalewatchers, the air was full of pointing fingers and indrawn breaths, and he couldn't see Connie anywhere.

The man at the wheel, presumably Larry, didn't crowd the whales. Pete could feel the engines cut down to nothing; *The Pequot* sat back and lolled.

And so did the whales.

Like dancers in an underwater ballet one black back after another rolled over the surface and slid below with a farewell flick of the tail, only to reappear a few yards farther on. Was he seeing the same three whales over and over again, or was there a whole platoon of them down there? "How many are there?" Pete asked Brady.

"Six. No, seven. That's Ruffles coming up right there. See the ragged edges on her tail? And there's Stripe. She's named after that scar from a line entanglement."

Pete didn't see any ruffles. He didn't see any stripe either. "I don't—"

"Here." Brady handed him his binoculars. Pete raised them. A huge nose and lips covered with what looked like warts leaped out at him, and suddenly Pete and Ruffles (or was it Stripe?) were eye to eye. Pete stepped back and almost dropped the binoculars.

"Beautiful, aren't they?" said Brady.

"Yes," said Pete.

Warts and all, they were.

Brady reclaimed the binoculars and peered out to sea, his body straining against the rail as if every inch closer meant another secret unraveled. "I haven't seen Stripe in two years," he said. "I'm glad she's all right." He pulled out a notebook, wrote something down and sighed. "It's like sending your kid off to college. They go north for the summer, and then in the winter they go south. Like spring break. So much can happen to them. They get tangled in fishing gear. They get hit by boats. Their food source gets fished out or killed off by pollution. *They* get killed off by pollution. They—"

Brady's voice trailed off, but the air hummed with the voices of the other passengers. *Over there . . . no, here . . . fifty feet, at least . . . teeth . . . they don't have teeth . . . God, did you see that tail . . .* Pete listened for one voice in particular, but he didn't hear it.

Someone yanked at his sleeve. Tweetie, at least, had managed to tunnel through the crowd and squeeze next to Pete at the rail. "Do you see them? Do you see them?"

"I see them."

Tweetie leaped toward the rail and Pete lunged after her. He looked around frantically for her mother. He saw The Bird Couple, guidebook forgotten, leaning against the rail. He saw The Gigolo, intent now on nothing but the creatures from the sea, and Mr. Mutual Funds, without an audience, finally silenced, but Madeline Cunningham was not to be found.

Neither was Connie.

But Brady Pearson was still with them. "They're starting to dive," he said. "They won't come up for a long time. When they do, they'll be miles away. Here, Tweetie, take a look." He hung his binoculars around Tweetie's neck. Was he out of his mind? He turned away to answer a question from one of the singles set about the gulp-feeding methods of humpback whales, and Tweetie and the binoculars were left to Pete. He grabbed Tweetie's shoulder with one hand, the strap of the binoculars with the other, and turned to look again for Connie.

"Stop jiggling," said Tweetie.

"Stop jumping," said Pete.

"You sure are cranky," said Tweetie.

Yes, he was.

The whales were leaving, and Connie was gone.

Chapter
13

A few evenings after we sailed, I was suddenly startled, by a most tremendous crash upon deck.

It hardly seemed possible that breakfast could be worse than dinner. Connie had peeked out of her porthole at daybreak and had seen the sea so still it seemed ominous. How could there be no wind, no waves at all? She showered, dressed, opened her door, and saw Jackson Beers coming out of Madeline Cunningham's cabin.

She went back to bed for an hour.

When Connie finally struggled into the dining room she was the last one to arrive. She looked around for Pete, and was dismayed to see him at the table with Jackson Beers and the Cunninghams again. Polly was nowhere in sight. Connie gave a moment's thought to sitting with her back to them at the crew table, but the only empty chair was the one next to that sack of inertia, Larry Morant. Instead, Connie opted for a seat across and down one from Pete.

This morning their table was served, not by the efficient Janine Moss or the slapdash Heather Seasons, but by the third cruise attendant, Gilby Peebles. What was this, whoever drew short straw got Jackson? Or had Janine and Heather ganged up on Gilby and told him if they had to serve Jackson Beers one more time, they were swimming home?

Gilby Peebles was young and clean-cut and looked like he might run for office some day. Apparently he didn't plan to start then, not with Jackson's vote, anyway. "Eggs," he announced and slapped the plate in front of him. Jackson examined the plate critically, but by the time he looked up, Gilby was gone.

Pete seemed out of sorts. It made Connie nervous. Last night she had felt so close to it, so close to finally saying whatever that thing was that still needed saying between them. What happened? The whales? Tweetie? The look in Pete's eye? Whatever it was, it had driven every thought out of her head and into the foam. She'd been separated from Pete in the crowd, and the odds of her catching him without Tweetie in the next couple of hours had seemed slim. Connie was damned if she was going to fight an eight-year-old for him. Her determination had drained away. She had watched the whales in quiet wonder, and had gone to bed alone.

Connie snapped out of her reverie as Brady Pearson stood up.

"Excuse me, please, I have a brief announcement. At two o'clock, for those of you who are interested, Stephanie Schrock, our resident naturalist, will give a brief presentation in the Seaview Lounge on the underwater communication systems of whales. Once again that's at two o'clock today, in the Seaview Lounge." Brady Pearson sat down next to Stephanie Schrock. For some reason Stephanie looked annoyed. Conversation resumed, or, in the case of Jackson Beers, it kept on going.

"Of course she was in quite a mood," Jackson was saying to Pete. *"Quite* a mood. Hormones, that kind of thing. We go through this every now and then. Once a month, I'd say." He chuckled.

Connie watched Pete's eyes go from brown to black.

"But of course she came to her senses. As usual. No harm done." Jackson speared a runny egg. He didn't seem to notice Pete's face.

Or Madeline's.

"Put that down, Tweetie," she snapped. "You've had enough donuts."

"One more." Tweetie lunged for the plate. Madeline made a halfhearted grab for the donut and gave up.

"It's a common enough mistake," said Jackson. "Letting your children wear you down. Lazy parenting, I call it. Anyway, as I was saying, Pete——" He turned away from the murderous look in Madeline's eye. "We're back to status quo. The ring is back on, this journalism foolishness is off." Jackson chuckled. "I must say, Sam Lederman was surprised. He came by the cabin last night, to console the lonely lady, I suppose. He seemed quite shocked to find me there."

Madeline Cunningham threw her napkin into her orange juice, pushed back her chair, and ran from the room.

Pete followed suit.

Connie followed Pete. She was thinking of becoming a sprinter. She was getting to be pretty quick off the mark. She found Pete at Polly's door.

Polly looked terrible. She had only opened the door wide enough for her face to show, but the face was enough. It was blotchy red, with puffy eyes, mangled mouth, and runny nose.

"This is getting beyond the point of ridiculous," said Pete. He sounded furious.

"Go away," said Polly. "Leave me alone."

"Just tell me if what he said is true. Are you back with him or not? Just tell me that."

"Pete, I'm asking you. He's going to come back here any minute. Go away."

"Good! I'll talk to him. I'm not—"

Polly reached an arm around the door and grabbed Pete's wrist. "Don't do anything, Pete. Stay out of this. *Out.* You don't know him. You'll make it—"

There were steps in the corridor behind them.

Polly's face went white.

"Ah. The loving family come to call," said Jackson. "I assume you're all reveling in the good news?"

Connie saw Pete turn. She saw his face go a shade of red she'd never seen before. She saw his right foot move forward and felt the surge in his body. She grabbed his shoulder, but it was Polly's voice, not Connie's body, that stopped him.

"Pete. Don't be a fool."

Pete stopped as if Polly had hit him.

Polly reached for Jackson's arm and pulled him into the cabin. She was actually smiling at him. Then Polly turned and Connie caught a better look at her face.

Her mouth may have been smiling, but her eyes were full of hate.

* * *

Pete gripped the rail and stared at the deathly still ocean. There was so little air he could hardly breathe. His eyeballs burned. Every now and then he opened his mouth to say something to Connie, silent beside him, but nothing came out. Who knows how long he would have stood there in a dumb rage if Emmett Grey hadn't tapped him on the back.

"Got a minute?"

Pete turned around.

Emmett looked awful. His face looked puffy and his shirt wasn't tucked in right. "My cabin?"

Pete left Connie reluctantly and followed Emmett to his cabin. Emmett pushed open the door and pointed to the bare white wall over his bunk.

The harpoon was gone.

"What the—"

"I'm starting to get seriously concerned about this," said Emmett.

Pete stared at the empty hooks on Emmett's wall. "How could somebody walk off with two feet of iron? Wasn't the door locked?"

"No," said Emmett. "At least not while I was asleep."

"You were in here, asleep, when it was taken?"

Emmett nodded. "We'd finally found a few whales. Stephanie and Brady were feeling pretty good, I thought it might be an excellent opportunity to patch things up a bit. I arranged for Larry to carry on at the wheel. I grabbed a bottle out of the lounge and invited them in for a drink."

"In here." Pete looked around. Besides the bunk there were built-in wooden chests with cushioned tops along two of the walls. It looked comfortable enough.

"Yes," said Emmett. "I wanted to get the two of them alone. It went okay but not terrifically. Brady

90

pretty much gulped his drink and left, and the minute he was out the door Stephanie started in on him. I urged her to stay, thinking that if I worked on her first I could square Brady away later. Well, we got off the subject of Brady, finally, and I—" Emmett rubbed his head. "Stephanie finished her drink and left, and I was so beat I didn't get up again, not even to lock the door. When I woke this morning the harpoon was gone. Judging by the way my head feels, I think the guy lobotomized me with it on his way out."

Swell. A hungover captain. "So the harpoon was still here when Stephanie Schrock left. What time was that?"

"It was well after midnight. I don't know just when. And it was gone at six this morning."

So the harpoon was stolen sometime between midnight and six. Pete didn't figure there were going to be many witnesses roaming around then. "I just don't see what I can do about this, Emmett. I think you're going to have to search the place and find the harpoon. It's two feet long, it's not that easy to hide."

Emmett yawned. "Right. I just thought you ought to know. I don't suppose you've come up with anything interesting on the other thefts?"

Pete shook his head. He'd been preoccupied with other things. He hadn't had much time to think about Libby's watch, and he'd been inclined to agree with Madeline about Tweetie's twenty. But now?

"Right. Well, thanks anyway." Emmett wrestled his shirt into his pants, rubbed his head, and proceeded to the wheelhouse, leaving Pete's confidence in his captain badly shaken. Oh well, he thought. They were God knows where in the middle of the ocean. What could he possibly hit?

* * *

Pete was late for the lecture in the lounge. Actually, he hadn't felt like doing much of anything, and if Connie hadn't knocked on his door and half-dragged him out of his dumps, he probably wouldn't have bothered.

He would have been better off if she'd left him alone. It wasn't that Stephanie's speech wasn't interesting. She had drawn a good crowd that included all factions, and she managed to keep the pages in the guidebooks unturned, and most of the mouths shut. At another time, in another mood, Pete would have been spellbound by her tales of 150-foot blue whales, bigger than any dinosaur, singing to each other from continents apart. At the close she made what Pete thought was a very modest and tasteful mention of her forthcoming book on the subject, and asked for questions.

At once, Jackson Beers rose. "I presume you began this book before you found out about the navy?"

"The navy?"

"The navy. Surely you know that they've diverted their cold war underwater microphones from the Soviet subs and directed them toward the whales? Surely you know that in a single hour they can tap more whale sounds than you or any other whale researcher has ever tapped in the whole history of the study of whales? Wouldn't this make your information a bit obsolete?"

Stephanie Schrock didn't speak, but from where Pete was sitting it seemed that she began to . . . well . . . vibrate.

It was six-thirty, and the bow of *The Pequot* was bare as the passengers scattered to prepare for dinner.

Pete huddled in the wheelhouse with Emmett Grey, silent and glum. The ocean lay before them still as glass and glittering half-gold, half-silver in the late-day sun. Every now and then Emmett brought up the subject of the harpoon, or the money, or the watch, or the camera, but Pete didn't give him much of a response. Finally Emmett stopped talking altogether.

There was a scraping, scuffling sound on the roof. Something big and brown flew past the pilothouse window and landed with a thud on the deck below. Pete felt the tremor of it through his feet. For half a moment Pete and Emmett looked at each other. Then Emmett reached down and flicked a switch from a position marked "hand" to one marked "auto." They bolted out the door and down the ladder.

Jackson Beers lay on the deck. His head was thrown back, eyes and mouth open wide. His back was arched at an awkward angle, one leg bent under him, arms askew. Pete reached him first. He gripped Jackson by the shirt, intending to roll him off his leg, but it wasn't the leg that had contorted Jackson's torso.

About a foot of Emmett Grey's iron harpoon protruded from Jackson's back.

"Jesus," said Emmett. He grabbed the iron shaft and yanked. It took a couple of pulls. There was blood, but not as much as Pete expected. Emmett called Jackson's name.

Nothing.

Emmett put his hand on Jackson's chest, then he put his head there.

He straightened Jackson's neck, pinched his nose, and pressed his mouth over Jackson's.

Pete saw Jackson's chest rise and fall. He felt for the carotid artery. "I think there's something. Maybe. Not much."

Emmett slid around to Jackson's head while Pete felt along Jackson's chest until he located the proper area with an index finger. He flattened his other hand next to it and pressed down, elbows straight.

Pete's adrenaline must have kicked in. It seemed that even as he concentrated over Jackson he could see and hear everything going on around them at the same time. Others had arrived, probably drawn by the thud of Jackson hitting the deck. Someone screamed. Someone else cried, "Oh God!" It kept on, it seemed forever. "Oh, no, oh God." The air began to hum with the buzz that shock and fear generates.

Pete finished fifteen chest compressions and nodded to Emmett. Emmett breathed into Jackson. Two breaths. Fifteen more compressions. Two breaths.

Pete felt Jackson's neck again. This time he looked at Emmett and shook his head. He heard the now-familiar sound of someone vomiting. The crowd noise increased to a dull roar, and as the news spread, there were frightened exclamations, more shrieks.

Emmett kept going.

So did Pete.

"Pete," Connie was beside him. "What can I—"

"These people. Keep them back. Where's Sam? Or Ned?"

Connie shook her head. She shooed the crowd back.

Pete felt for Jackson's pulse again. Still nothing.

It seemed to last forever. Pete checked the carotid pulse periodically, shaking his head each time. After an eternity Emmett sat back on his heels and said it.

"Dead."

Pete dropped his weary arms. His eyes met Connie's.

Then he looked across the dead body of Jackson Beers and saw his sister.

Chapter
14

Committed his body to the deep.

A stunned silence fell over the deck, or at least over most of it. Somewhere, someone was still sobbing. Emmett Grey straightened up and cleared his throat. "Please. Everyone return to your cabins."

There was a lot of murmuring, but not much movement.

"Please," said Emmett again. "Return to your cabins. We'll be communicating with each of you, but right now it's imperative that the deck be cleared."

The sobbing picked up steam. There was a wail or two, and then a voice that sounded like Mr. Mutual Funds. "What in the—"

"Now," Emmett snapped.

The sobbing stopped. The crowd began to move.

Emmett spotted Sam Lederman and Ned Tate and waved them over. He spoke to them quietly. The two of them hefted Jackson and carted him off. Emmett picked up the harpoon with a rag from his pocket and vaulted up the ladder to the wheelhouse.

Pete looked around. It seemed that every single passenger had been on the deck, but Pete concentrated on Polly. Connie was trying to lead her away, but Polly continued to stand and stare at the spot where Jackson had fallen. She wasn't crying. She wasn't shaking. She wasn't even particularly pale. She looked up and caught Pete watching her. She stared at him dully for a second or two, and then she laughed.

"If you could see your face," she said. "If you could only see your face!" She laughed again.

"Shock," said Emmett at Pete's elbow. "Give her a brandy. Here." He shoved a small silver key into Pete's hand. "Give her the good stuff. Behind the bar on the right."

Pete crossed to Polly and took her other arm. He and Connie herded her into the lounge.

Pete slid behind the bar, looking for Emmett's liquor cabinet. He found it right where Emmett said he would—behind the bar, to the right. The silver key worked—inside Pete found not only good brandy, but Napoleon brandy, a pristine bottle, unopened. He cracked the seal, poured a healthy swallow into a snifter, and shoved it in front of Polly.

"Is this the wake?" she asked. "Rather a small turnout, wouldn't you say?" She tossed down the brandy and raised her glass in the air. It looked like a toast.

Pete shot a look at Connie.

"Get me one of those," said Connie.

"Yeah," said Polly. "This is a wake. Pour 'em out, Pete."

Pete took down one more glass and poured a dollop into it. He needed Connie with her wits about her. But Polly took the bottle from him and generously topped off both glasses.

"We've come to bury Caesar, I take it, not to praise him?" Polly raised her glass again, then seemed to see it up there in the air for the first time. She dropped her hand to the bar. "It looked awful, didn't it?" she said. "That harpoon in his back?"

Pete and Connie said nothing.

"Did the harpoon kill him? Or was it the fall?"

"I don't know," said Pete. "I'm pretty sure there was a pulse at first. Not much of one, but a pulse."

"He died before our very eyes, then," said Polly. "Just think of that." She drained the brandy and played with the empty glass for a second or two. "And you tried to save him, Pete. Just think of that."

Pete shot Connie a desperate look.

Connie looked helplessly back.

"Polly," said Pete. "I'm sorry about this. You know that."

"I know," said Polly. "I could see your dismay the minute you looked up from his dead body." Polly laughed loudly, just as Emmett Grey walked into the lounge.

Polly's laugh cost Emmett a step, but he recovered well. He continued on to Polly, put his arm around her and kissed the top of her head. Was it just Pete, or was everything off today? It could have been a kiss of condolence, sure, but it could equally have been one of congratulations.

"I've asked the chef to set up a quick buffet in the dining room. Polly, if you'd rather not face the hoard, he can send something up to you."

"Yes," she said. "Thank you." Either the brandy or Emmett seemed to have suddenly deflated her. She slid off her stool and started for the door. "I think I'll go to my room now."

"Wait," said Pete, starting around the bar.

"I'll go with you," said Connie.

"No," said Polly. "Please. I . . . for now, I think . . . alone."

Pete and Connie looked at each other.

"She wants to be alone, I'd let her be alone," said Emmett.

Polly smiled gratefully at Emmett and left, alone.

Pete moved the glasses around on the bar.

"Pete, I know this is no time to pester you," said Emmett. "And I'm sorry. But I need your help again."

"What do you mean 'again'? I haven't exactly cleared up those thefts."

Emmett shook his head. "I've got a few more important things than the thefts to deal with now. The radios are out."

"What?"

"Both of them. And the ship-to-shore phone. Someone's ripped out the wires."

"But why?" asked Connie.

"I don't know," said Emmett. "All I can do is guess. Without the radio I can't reach the Coast Guard. I can't tell anyone what happened to Jackson. Someone wants to buy some time, I'd guess. That's where you come in, Pete."

Pete and Connie looked at each other again.

"I'd like to cover what bases I can. I've instructed everyone to stay off the roof, I've wrapped up the harpoon, I've taken care of the body. I'd like you to begin a systematic questioning of each person on board. To the best of my knowledge Jackson was killed at approximately six-forty-two. Who was where at six-forty-two tonight? Who saw what when? Someone should document everything for the police. What's occurred. When it occurred. What everyone saw. Where everyone was, while it's still fresh in their minds. As captain of *The Pequot* I'm authorizing you, Pete. Hiring Factotum. Person employed to do all kinds of work."

Pete shook his head. "No way, Emmett. This is my sister's fiancé who bought it, in case you forgot. I've got a few more things to worry about than documenting this for the police. Do you know how many people there are on board? Do you have any idea how long something like that would take?"

"That's exactly my point. And I've got bigger problems to deal with, as you know. And since you're the only one who has an alibi right now—"

"What alibi?"

"You were with me, remember?"

Pete stared at Emmett. "I hope this is a joke."

"No joke, Pete. No joke."

"So hit a port. Any port. A couple hours one way or the other won't—"

"I see you haven't noticed," said Emmett.

"Noticed what? Jesus Christ, if you—"

"The ship," said Connie.

"Exactly," said Emmett.

"The ship *what?*" snapped Pete. But then he felt it. And heard it. The wallowing. The silence.

"We're not going anywhere," said Emmett. "Not for a while. Someone's ripped up the oil and fuel hoses, too. And just as an afterthought, I might add that the emergency flares are missing from the bridge and both lifeboats. The EPIRB is gone, too."

"The what?"

"Emergency position-indicating radio beacon. A nifty little device that signals the location of our craft to any rescue personnel. So you can see that I need you, Pete. We were due back in Southport in three days, and I assume that if we don't show up they'll come looking, but until then, who knows how long we'll be drifting out here? I need you, right now, this minute in fact, to start some cabin-to-cabin interviews. I've asked everyone to assemble briefly in the dining room for the buffet. I'd like you to go with me. I'll make an announcement that you've been hired to do some documentation for the police. After the meal I'll ask them to return to their cabins, and you can begin."

"And what will you and the rest of the crew be doing? I still don't see where I—"

"What will we be doing? The radios, Pete, remember? The engine hoses? Add to that the job of appeasing a boatload of angry and frightened passengers. That should keep us busy enough."

Pete groaned. "I need to talk to my sister."

"Fine." Emmett reached into his pocket and handed Pete a notebook and pen, along with a long and level look. "I suggest you record everyone's activities between the hours of five and seven. It's reasonable that you'd want to start with Polly."

Pete's hand froze halfway to Emmett's book and pen.

Start with Polly?

"I think it would mean a lot to Polly if she knew that you were helping with this," said Connie.

Pete looked at her in surprise.

"So is it a deal?" asked Emmett.

Pete felt a gentle palm come to rest in the middle of his back. "It won't be so bad," said Connie. "Start with me. Ask me where I was this afternoon between, say, five and seven."

"I don't—"

"Okay, I'll tell you. Polly and I were in her cabin. The whole time. And neither of us saw anything. See how easy it is? So write that down." Connie took the notebook from Pete and opened it.

"There you are," said Emmett, sounding relieved. "Polly and Connie accounted for. And Connie can help you, can't you, Connie? You're part of Factotum, right? What do you say?"

The only time Pete had heard an idea as rotten as this was when Polly asked him to go on this trip in the first place. But Connie was watching him, and he could tell that for some reason she was willing him to say yes. "Oh, all right."

Emmett sighed. "Good. I'm going to the dining room now, and I'd appreciate it if you'd join me as soon as you can." He preceded them from the lounge.

For some seconds neither Pete nor Connie spoke.

"Polly," said Pete, finally. "I don't care what Emmett says, I don't feel right about leaving Polly alone. Would you check on her?"

Connie nodded.

Pete followed Emmett out of the lounge.

* * *

"Hey," Pete said to Emmett, just outside the dining room door. "What did you mean, you've taken care of the body?"

"We committed him to the deep."

"What? You can't—"

"The deep freezer."

Pete groaned.

Chapter
15

Cannot get into the harbor tonight.

The dining room was a den of anarchy. White faces, red faces, shaking voices, vigorous voices, all competed with each other for breathing space, air time. Only The Sourpuss seemed oblivious, or if not oblivious, at least changed. He stood alone, an island in a sea of angry faces, beaming incongruously, suddenly A Happy Man.

Emmett Grey got two hands in the air and raised his voice, he was finally able to pierce the tumult enough to quiet it down. But before he could begin his speech, Mr. Mutual Funds jumped into the lull Emmett had provided him.

"We'd like to know what in tarnation's going on around here!"

"And that's why I'm here," said Emmett calmly. "To explain what's going on, as least as far as I am able. At this time, this is what we know: Jackson Beers, a passenger on this ship, was killed either from a wound incurred by an antique whaling harpoon, or from the fall resulting thereof, at approximately six-forty-two this evening." Emmett slid an eye toward Pete. Was Emmett *enjoying* this? "I'm afraid we have no more information about this unfortunate incident at this time, but I assure you an investigation is already underway. We are most fortunate to have with us on this trip a person who has worked extensively with the police in similar matters." Emmett waved a hand at Pete. Pete could have killed him. "Peter Bartholomew will be in charge of sorting out what facts we have. He will also be in charge of collecting any additional information as he sees fit. He will be speaking with each of you shortly. You are all, in effect, witnesses of sorts, and Pete's intention in speaking with you will be to find out where you were and what you may have seen during the period in question. I would appreciate, and he would appreciate, your full cooperation."

"That's it?" yelled Mr. Mutual Funds. "And what's that supposed to mean, 'worked extensively with the police in similar matters'? Is this man a policeman or not?"

"No," said Pete. "I'm not. I've been hired by the captain to ask some questions. That's all."

"Well, you can ask somebody else your bloody questions, I'm not talking to anyone but the police. When are we hitting port? Or are they flying out? I want to know the timetable, here!"

"I was coming to that," said Emmett.

Pete wondered if he was. From where he was standing he could see Emmett's Adam's apple bob up and down. "We appear to have a small problem with a fuel line."

Immediately cries and murmurs and exclamations swooped around the room, rising and falling like a roller coaster.

"What!"

"What does he mean?"

"A fuel line?"

"We're not moving."

"I *told* you we weren't moving."

"Are we going to explode?"

There were several gasps.

Emmett raised his hands again. "Please! Please. Everyone. Quiet down. There is no danger. *No danger,* is that clear? I told you I would tell you what I know and if you'll allow me, I would like to do that now."

Pete had to admit that the captain had a certain something. Slowly the crowd settled down.

"There is no leaking fuel. There is a damaged fuel line, and as I told you, it is presently undergoing the necessary repairs. I anticipate our delay to be brief, but since I cannot say for certain how long it will be, I don't want to promise you that we will be under way at any specific time."

"I have a meeting first thing Monday morning!" hollered Mr. Mutual Funds, and that started everyone up again.

"Monday!"

"We're stuck out here till Monday?"

"I have to get home!"

"I have three cats!"

"Who cares about cats? We're stuck in the middle of nowhere with a killer!"

"Call the Coast Guard. What do we pay them for, anyway?"

The call swept the room like wildfire.

"Coast Guard!"

"They're calling the Coast Guard."

"Thank God, they're calling the Coast Guard!"

Pete watched Emmett. He could see him debating whether to leave them with the lie, but when he raised his hands for the third time, Pete had a feeling that truth would out.

"You've all heard the expression that bad things come in threes," said Emmett. "Unfortunately, we have a third small problem."

Silence fell.

"The radio cable. I'm afraid the radio is also temporarily malfunctioning. I am unable, at present, to call the Coast Guard. Or anyone. I assure you every effort is being made to—"

"No radio!"

"They can't call the Coast Guard!"

"No Coast Guard?"

"What about flares? Don't you have flares? Shoot off some flares!"

Emmett's nerve seemed to fail him at the thought of admitting to a fourth disaster. He kept silent. Thank God nobody among the passengers seemed to know what an EPIRB was.

"I anticipate that the radio and fuel hose will be working in short order. But it is on account of these temporary delays that I have authorized Pete to compile some information while it's fresh in your minds. To that end, I must ask that after you finish your meal you return to your cabins, and Pete will speak to each of you there. Thank you."

Emmett clapped a hand onto Pete's shoulder and steered him out of the room.

Behind them, the noise in the dining room grew from a dull roar to a din.

Pete didn't consciously head for the spot Jackson had fallen from, but that's where he ended up. He walked around to the lee of the wheelhouse, found the ladder that led to its roof, and climbed up. It was the highest spot on *The Pequot*.

As Sam Lederman had told Jackson, the top of the wheelhouse was off-limits except for crew. Pete had never seen anyone up there, but the narrow ladder was in plain sight, behind the wheelhouse, and anyone could have decided to climb it. Jackson had, obviously, and just as obviously, someone else had seen him and followed. Or maybe Jackson had been brought to the roof by someone, someone with murder in mind. Pete imagined the various excuses that might have convinced Jackson to climb the ladder to the roof. Immediately behind the enclosed area were several sturdy-looking antennae and the radar tube, and at the extreme rear, the lifeboats. As Jackson had indicated, it would be an ideal spot to watch for whales, and the various equipment up there might have attracted someone like Jackson who seemed to need to know everything about everything so that he could find fault with it all.

Pete looked down. From the roof to the deck where Jackson had fallen it was just about a two-story drop. The fall could certainly have killed him if he landed just right. Or just wrong. But did it matter? Jackson would never have fallen without the help of that harpoon.

How many of the passengers might have come up here to look for whales? Pete wondered. Not many on the rough days, but today had been clear and calm. The ladder to the wheelhouse roof ran up behind the wheelhouse. He and Emmett, inside the wheelhouse, would have seen nothing, but what exactly had they heard? Pete tried to recall something more distinct than the vague scuffling sounds he'd heard just before Jackson's fall, but he had been so lost in his own misery he had paid little attention to the outside world.

And Emmett Grey had been hungover.

Swell.

Pete walked around the perimeter of the wheelhouse roof. Below him he saw the lifeboats on the roof over the staterooms, but no one walking along the rail from bow to stern could see the wheelhouse roof. No one standing at the distant stern could see it. He descended the ladder to the stateroom roofs where the lifeboats were. Only a person on the bow could have seen the wheelhouse roof from below, and when Jackson fell, the bow had been empty. It had been six-thirty, almost dinnertime, and everyone had gone to their rooms to change. Perfect timing.

But just to be sure of his facts, Pete went down the ladder and circumnavigated the ship's deck below. He had been right. The wheelhouse roof was invisible from all locations except the bow.

Pete hung a left into the portside corridor and knocked on Polly's door.

Connie opened it.

Polly was lying on her bed, staring at the ceiling. "Connie says you have a job," she said.

"It's your fault," said Pete. "If you hadn't gone blabbing to Emmett about Factotum and all those murders on Nashtoba, he never would have picked on me."

There was no response from the bed.

Pete looked at Connie. She jerked her head toward the door and pointed to herself. *Go?* Pete shook his head desperately. *No.* He sat down on the corner of the bed.

"So you're here to take my statement?"

"No, I'm not," said Pete. "And I don't have to take this job if you don't want me to."

"Hell, why not?" said Polly. "Besides, Connie told me my whereabouts are already accounted for."

"Yes," said Pete.

Polly raised her head and looked at him.

"I think I'll go," said Connie.

Pete gave Connie one last fleeting look, but she didn't see it. She was already gone. The minute the door latched behind her Polly sat upright. "He's dead," she said. "Can you believe it? He's *dead.* It's so easy, isn't it? Just like that. This morning I was engaged to him, and now—"

Pete waited, bracing himself for the tears that were sure to come.

Polly's mouth quivered, her lips parted, and she laughed.

Again.

Chapter
16

Our ship lay some distance of the shore . . .

Janine Moss arrived with Polly's dinner and Polly shooed Pete out. Not that he wasn't happy to go. He couldn't seem to say anything right to Polly these days. Was it his fault, or hers?

Outside Polly's cabin, Pete turned left. He didn't want to think about Polly. He had long ago learned that for him the best antidote to thinking was working, and as luck would have it, he now had plenty of work to do. The passengers were waiting. Pete decided to start where he was, next door to Polly's cabin. Libby Smith.

Pete was surprised to see that Libby Smith's cabin was the duplicate of Polly's luxurious accommodations, complete with double bed. She must have liked her space. She stood square and trim, with her back to her stateroom window, hands folded in front of her, looking surprisingly unrattled by the prospect of a murderer on board. Pete sat on the corner of her bed with his pad on his knee.

"And how did you land this despicable job?" she asked Pete.

"I have a sister with a big mouth. I accidentally got involved in a few crimes back on Nashtoba and Polly seems to have convinced the captain that this makes me the man for the job."

"This Factotum. You do this alone?"

Pete shook his head. "Connie's in it with me. There are two others back home."

Libby Smith looked puzzled. "Connie? You mean your—"

"Ex-wife. Yes." Pete was used to feeling foolish every time this subject came up, but this time he felt something else besides foolish. He had temporarily forgotten that Connie *was* in it with him, and now he felt . . . what?

Less at sea.

Pete cleared his throat. "As to the events of earlier this evening, I need to log your whereabouts, and what, if anything, you might have seen."

"My whereabouts were here. In this room. From three o'clock on."

"Alone?"

"Alone." She smiled at him, crisp and clean. "But thank you for asking. You may have noticed I'm not much at mixing."

"I haven't noticed that at all," said Pete. "I think you could, and do. When you want to."

"Ah. Yes. When I want to." Libby Smith crossed to the bed and sat down. She sat much the way she stood—ankles together, canvas shoes even at the toes, crisp, unfaded denim skirt anchored at the knees with her hands. "I'm a very private person," she said. "Too private, I suppose. Does it seem odd to you, someone that private on a trip like this?"

"Yes," said Pete.

Libby smiled. "Yes. It does to me, too. I do this as an exercise. My husband and I—" She stopped and straightened her already straight skirt. "We stuck to ourselves, my husband and I. Out in the woods, away from everyone, on our little pond. It was enough for us. It was more than enough. And it was more than most people ever get. But then he died."

Pete said nothing.

"Oh, I was lost. *Lost.* The first time I did it, it took every bit of strength I had to finally drive down that long road and up to the dock and sign on this boat. I knew if I came on a cruise I'd have to talk to people, you see."

Pete smiled at her. "Good thinking."

"Yes, it was." Libby Smith sounded proud of herself. "But I can only pull it off for so long. Then my resolve leaves me. That's when I retreat to my cabin to hide."

"Like today?"

"Like today. And many other days. And many trips before this one. And when I finally get home, what a joy to see my lonely woods and still pond and empty house! I crawl back into myself again, and stay there until I know it's time to crawl back out again, or—"

"Or what?"

"Or die." Libby Smith stood up and strode to the window. You actually could stride in this cabin. "So there you have my life story. With one difference. This time when I go home I won't be crawling into my shell. I've decided to donate our woods to the conservation trust, to turn the beach on the pond into a park in my husband's name. When I go home I'll have work to do this time, and maybe the next time I come home from one of these trips they'll be people around, enjoying my husband's gift to them, enjoying our woods and pond."

"On jet skis?"

"No," said Libby Smith. It was one gentle word, but it carried all the strength of steel. She turned around. "So! Enough of all that. I don't suppose you've found my watch?"

Pete had all but forgotten about the watch. "No. I'm sorry."

"Oh." Libby Smith seemed to lose interest in further talk. "Is there anything else?"

Pete considered. Libby Smith's cabin was almost below the lifeboats. "Did you hear anything unusual while you were in here this afternoon?"

Libby Smith shook her head. "I don't recall hearing anything out of the ordinary until . . . until all the commotion outside. When he . . . died."

"And then you came out of your cabin?"

"Yes. Then I came out, and went on deck with everyone else."

"Did you see anyone in this corridor?"

"Yes, I did. That very unique young lady, Jenny Sears, was talking to Mr. Pearson at the door to his cabin. I remember noticing her in particular, because when I came up to my room at three, she was just going in."

"Into her room? Which one is hers?"

Libby Smith gave Pete a long, cool look. "I believe her cabin is on the other side. The cabin she was entering was Mr. Pearson's."

"I see," said Pete. He opened his notebook and wrote it down. Then he stood up.

"Before you go," said Libby, "how is your sister?"

"Oh," said Pete, "I'm sure she'll do okay."

Libby removed a piece of lint from her sweater and smiled, but whether the smile was over the report on Polly or the successful removal of the lint, Pete couldn't say.

Brady Pearson's cabin was next in the row, but Pete hesitated in front of it. What exactly had Emmett said? Was he to interrogate only the passengers? And would the scientist be considered a passenger, or a member of the crew? Pete decided to speak with Brady anyway. Libby Smith had raised a few questions Pete would like to have answered.

Brady's cabin may have been in the same row as the classy ones, but it didn't fall under the category of "stateroom," by any means. It was much smaller, lit only by a porthole, and situated so far aft as to run afoul of the diesel fumes. Above the cabin was the lifeboat area. A visibly shaken Brady Pearson opened his cabin door to Pete's knock, and ushered him inside.

"We're still not moving," said Brady.

"No," said Pete. "I'm sure we will be shortly. A small problem with one of the hoses, I'm told."

"And the radios. And the phone."

"Yes," said Pete. "But I'm sure—"

"Do you have any idea where we are?" asked Brady in the kind of voice that caused Pete to marvel at, in hindsight, Libby Smith's calm.

"No, I don't know where we are," he answered, "but I assume it's the expected location."

"No, it isn't. Not unless we're chasing a couple of

right whales. We don't, as a rule, go farther than Billington Swell. We certainly never leave the Bank. Right now we're at least one hundred miles east of the Bank's northeast peak."

Wherever that was. And if they were one hundred miles east of the Bank's northeast peak, how far was that from Nashtoba? Something told Pete it was best not to ask. "I'm sure the hoses will be fixed soon," he said.

"Are you? And will that be before or after someone else gets killed?"

Pete decided to consider the question rhetorical. "You know why I'm here?"

Brady nodded. "You want to know where I was tonight, what I saw."

"Between five and seven."

Brady rubbed his forehead as if it ached. "I was here, in my cabin. Alone. When I opened the door to go to dinner around seven someone told me what happened. I went up on deck with everyone else. I don't know why. Instinct, I suppose. I saw nothing except . . . the body."

Pete wrote it down. "You say you were here alone?"

"Yes," said Brady.

"And who was it who told you what had happened?"

Brady Pearson rubbed his head again. "Who was it? Jenny Sears, I believe."

"And this was around seven?"

Brady nodded.

"You heard nothing before then? Nothing from up above?"

Brady shook his head. "Nothing. I heard nothing. I was working. I'm a bit oblivious when I'm working."

Pete looked in the direction of Brady's pointing

finger and saw sheafs of papers strewn over his bunk. "Do you use the top of the wheelhouse as a lookout for whales?"

Brady Pearson met Pete's eyes levelly. "Yes, I do. The scientists do."

"Meaning you and Stephanie Schrock?"

Brady hesitated, but said just as levelly, "Yes, Stephanie and I do."

"Anyone else?"

"I don't know. Although there was nothing posted, that area was intended to be essentially off-limits to the public."

"Jackson Beers?"

"I never saw Jackson Beers go up there, no."

Pete sighed. There were probably plenty of other questions to be asked, but he couldn't think of them. He had done what Emmett had asked. He had established where Brady was, established what he had seen, which certainly wasn't much. Now what?

Then Pete remembered the harpoon.

"The harpoon that killed Jackson Beers appears to have been missing from the captain's cabin since six or so this morning. The captain says you and he and Stephanie Schrock shared a drink there last night. Do you recall what time you left?"

"Fairly early. I don't know just what time. I believe Emmett had some sort of . . . diplomatic goal in mind. It seemed fairly clear to me early on that it was not going to be met."

Pete considered for a minute exactly how far his "job" should carry him into areas like this, but since Brady brought it up, Pete decided to pursue it. "Would you care to talk about that? Do I gather that things weren't just as they should be between you and Stephanie Schrock?"

Brady Pearson gave Pete a closer scrutiny, and then sighed. "All right. Here it is. Stephanie Schrock seems to feel, for reasons clear only to herself, that somehow or other I'm undermining this last-word-on-whale-speak book she's writing. She feels, mistakenly, I assure you, that grant monies have not been fairly apportioned in her favor, and she also feels that the Institute, and myself as one of the scientists at the Institute, should be plugging her book in a more substantial way. Further than that I would not wish to say. Only perhaps to add that I'm not the only one she feels is out to sabotage her, so to speak. She has a long list, and I'm sure Jackson Beers has a place on it."

"Because of his plans to sabotage the grant?"

Pete's question seemed to startle Brady. "I . . . no. That is, I really couldn't say. I was more inclined to consider what went on in the lounge today. Did you catch that remark by Beers about the navy?"

"I caught it, yes." Pete returned to last night. "So you left the captain's cabin when you saw that nothing was going to be gained?"

"I left the cabin after one drink. I'm not much of a drinker, and brandy in particular doesn't agree with me." Brady rubbed his head again. "I was extremely tired. But I might have lingered if I'd seen any point."

"And the harpoon was on the wall when you left?"

"The harpoon was on the wall when I left."

"About this harpoon. I take it you've been around Jenny Sears enough to gather she's not too crazy about Emmett's choice of decor."

Suddenly Brady Pearson looked uncomfortable. "Yes, I've gathered that."

"And what's your feeling on the matter?"

Brady coughed. "I try not to fault my ancestors

simply because they lacked the knowledge and sensitivity of the present."

"And did you tell Jenny Sears that?"

"Jenny Sears never asked me how I felt about Emmett's harpoon."

"She assumed she knew how you'd feel?"

Again, Brady seemed startled. "I don't know. We didn't discuss it."

"And you said the first person you saw this afternoon was Jenny Sears. This was at—" Pete fumbled for his notebook.

Brady took his time filling the gap. "Seven," he said. "Around seven."

"Okay," said Pete. "I guess that's it. I take it you scientists knew about Emmett's harpoon before last night?"

"Of course."

"And I assume the crew knew about it."

"I would assume."

"Would you care to hazard a guess as to how many passengers knew about it?"

Brady's strained face cracked open in a thin smile. "By the time Jenny Sears got through? All of them."

Stephanie Schrock's cabin sat back-to-back to Brady Pearson's, its mirror twin. Stephanie let Pete in, then stood facing him with legs apart and arms folded. Her face, previously tanned and chiseled, looked pale, but she was anything but subdued. In response to Pete's awkward introductory remarks she got straight to the point.

"I know, I know, I know. You have questions, and I'm supposed to answer them. And I have a few of my own. We have a maniac on board, is that it?"

Pete coughed. "I don't know what we've got on board. I've been sent here to ask questions, that's all."

"Right," said Stephanie. "So what do you want to know? I was in my cabin. I heard all the commotion. I went out on deck and there he was. Dead. Murdered. I suppose it has occurred to you that we're all trapped out here? With a killer? Has anyone told you, in your official capacity, just when we might expect to get moving again? I can't believe this. Although, why not? It's perfectly in keeping with everything else that's been going on. God, if I could have picked a worst-case scenario! So have they told you when we can expect to move?"

"No, they haven't," said Pete. He hurried on before Stephanie Schrock could start in on just how many miles away all the swells and peaks and banks . . . and islands . . . were. "When exactly was all this commotion you speak of? What exactly did you hear?"

"When was it? When he crashed onto the deck. I heard the crash, I heard doors, and people, and voices. The usual mass hysteria."

And yet Brady, next door, hard at work, had heard nothing?

"And how long were you in your cabin prior to all the noise?"

"Two hours, maybe. No, three. After the session in the lounge I'd had it with people. I wanted quiet, rest."

Pete didn't want to get into the session in the lounge, that was for sure. "Did you hear anything during that time? Anything above you, from the roof?"

Stephanie Schrock shook her head. "No murderers stomping around, if that's what you mean."

"Anything that sounded like someone messing with the lifeboats?"

Stephanie's eyes widened. "What's wrong with the lifeboats?"

"Nothing. The lifeboats are fine." Pete saw no need to add that the emergency flares weren't. "Now about Emmett's harpoon."

Stephanie seemed to catch sight of something out the porthole. She peered out it for some time.

"I understand you and Brady Pearson and Emmett Grey shared a drink last night in the captain's cabin."

Stephanie whipped around. "No one told me you were entitled to grill people on where they were last night, too."

"Not per se, no. But I understand you were the last to leave, and sometime after you left the captain's cabin, the harpoon, the murder weapon, was stolen. I need to—"

"The harpoon was on the wall when I left the captain's cabin. That's all I have to say." Stephanie looked out the porthole again.

"What time did you leave his cabin?"

"I have no idea. Now is that all?"

"Emmett said it was sometime after midnight, but—"

Stephanie spun around again. "Oh, he did? And whose story are you checking, his or mine?"

Oh, Pete was going to get Emmett for this! "Neither. Emmett was vague as to the time. I only want to narrow it down."

Vague. I'll bet he was vague! I'll tell you when I left. I left after he passed out."

Passed out? The captain of the ship, *passed out?*

"What time did—"

"Look. I told Emmett I'd stay for one quick drink. Some special French brandy he's supposed to use on traveling dignitaries or some such rot. He thought it was a big deal. It wasn't. I didn't even finish it. But Emmett had a couple, and I stayed while he had them. I was talking to him. I had a few things I wanted to say about what was going on around here. The next thing I know he's kilted up against the back of the bunk, snoring. I'm not used to being passed out on, all right? So I left."

"What time—"

"Is this really necessary? I don't know, all right? Twelve-thirty. All right, maybe closer to one o'clock. And the harpoon was *on the wall.*"

"Thank you," said Pete. "If you don't mind I have just one more question."

Stephanie Schrock looked like she minded plenty, but Pete sucked in some more oxygen and blundered on.

"Jenny Sears has made it pretty clear she doesn't care for the way the captain decided to decorate his cabin. How do you feel about it?"

"Feel about it? Emmett Grey's cabin? I assure you I'll never set foot in it again."

Pete winced. "I'm talking about the harpoon," said Pete. "Other than its particular location, did you object to the harpoon itself?"

"The harpoon? No. I don't waste my time getting worked up over things."

It was too good an opening to pass up. And besides, Pete felt it was only fair to give Stephanie Schrock the same amount of air time he'd given Brady Pearson. "But I gather an occasional person could get you worked up? Brady Pearson, for example? Apparently the captain had the two of you up to his cabin for a purpose."

Stephanie Schrock made no pretense of looking for things outside portholes this time. Her eyes drilled into Pete's as if she were mining for brain cells, but she appeared to come up empty. "A day may come when I'd feel comfortable discussing Brady Pearson with you," she said. "Right after your sex change operation, perhaps."

Pete coughed.

"Try walking a few million miles through man's turf in a woman's shoes. *High*-heeled shoes. Now are you quite through?"

Pete was through.

Thank God.

Chapter
17

Nothing worthy of note has transpired since my last date.

It took Pete all night to talk to the remaining passengers. He asked each of them where they were—in their cabins, mostly—and what they saw—nothing, mostly. The single set could tell him every detail of what clothes they were putting on, or taking off, and with whom. Some of the retirees, including Mr. Mutual Funds, were napping before dinner, but a small group had gathered in the Seaview Lounge. The Sourpuss's career as A Happy Man seemed to have been short-lived—he scowled and seemed unable, no matter how much Pete prodded, to remember where he'd been or what he'd been doing all day.

Pete's questions to each of the passengers took a few

minutes, at worst. It was all their questions, and suggestions, that took up all the time.

"I heard somebody else has been killed."

"I want a guard posted at my cabin."

"I need protection. I need a knife. They should hand out the knives from the kitchen."

"Haven't they fixed the fuel line yet?"

"Haven't they fixed the radio?"

"Why haven't they fired off the flares?"

"Who did you say you were, again?"

And, over and over again, "I hate to speak ill of the dead, but—"

No one had cared for Jackson Beers. Their reasons were varied, offered freely, and taken as a whole, all-encompassing. If Jackson had set out to make everyone hate him, he couldn't have done a more thorough job. In a million little ways he had set teeth on edge, people on edge. He had whispered about people. Out loud.

Jackson had expressed the opinion that one man's wife was dressed too provocatively for a happily married woman.

He had commented on a husband's roving eye.

He had engaged one of the fading flowers in a discussion on plastic surgery.

He had questioned a fifty-year-old about Medicare.

He had told most of the single young men that the deckhand, Ned Tate, was gay. He had complained about the food. He had told anyone who would listen that the ship was falling apart, the cruise attendants were sloppy, the cruise director was inept, the first mate had altered the course, and they were lost.

Everyone disliked Jackson.

Everyone had seen disaster coming a mile away.

It was just that nobody had seen it up close.

And Brady Pearson was right. Thanks to Jenny Sears, everyone knew about the harpoon on the captain's wall.

There was only one passenger who didn't answer Pete's knock, and that was Jenny Sears. There was only one door Pete couldn't bring himself to knock on, and that was Madeline Cunningham's. Pete was already sick of the job, and with each passing minute, he was getting more annoyed with Emmett. Besides, if there was one person he didn't want to talk to, it was Madeline Cunningham. He decided he needed a break. He headed for the stairs, retreated down his narrow corridor, walked up to Connie's cabin, and tapped on the door.

She opened it yawning and riling up her hair. "Good, it's you." She plunked down cross-legged on her bunk and backed up, making room for him.

Pete sat down facing her, cross-legged, too. He thought he'd come because he wanted to talk, but now that he was here he realized he just wanted to sit there.

"Any news on the engine? The radio?"

Pete shook his head.

"So what have you found out?"

"Nothing."

"Nothing?" she repeated.

"Nothing." He told Connie about all the nothings he'd found, but he left nothing out, not even Libby Smith's struggle with her grief. "She sure misses her husband," said Pete. "She was more worried about getting back the watch he gave her than she was about the murderer."

"So someone stole the harpoon after Emmett passed out, between one and six, you say."

"If Stephanie can be believed. Even if she can't,

Emmett was awake till midnight or so, and the harpoon was on the wall at least till then."

"Hmm," said Connie again.

Pete shifted on the bunk just as the boat rolled, and Connie pitched forward. Pete caught her. Suddenly Pete felt an old familiar sensation, as if the barometer had plunged. He could hear Connie breathing. He could *feel* her breathing.

She straightened up. "So," she said again, but differently this time. "Do you think those other thefts were just the lead-in to this one, to get everyone so used to theft that nobody would think it odd when the harpoon disappeared?"

Pete hadn't thought of that. He hadn't thought of much. He couldn't think so hot right now. "I don't know," he said. "Connie—"

"How about alibis?" asked Connie.

"A group of passengers were together in the lounge, and most of the couples were with each other in their cabins. There was some heavy Love Boat action going on with some of the singles. Emmett gives me an alibi—"

"And that gives Emmett one from you."

"And you and Polly alibi each other."

Connie stood up suddenly. "Polly," she said. "We're forgetting Polly. You're right, you know. We shouldn't leave her all alone. Maybe I'd better bunk in up there."

Pete stood up, too. "Connie."

She turned away. All he could see of her was the smooth angle of one cheek and the bristle of pale brown hair. "Hey." He drew her face around until she was facing him. At least most of her was facing him.

Her eyes skated away.

* * *

Pete went up on deck.

The ship might not have been moving forward, but the wind was back, and it moved the ship from side to side. It left Pete with a rolling, dipping, generally unpleasant sensation beneath his feet. He made four full turns around the deck, trying to overcome a sudden, throbbing loneliness, an increasing uneasiness. He saw no one. True to the captain's instructions, they were staying in their cabins. Pete climbed to the wheelhouse, where he found Emmett Grey, alone.

Emmett sat at the wheel of the dead ship, peering grimly at one of the dead radios. He made a poor attempt at enthusiasm when Pete came in.

"Ah! Factotum. Coming to report?"

Pete looked through the wheelhouse window and studied the boiling black sea below. "There's nothing to report."

Emmett cast Pete a sideways glance. "How is Polly?"

Pete shrugged. "Connie's staying with her."

Pete wished his peripheral vision weren't so good—he could tell he was getting another look from Emmett.

"So," said Emmett. "Anything else? Who else have you talked to?"

"Stephanie Schrock."

Emmett ducked down to get a closer look at the radio. "Oh? And what did Stephanie have to say?"

"Her version of last night's events differs from yours in one minor detail. She says you passed out on her and she let herself out."

Emmett sat up. He pinched his forehead between his thumb and fingers, kneading it for a second or two.

"Oh, hell. I was afraid of that. It's true I don't exactly remember her leaving, but . . ." Emmett trailed off.

"Does the Coast Guard know about this habit of yours? Getting blotto and passing out?"

"I had two good slugs of that brandy, Pete. *Two*. I can handle plenty more than that, but I don't try, not when I'm on board. As it was, Larry was on duty, not me."

Pete couldn't see any point in getting nervous about a drunk captain while the ship was standing still, but that did remind him to ask Emmett something else.

"Any luck on getting this thing moving?"

The captain shook his head. "Not yet. But Ned and Sam and Larry are all down there trying to improvise some hoses."

"You don't carry spares?"

"Apparently not," snapped Emmett.

"And the radio?"

Emmett shook his head.

Pete groaned. "So this is high-class sabotage. Doesn't this narrow things down?"

"There's nothing high-class about any of this. It's amateur destruction, that's all."

"Even the EPIRB?"

"That, too. It's mounted on the outside wall of the wheelhouse, clearly labeled."

"And the hoses?"

Emmett considered. "If I didn't know anything about engines and I wanted to stop this ship, that's probably what I'd do. To the uneducated eye, the hoses would look like the most vulnerable thing down there. Anyone could walk into the engine room, see the hoses, and hack away."

"And if you did know something about engines?"

129

Emmett squinted at Pete. "Meaning?"

"You said to talk to everyone. I assumed that included the scientists. Does it include the crew, too?"

For one full loll and dip of *The Pequot,* Emmett continued to squint. "You're talking about someone in particular?"

Pete shook his head. "You said I'm supposed to record where everyone was, what everyone saw or heard, while it's fresh in their minds."

"And when I said 'everyone' I meant 'everyone.' I just don't much care for that gleam in your eye, Pete. If you think—"

"I'm not thinking, I'm recording. See?" Pete pulled out his notebook.

"Okay," said Emmett. "In my opinion, if I knew something about engines, the hoses are the last thing I'd bother with. But to answer your question, yes, I expect you to talk to the crew."

Pete propped the notebook on his knee. "Okay. I'll start with you. You were here, in the wheelhouse, when Jackson was killed. With me. All I saw was a brown streak in front of my eyes. What did you see?"

"A brown streak in front of my eyes."

"And hear?" Pete again tried to remember what he had heard, but the vague scrape and shuffle refused to become anything more definitive than that. He had heard no voices. "Did you hear voices? They were right over us, you know."

"I know that." Emmett was starting to sound a little testy. "I had a head like a bowling ball. I don't remember hearing anything, other than the roaring in my ears."

Pete groaned.

"So let's look at it from this end," said Emmett. "Someone murdered Jackson. Why?"

"Do you want all the reasons or just the good ones?"

"Okay, okay. Skip that. So he gets killed. For whatever reason. Then what? What came first?"

"The radio?"

"The radio," said Emmett. "It must have happened when we were on deck with Jackson. How long would you say we were down there, thirty, forty minutes?"

Pete nodded. "Plenty of time for the radio. The engine, too?"

"To slice up some hoses? Sure."

"I still don't get the reasoning behind all this stalling. What's the point? He can't keep us out here forever, and he can't escape. Or can he?"

Emmett shook his head. "It would be impossible to launch a lifeboat without us immediately knowing. And besides, everyone's accounted for."

"Not everyone. I can't find Jenny Sears. At least she didn't answer her door. And I haven't looked for Madeline Cunningham yet."

"Jenny Sears was out on the bow a while ago. I told her to return to her cabin; I imagine she's waiting there now."

Pete didn't find the thought especially alluring. "So why's the murderer stalling us?" he asked again.

"Maybe he's not through," said Emmett.

Pete groaned again.

Chapter
18

So ends this long and tedious day.

The bottle of Napoleon brandy they had used for medicinal purposes in the lounge had somehow ended up in Polly's cabin, and although Connie hadn't exactly marked the level on the bottle, it had been untouched when Pete opened it, and there was a hell of a lot less of it now. Oh well, she thought, maybe it's just as well. This way Polly might sleep. Connie passed on the stuff herself. She could already feel it in her guts every time *The Pequot* leaned away from a peak, or rolled down into a trough. She took a Dramamine, figuring she and Polly would probably conk out together.

The only trouble was, Polly didn't look like she was going to conk out any time soon, brandy or no brandy.

She sat leaning against the wall with her feet straight out in front of her, her profile to Connie as she talked.

And talked.

Polly had somehow worked herself around from the way things had ended up with Jackson the way things had begun.

"That's how I met him," she said. "He came into the hardware store to return a saw and buy some nails and I screwed up the whole thing—I rang it up wrong on the register and gave him too little change and by then I was so nervous I went to hand him the box of nails and I dropped them all over the floor. They were roofing nails. It's funny that I remember that, isn't it? Roofing nails. They went everywhere. But Jackson was so nice. He helped me pick them up."

The sport, Connie thought.

"There we were, down on the floor picking up all these nails, and all of a sudden he takes my hand and turns it over and puts his nails in with my nails and closes his hand over my hand and he gives me this look, you know the kind of look I mean? The kind of look that makes you feel all . . . all . . ."

All pukey?

Polly sighed. "It was nice." She fell silent.

And then she started to cry.

Pete left the wheelhouse, dropped down the ladder, and swung himself around the corner, smack into Jenny Sears.

They both yelled, but Pete figured he had more of a right to—Jenny Sears looked like death, her white skin stretched tight over her skull and her black hair, despite the wind, heavy and still.

"I need to talk to you," she said.

133

"Me, too," said Pete, wishing like anything that he didn't.

"Come," said Jenny Sears. She backed up, beckoning Pete with a long, yellow nail.

Pete followed.

Slowly.

Jenny Sears led him to her cabin. She shut the door behind Pete. She came toward him.

Pete backed up.

"It's about your sister," she said.

"My sister?"

"Your sister. I want you to tell your sister not to cry. There's no telling what the spirits hear, and it would be wrong, it would ruin everything, if he heard her cry."

"Spirits?"

"His spirit will linger here. Surely you know that. He was not a peaceful man, and he did not have a peaceful end. Those are the spirits that wander. He's still here, I know it." Jenny Sears looked around the room. Pete considered telling her to look in the freezer.

"Okay," he said. "I'll pass the word. Now if you have a minute, I do have a few questions I'm supposed to ask you, as the captain said." Out came the notebook again.

Jenny Sears watched and waited.

"First of all, where were you earlier this evening, between five and seven P.M.?"

"Here," said Jenny Sears.

"Alone?"

"Alone."

"From when to when, would you say?"

"From after the lecture. I had taken some notes that I needed to organize."

"And you were here until when?"

Jenny Sears examined a particularly repulsive nail. "Dinnertime. Until just before dinnertime."

"No stops along the way?" asked Pete. Libby Smith had said Jenny Sears entered Brady's cabin at three.

"No. From the lecture I came straight here."

"And how and when did you hear what had happened to Jackson Beers?"

It seemed to Pete as if she started to smile and then tried not to. "I left my room shortly before dinner to check the bow for whales, but when I heard what happened, in the halls, I changed my mind and returned below."

Pete tried another tack.

"But during that trip you must have seen . . . someone?"

"Yes," said Jenny Sears. "As I was heading down the corridor from the bow, Brady Pearson opened his door. I told him what happened."

"And this was when?"

"Close to seven," she said.

"And that was the only time you saw him, or anyone, after the lecture in the lounge?"

"Yes." Jenny Sears looked straight at Pete without flinching.

Was she lying? Or was Libby Smith lying? Libby hadn't flinched, either. Practiced liars never did. It was the amateur liar who couldn't look you in the eye when he lied.

And just like that Pete was back in Connie's cabin, turning her to face him, watching her eyes skate away.

"I tried to tell Pete," said Polly. "I tried to tell him about Jackson, but you can't tell Pete anything."

Connie opened her mouth to say something, but

then closed it without speaking. She'd been doing that a lot lately. It wasn't easy, either.

"After the hardware store, after that thing with the nails, Jackson kept coming back. He said it was because he was fixing up his grandfather's house, but I knew it was because of me."

It made sense to Connie. She couldn't picture Jackson Beers fixing up his grandfather's house. She couldn't picture Jackson Beers having a grandfather.

"What does Jackson do, anyway?" asked Connie. "What did he do, I mean?"

"Rugs," said Polly.

"Rugs?"

"He sells rugs. He *sold* rugs."

"That's all?" asked Connie.

Polly's amber cat's eyes swung around.

"I mean to say," said Connie, fast, "with the number of subjects he seems to have felt comfortable discussing, I just wondered where he got it all."

"Talk radio," said Polly.

Connie started to say something else and stopped herself so fast she started coughing.

"And the newspaper. He'd get mad if I took a piece. He'd say 'stick to the TV page, that's all you'll ever—'"

Polly stopped talking.

Connie coughed some more.

"It's Pete's fault," said Polly. "He addicted me to those old movies. I still look for them like it's some kind of a contest or something."

"So what? There's nothing wrong with that. It's not—"

"I read the paper. I just read the TV page first, that's all. So Jackson reads the first page first. Pete reads the sports page first."

"Not anymore," said Connie. "Now he reads the obits first."

For a minute Polly stared at Connie. Then she burst out laughing.

And then she was crying again.

Pete couldn't stall any longer. He went below and rapped sharply on Madeline Cunningham's door. When Madeline opened it, Pete was dismayed to see that Tweetie was there, sitting upright in her mother's bunk.

"I know why you're here," said Madeline. "We can talk in your cabin." She tipped her head in Tweetie's direction. It looked like Tweetie had been crying.

It looked like Madeline had not.

"Tweetie, get under the covers," said Madeline. "I'm going across the hall to talk to Pete. I won't be long."

Tweetie slid under the covers. Madeline gave her a hug, and it seemed to Pete that Tweetie hung onto her for an un-Tweetie-like length of time.

"Good night, Tweetie," said Pete.

Tweetie hunkered under the covers and didn't answer.

Pete and Madeline crossed the hall.

"She's been so frightened since this happened," said Madeline. "I've tried to reassure her that what happened to Jackson wasn't going to happen to her, but I'm letting her sleep in with me tonight. She didn't want to be alone."

Pete suspected Madeline didn't either. She sat on Pete's bunk and hugged her arms as if she were cold. "And she's worried about the ship. I've tried to tell her that it's going to be fixed soon, but she seems unconvinced. I told her even if it wasn't fixed soon, in this modern day and age being out to sea is like being in the middle of a mall, or something. Someone will see us any minute. And it's not like this ship could possibly go down."

It wasn't a question, so Pete didn't answer it. Neither did he mention *The Titanic.*

Madeline Cunningham shivered. "I find this whole thing absolutely terrifying. And so . . . so sordid. My part in it being one of the more sordid, I suppose."

It wasn't the beginning Pete had expected. It certainly wasn't the beginning he wanted. "All I need to know is where you were between five and seven this evening, and if you saw anything during that time, or if you saw anything unusual earlier in the day."

"Today was not what I would call a particularly good day," said Madeline. "Of course you noticed I made a fool of myself at breakfast."

Pete blinked. His sister's fiancé had been murdered this evening, and Madeline Cunningham wanted to know if Pete had noticed she'd made a fool of herself at breakfast?

"I made a fool of myself, all right. Afterward I stayed in my room most of the rest of the day. Although later on I did see Jackson, not far from where he apparently got killed. I suppose you'd like to hear about something like that?"

"Please," said Pete. It was the closest he'd come yet to anyone seeing anything.

"To tell you the truth, I set out to find Jackson. I hunted him down." Madeline smiled a tired smile. "Poor choice of words. I did not bring a harpoon. But I did finally locate him, not far from the spot of his eventual demise." She shivered. "He was actually standing near the ladder to the wheelhouse roof."

"What time was this?"

Madeline shrugged. "I don't know, exactly. Four o'clock? Five o'clock? His hand was on the ladder rail. He was ready to go up, but when I called to him, he turned around."

"You spoke to him?"

Again that tired smile. "I intended to tell him off. But the minute he turned around and I looked at him, really looked at him, suddenly I just didn't care anymore. He wasn't worth it. He never was. I told him to stay out of my way, something like that, and I left."

"Did he go up to the roof?"

Madeline shrugged. Everything about her seemed tired. Her shoulder barely moved up and down. "I think he would have, but just then there was some noise in the wheelhouse. I think they were changing shifts. I think Jackson thought the captain might come by, so he turned around. He wasn't supposed to be up there."

"Did you see anyone else?"

"Not that I recall."

"And what did you do then?"

"I went to my cabin, and it was debatable whether I would have surfaced again, even for dinner, if Jackson hadn't been killed."

"How did you know he was killed?"

"Tweetie told me," said Madeline. "Of course."

Of course.

"The poor thing. She was rambling around the ship as usual, and apparently she caught wind that something was up. She ran out on deck and saw the whole thing. The body with the spear, I mean. You can see why she'd be upset."

Pete could see why anyone would be upset. "One

last question. Have you ever been up on the roof of the wheelhouse?"

To Pete's surprise, Madeline said, "Yes."

"Often?"

"Yes," she said again. "With Jackson. He took me up there to look for whales, to show me how the radar worked. He said they had the cheap kind."

That figured.

"Did you ever run into anyone else up there?"

"Oh, yes," said Madeline. "The scientists. And that peculiar-looking woman with the long black hair. What is her name?"

"Jenny Sears?"

"Yes. Sears. And once I saw Mrs. Smith loitering around the foot of the ladder. I think she was looking for a place to hide, myself, but I didn't actually see her go up."

"Okay," said Pete. "I guess that's it." He stood up, and Madeline followed suit, but she turned around when she got to the door. "I'd like you to give your sister a message from me, if you would."

"It depends what it is."

"I'd like you to tell your sister that I didn't mean to hurt anyone. I certainly didn't mean to hurt *her.*"

"Then why did you?" Pete blurted before he could stop himself.

Madeline only shrugged. "Who knows. Maybe it's been too long since somebody looked at me that way. Maybe it's been too long since anybody cared. Maybe *I* don't care." She jerked her head in the direction of the hall. "Even my daughter. Lazy parenting, isn't that what Jackson called it?" Her voice was so bitter that Pete had to resist the urge to back up.

"Forget about Jackson," he said. "Go to bed. Get some sleep."

"Will you tell your sister what I said?"

"Someday, maybe. Not now."

"I see," said Madeline. "Yes, I . . . fair enough. Thank you, anyway. Good night."

The minute the door closed behind her Pete started to feel sorry for her.

A minute after that, Pete began to wonder if that hadn't been the point.

Connie yawned for the tenth time in five minutes.

"Are you tired?" asked Polly.

"No more than one would expect," said Connie. As answers went, it was something of a masterpiece.

"Go to sleep," said Polly. "This brandy'll knock me out soon. The minute I start to feel sleepy I'll just brush my teeth and turn out the light. It's funny how my mind is racing and racing. I keep wondering about Jackson, about what he saw in me. There sure wasn't much he *liked* about me, I can tell you that."

"Hm," said Connie. She wanted to address that point further, but all of a sudden she couldn't keep her eyes open, or activate her mouth.

"It sure wasn't my looks," said Polly. "He wanted me to grow my hair long. And wear dresses a lot. And he absolutely hated my mouth. He told me I should practice controlling its mobility." Polly jumped out of bed and peered into the mirror, moving her mouth. "Although I suspect he sort of liked my teeth." She gritted them and grinned into the glass, turning left and right. "I wonder what it was," she said.

"Hm," said Connie again. She closed her eyes. They felt like someone had Superglued them. There was nothing on earth that could get her to open them again. She lay back against the pillow and listened in a half-stupor as Polly wondered many things about Jackson Beers.

Except the one thing everyone else was wondering about.

Connie's eyes flew open.

Chapter
19

*It created quite a sensation on board, to
think we were so far north.*

It was cool and gray the next morning. The water was
as black and as flat as a parking lot. Pete was glad, for
Connie's sake, that it was calm—it was not the most
pleasant of sensations to be riding in a wallowing ship.
He set off for the dining room bright and early, hoping
Connie and possibly Polly would already be there.

"Hey there, young fellow!"

Pete considered ducking back the way he had come,
but he considered it a fraction too late. Mr. Mutual
Funds gripped him by the elbow, turning him around.

Pete didn't take kindly to being turned around. He
pulled himself loose.

"Listen here, young fellow! You wait one minute,
here! I want to know what's going on. You seem to

have been given some authority on this ship and there are a few of us who'd like to have some answers. *Now.*"

"I have no authority on this ship. I suggest you talk to the captain."

"The captain has disappeared. And don't you try telling me you have no authority around here, I know what—"

"I have *no* authority. None. Zippo. Try the cruise director, Aura Caine."

"And where in the blue blazes is she? I've been looking for her every hour on the hour since we loaded on this crate. Are you aware that lives are at stake? Are you aware that a killer is at large among us and we're hundreds of miles out to sea without a paddle?"

"I'm sure they've got a couple of paddles around." Pete pushed away and entered the dining room. The atmosphere was brittle, to say the least. The singles club seemed to have lost interest in each other and watched him anxiously as he crossed the room. The retirees conversed painstakingly but watched him all the same.

Neither Polly nor Connie were there. For that matter, neither were any of the crew or either of the scientists. Pete grabbed a cup of coffee that he gulped standing and a donut that he ate climbing the stairs to Polly's cabin.

When Polly opened the door she reminded Pete of a towel that had been through the wash too many times and had started to fray at the ends.

"Okay?" Pete asked her. It was a dumb enough question. He wasn't surprised when Polly only shrugged.

"Look," said Pete. "I want you to understand something. I know you think I didn't like him—"

"*He* knew you didn't like him. Do you know what he said to me that night, when he came back to the room? He told me I'd embarrassed him in front of everyone. He told me I had to make it darned clear to everyone on the boat that things were back on. I made him look like a fool, he said. That's what bothered him, that I made him look like a fool. Then he started talking about you, about how he knew you didn't like him, about how you were trying to break us up. He said you should just give up on the whole idea, that *he* was going to win, not you."

"I wasn't looking to *win* anything," said Pete with more heat than he had intended. Polly's agitation had made him forget for a second that Jackson was dead. "I had nothing to do with this. Winning had nothing to do with this. Except for you. I just wanted you to—"

Polly waved a hand. "Winning had everything to do with it, to him. It was all about winning. About control. He wasn't going to let you win. He wasn't going to let me win. That night, that night when I gave back the ring, I thought it was only because I did it in front of people that—" Polly began to shake. "It was worse the next morning. He made it all clear to me the next morning, who he was, what he could do. I never saw it before. . . . He swore he'd never let me go, he'd never leave me alone."

Pete cleared his throat. "It's going to be all right, Polly."

But Polly shot forward. "He wouldn't have let me alone. He wouldn't have let me go. If it is going to be all right, it's because he's dead, that's all."

"Polly—"

Polly looked at him and laughed. "Oh, God, that face again! So what do you want, anyway? Connie?

She went below to change. If you hurry you'll catch her."

"I'm not looking for Connie."

"Go on. Get out of here."

Pete gave up and went. He wasn't too surprised to find himself standing in front of Connie's door soon after. What did surprise him was the door itself, or more exactly, what was decorating it.

Hanging from the knob was Connie's camera.

Pete removed the camera and knocked.

Connie opened the door. "My camera! Where'd you find it?"

"On the door," said Pete.

"On the *door?* What was it doing on the door?"

"Someone must have found it."

"So why didn't they knock?"

"It wasn't there when you came down before?"

"I'm not blind."

"So maybe they thought you were sleeping."

"So how'd they know it was mine? I've seen about sixty of these things around."

"I don't know," said Pete. "But if somebody heard you lost it—"

"I didn't *lose* it. It was stolen out of this room. Something's weird about this."

"So they heard it was stolen."

"It's weird," said Connie. Then she looked harder at Pete. "What is it, Polly?"

Pete nodded. "It gets worse every time I try to talk to her."

"Maybe it would be better if you stopped trying to talk to her," said Connie. "Let's try something easier, like breakfast."

Pete shook his head. "I have to get to work."

"Oh? What's next?"

"The crew."

They weren't hard to find. Pete decided to start at the top and work down, and the first thing he found was Larry Morant in the wheelhouse, half upside down and inside the cabinet, playing with the radios.

"Any luck?" asked Pete.

Larry jumped. Then he turned around, looked at Pete, and gulped the usual mix of indecipherable sounds.

"Have you found the problem?"

Larry seemed to collect himself. "Into pablum, soda fix it," he said. At least that's what Pete thought he said.

"What?"

This time Pete's ears were ready, and he was able to unravel the efforts of Larry's half-paralyzed tongue.

It wasn't the problem. It was how to fix it.

Of course.

Pete pulled out his notebook and began the grueling process of wrestling out of Larry where he'd been the night before, and what, if anything, he'd seen.

It turned out to be effort well spent. Larry might have been bashful almost to the point of paralysis, but he wasn't deaf or dumb. He had been in his cabin, the one he shared with Ned and Sam below the wheelhouse, when Jackson had been killed, and unlike the preoccupied Pete and the half-comatose Emmett, he'd heard plenty. He stumbled and started and blushed and burbled through his story step by step.

He had heard footsteps on the roof, yes, but other than the fact that two people had scuffled onto it and only one had scuffled off, he had nothing new to offer.

He had, however, heard voices on the ladder going up to the roof. Yes, he was certain one of the voices was Jackson's. And the other voice?

Larry didn't know who it was. All he knew was that it was a woman's.

After breakfast Connie snuck below for a nap, or at least she tried to take a nap, but the longer she lay there the more awake she got.

It wasn't as if she didn't know why. A murderer was running around loose, the ship was stalled, the radio was out, and Pete and Polly were both miserable. For one or two minutes Connie let herself continue to pretend that one or all of those things was what was bothering her.

Then she admitted it.

What was bothering her was that she had lied.

To Pete.

Connie never lied. So of all people to start out on, why had she picked the person she wanted to lie to least?

Because Connie couldn't stand to see him miserable anymore, and at the time, lying had seemed like the quickest way to fix it. It wasn't, of course. First of all, it hadn't worked, since Pete was still plenty miserable. And then there was the little matter of the lie rearing its ugly head every time he got within range. If Connie couldn't even look at Pete while she was lying to him, she wasn't going to be able to pull off much else.

There was only one thing to do.

She went to find him.

Pete headed next for the cabin shared by Janine Moss and Heather Seasons.

Janine's and Heather's cabin was even smaller than

Pete's, and opened directly into the hallway leading to the dining room. Pete wondered if it was by design or accident that the male and female members of the crew were separated by an entire deck. He rapped on the door.

Janine opened it. "Hello!"

"Hello," said Pete. He found himself smiling at her. There was something about Janine Moss that had that effect.

"Our turn, I guess?"

"Your turn. Sorry."

Janine ushered Pete inside and gestured to a seat beside her on the lower bunk, but since Heather Seasons was stretched out on the upper bunk and didn't appear to be budging, Pete opted for a position leaning against the wall opposite them instead. He needed to see both of them. Janine folded her hands and looked up at Pete expectantly. Heather continued to recline, halfheartedly blowing illegal cigarette smoke in the direction of the open porthole behind her head.

"I just need the basic stuff," Pete began. "Where you were yesterday from five to seven, and what, if anything, you saw."

Janine shivered. "I was in the dining room," she said. "Setting up with Gilby. So I didn't see anything. Except Gilby, of course." She smiled at Pete.

Pete smiled back. "And you, Heather? Were you setting up, too?"

"Galley," said Heather. That was all she said. She and Larry must get along great.

"We each take turns with galley duty," Janine explained. "Two of us set up, one of us helps Drew in the galley. Yesterday was Heather's turn."

Pete had totally forgotten about the chef, Drew.

He'd have to talk to him, too. "So you were in the galley from when to when, Heather?"

Heather rolled over onto an elbow. "I was in the galley from four-thirty to whenever it was Gilby came tearing in with the good news, Pete."

Pete was starting to feel he was in over his head. He turned back to Janine. "So Gilby was the one who told you about Jackson Beers being—"

"Dead," said Heather. "Gonzo. Run through like a shish kebab. I was trying to get Gilby to cover for me while I went up top for a butt, but he said *he* wanted to go up top for a butt, first. Then he came screaming back down with the news about Jackson."

Janine made a coughing, gagging sound.

"So none of you heard anything until Gilby came running in?"

Janine shook her head.

"Nada," said Heather.

"So other than Gilby and Drew, was anyone else around?"

Both heads, Janine's red flame and Heather's silver feathers, shook no.

"And neither of you left your respective posts until after Gilby told you Jackson was dead?"

"You got it," said Heather. "I didn't leave the galley till Gilby came to get me."

Janine swallowed audibly. "I didn't leave the dining room at all. Not even after Gilby came."

"Okay," said Pete. "Thank you." He closed his notebook and pushed away from the wall, but before he reached the door Heather slithered to the foot of her bunk and landed on the ground in front of him.

"Hey, wait a minute," she said. "You're an 'older man.' What do you think of this?" She raked her fingers through her hair. "I'm trying to promote the

150

natural look. You know, aging gracefully, that whole thing."

Natural look? Was she trying to tell him the gray was real? "It's certainly . . . dramatic," said Pete.

"Yeah," said Heather. "And, I mean, I don't get this age thing. Who says being young is so great, and being old is such a bad deal? I think older's better, you know? Especially older men."

Janine coughed, or gagged, again.

For the first time since he'd entered the cabin, Pete realized something wasn't right.

Chapter
20

No whales. I feel anxious to get another whale so we can boil, but perhaps we shall not get another under a month.

Pete found both deckhands in the engine room, covered with grease. Pete was kind of glad to see the grease—it implied that they had, at one point, been working. At present they were sitting on boxes, listening to complete silence, and staring into space.

"Any luck?"

Ned Tate and Sam Lederman just looked at him.

Pete pulled up a box and sat. "Okay. So what's the worst case? The engine never gets going. The radio never works. We're not going to sit out here forever. Someone's going to come along and—"

"Sure," said Sam.

"Right," said Ned.

"It's got to look kind of strange, this big boat just

sitting here in this one spot day after day. Someone's going to see it and—"

"Sure," said Sam again.

"Right," said Ned.

"Now wait a minute," said Pete, and that seemed to rouse Sam from his stupor.

"No, really," he said. "You're right, Pete. At first it won't look strange: a whalewatch boat that's throttled back to a standstill, floating around looking at whales. That's what they'll see. But after a while it'll dawn on someone that something's not right. There's no cause to worry."

"Right," said Pete.

"He's right," said Ned. "And when we don't show in port on schedule they'll be out looking for us. It's just that we thought if we could get us going we might as well."

Right, thought Pete. He flipped out his notebook. "Okay. You first, Ned. Where were you last night between five and seven when Jackson was killed?"

"On the other end of the spear," said Ned. "I wish."

"Ned," said Sam. He turned to Pete. "Nobody much liked Jackson. I guess you know that."

"Any particular reason why you didn't like him, Ned?"

Ned shrugged. "Nothing in particular. More in general, I'd say."

"So you didn't mind the rumors you were gay?"

Pete could see Ned's slow burn begin—first his neck went red, then his ears. "He told you that? He told you I was . . . I was—"

Sam looked away.

"He didn't say anything to me," said Pete. "A few of the passengers mentioned it. I only bring it up because—"

"He's bringing it up because you said you wanted to kill him," said Sam. "Come on, Ned. What's the big deal? Who'd believe Jackson, anyway? Tell the man where you were when Jackson was killed and let's get this out of the way."

Ned's skin reversed slowly, from red back to white. "All right. All *right*. When Jackson was killed I was on the stern rail, replacing a line."

"For how long?"

"I went out about six-fifteen or so. I was in my cabin before that."

"Alone?"

Ned looked at Sam. Sam looked back.

"Alone."

"And when you were working on the line? Did you see anyone? Anyone up around the lifeboats? I know you can't see as far as the bridge from the stern."

"I don't remember seeing anybody," said Ned. "I heard him land on deck, or felt him land, and I went forward to see what was up." Ned ran a hand through his hair and exhaled, slowly calming down. "The way I figure it, all that lifeboat business, the flares, the radio, the engine room, all that happened when everyone charged out on deck. You and the captain worked over Beers for a long time. All the time you were doing that, most everybody just stood on deck. Nobody moved. Whoever killed Jackson had all that time to make his rounds and—" Ned made a jettisoning motion.

"Okay. When you first arrived on the bow from the stern. You must have gotten there pretty fast. Who else was there?"

"Let's see. Beers was there." Ned attempted a grin. "You. The captain. A couple of passengers came pretty quick—the woman who wears all those weird stripes, the fat guy with the voice, the little kid."

"Who else? Who was next up?"

Ned looked at Sam again. "Polly. And that ex-wife of yours."

"Who else did you see?"

"That nice lady from Southport who lost the watch. What's her name?"

"Libby Smith."

Pete wrote it all down, but what did it mean? If you were first on deck did that mean you got there that fast because you'd just speared Jackson from twelve feet above, or did it mean you couldn't have been racing around slashing hoses and radios? Pete supposed there would have been plenty of time for any of those early arrivals to slip away unnoticed later, when everyone was waiting and watching to see if Jackson had breathed his last.

Pete turned to Sam and cleared his throat, but before he could ask anything, Sam spoke.

"How's Polly, anyway?"

"I don't know. All right, I guess."

Sam sighed. "I guess it was bound to happen."

"Jackson?"

"Polly and Jackson. After the way things went with Polly and me."

Pete hesitated. "I don't know anything about the way things went with Polly and you," he said. He wasn't sure he wanted to know now, but if he was ever going to get squared away with Polly on this boyfriend issue, he was going to need a lot of help.

Sam shifted the box under him and rubbed the side of his face. It left it greasier. "Nothing too unusual, I guess. I don't know about you, Ned, but—" Sam broke off.

Ned stood up. "If you're through with me I'm out of here."

Pete nodded.

The minute Ned was gone, Sam Lederman leaned in.

"It was a lifestyle thing with Polly and me. I'm out to sea all the time. I *want* to go to sea. I don't want to get . . . entangled, you know?"

Entangled. Pete thought of Jenny Sears. He pictured a whale lumbering through the ocean, trailing cast-off pieces of fishing gear. *My sister, the gill-net.*

"Polly was honest," Sam went on. "She made it clear what she was looking for, and finally I figured I'd better call it off before things got out of hand. While I was still able. The trouble was, Polly never understood. She's one of those romantics, you know? She couldn't come to grips with the idea that love wasn't so absolute, that I could care about her, and still go off to sea."

Pete shifted uncomfortably on his box. Maybe it was genetic, this problem with absolutes. "For what it's worth, I think she understands now," he said. "She said the two of you wanted different things, that's all."

"Oh, she understood in her brain. But in her heart she kept thinking something was wrong with her or I wouldn't have been able to leave her that way. See what I mean about Jackson? I left her ripe for some two-bit nobody like him, a guy who only feels big when everyone around him feels small."

Yes, thought Pete. And the more unsure of herself Polly became, the more powerful Jackson got. They would have spiraled down and down and down, until . . .

Sam gazed morosely at Pete.

"It's not your fault," said Pete.

"I know that."

Yeah, he knew it in his brain, maybe, but what about in his heart?

Pete flipped open his notebook. "So let's get this over with. Last night between five and seven, where were you, and what did you see?"

"I was here, in the engine room." Sam spread his hands wide. "And believe me, there's not much to see."

"You were alone?"

"Alone."

"And who told you about Jackson?"

"Nobody. I came out on deck on my way to the wheelhouse and I saw for myself."

"Who was there when you arrived?"

"Everyone," said Sam. "Or so it seemed to me."

"Can you name them?"

Sam named pretty much the same list Ned had, hesitating only fractionally before he named Polly.

"But about Polly," he said. "If there's something I can do for her I'd like to do it."

Pete couldn't think of anything.

Unless, of course, Sam had done it already.

Pete was nowhere in sight. Connie found Tweetie, though, alone on the deck, peering through the rails.

"Hi there," said Connie.

Tweetie didn't look exactly thrilled to see her. "Hi," she mumbled.

"Any whales?"

"On this crummy boat?"

Connie peered out at the pewter water, then up at

157

the sky. There was no light in it at all. Connie leaned out over the rail. "Are you sure? Did you look over there?"

Tweetie looked where Connie pointed. "I don't see anything."

"Me either," said Connie. "I guess it was just a wave."

"There aren't any waves."

"Oh. Then it must have been a whale."

Tweetie frowned at Connie. Then she turned her attention back to the sea. Connie was left to dive deep into her own black thoughts.

It was the thievery that bothered her, or to be more exact, the reappearance of one recently thieved item —her camera. Connie could understand theft. What she couldn't understand was the sudden abandonment, with no apparent reason, of the fruits of the theft. Had someone taken her camera, used it, and decided to return it when he was through? Unlikely. Maybe the thief had become fearful that the possession of the camera would incriminate him. But why would the thief fear incrimination now? What had happened to make him afraid of getting caught with the camera now, that hadn't made him afraid three days ago, when he took it?

Jackson Beers had been murdered with a stolen harpoon, that's what had happened.

Yes, that made more sense. The thief had taken Libby's watch, maybe even Tweetie's twenty, Connie's camera, and Emmett's harpoon. The murderer (the thief?) had killed Jackson with the harpoon, and any minute now he expected the captain, as part of his murder investigation, to order a search of the ship to look for the other stolen things. In an attempt to cover his tracks, the thief begins to get rid of the stolen items one by one. He wouldn't have to worry about Tweetie's twenty, since no one would know which particular twenty was Tweetie's, but the watch and the camera would certainly be incriminating if found on the thief. So the camera was left on Connie's door, and if Connie were right, the next step would be to drop the watch off at Libby's.

There was only one problem with Connie's theory. It was just as risky to be caught returning an item as it was to be caught stealing it. What kind of an idiot would risk something like that, when the world's biggest garbage can was simmering and stewing around them on every side?

"Hi," said a voice behind them, and as if every one of her questions had just been answered, all the knots in Connie's body and brain melted away. Pete.

"Any whales out here today?"

"On this crummy boat?" asked Connie, nodding toward Tweetie.

"It's Emmett's new strategy," said Pete. "Since he can't find them, he's going to sit still and let them find us."

Tweetie didn't seem to enjoy Pete's humor. She turned away from the rail.

"Hey, you're not giving up?"

"Whales are dumb." With that, Tweetie left them.

A raindrop slapped the back of Connie's hand.

"It's raining," said Pete. "We'd better go in."

"No," said Connie. "Please."

Pete looked at her in surprise.

"I've been looking for you. I want to tell you something." Connie flipped up the hood of her sweatshirt against the peppering rain, took a deep breath and looked straight into Pete's eyes. "I wasn't with Polly when Jackson was killed."

Pete didn't look too shocked. Actually, he looked sort of relieved. He shrugged his shirt collar up to deflect the accelerating rain, moving close enough so his shoulder nudged hers, but said nothing.

"I panicked. That's all it was, idiot panic. You were so miserable. I could tell you were worried about her. I just wanted to ease your mind. I couldn't stand to see you go through any more pain. I figured if you knew Polly was out of it, you'd be okay. I just wanted to help you. I'm sorry." Her words seemed to come out in torrents. She knew these words weren't the magic ones she'd been after, but she let them come. "I hate to lie. You know how I hate it. I know this is old history now, but you know that fling I had with Glen Newcomb? I broke my promise to you, I acted dishonestly, but I never lied to you. That's why I left you. I couldn't lie about it. And I couldn't tell you what I'd done. I never meant to leave you, Pete. I was just so . . . so . . . you're so self-contained, you know? And I'm not. I was lonely. And angry. I tried to hurt you. I didn't know how to reach you, I . . ."

Pete must have moved. The next thing Connie knew they were holding on to each other like crazy.

After a while Pete's jaw moved against her temple. "And what about me? I refused to see that something wasn't right. I bleeped out all the bad parts." He pulled away and peered at her. "But it *is* old history. We're past that now, aren't we?"

Connie nodded. She leaned back into Pete's soaking shirt and he refolded his arms around her. She could feel a new calm in him.

"You don't know what a relief it is to have told you this," she said. "And that stupid lie. Did you know it was a lie?"

"Not at first—then the next time the subject of

Polly's alibi came up, you wouldn't look me in the eye. So I got to wondering if you'd made it up, and that's what bugged me about it. I figured you'd only lie if you thought Polly did it. It scared the hell out of me."

"There was that one split second where it seemed like lying was the best thing to do. I felt responsible, you know? Here she was, whipped into this total state of self-immolation. Then I come along, and what do I do? I start talking to her about her goals. I tell her Jackson will never help her reach them. I tell her she doesn't have to put up with him. I tell her to stick up for her rights. I—"

Connie stopped talking. She could feel it through her sweatshirt—the calm had left Pete's body. He dropped his arms. She turned around.

Now he looked shocked.

What had she done? What the hell was she saying? That she had goaded Polly on. That she had urged Polly to act.

That she *did* believe Polly killed Jackson.

Chapter
21

*At seven o'clock the watch went below
for three hours.*

Connie pulled on a dry sweatshirt, roughed up her hair with a towel, and then threw the towel to Pete. Pete swiped at the back of his neck and threw the towel over Connie's sink.

"I know what it sounded like," said Connie, plunking down on her bunk, "but I don't for one minute think Polly killed Jackson."

Pete sat down beside her. "Why not?"

"Come on. You think she harpooned him?"

"I think we at least need to think about it. What you said before—"

"Forget what I said before! I'm trying to tell you! I was just running off at the mouth and I didn't—"

Pete caught Connie's flailing hands in his and held

onto them. "No," he said. "We've made this mistake before. Isn't that what we were just talking about? Saying one thing, hearing one thing, and trying to pretend it's something else? You said you felt responsible because you encouraged Polly to stand up for herself. Let's just accept that, all right?"

Connie didn't look too accepting. He gripped her hands harder. "Connie. I've had the same thoughts about Polly, I even sort of knew you did, but I couldn't admit it until you said what you said. So let's just go with it for a minute, all right? It wasn't just you. Maybe you opened Polly's eyes a little to what life with Jackson would be like. Maybe I did, too, I don't know. But we know Jackson opened her eyes with all that idiot stuff with Madeline Cunningham."

"Okay, okay."

"Okay. So you decide to help Polly by—"

"I decide to help *you*. I didn't want you going crazy thinking your sister was a killer. See how well it worked?"

"You have helped me," said Pete. "I couldn't do this without you. Any of it."

Connie's green eyes widened in disbelief. She didn't believe him. Why not?

Pete thought of all the times he had tried to tell Connie how much she meant to him. He'd told her he loved her plenty of times. Even, once, sort of, after she'd come back. But had he ever said anything about how much he needed her?

Pete swallowed. It was easier to love than to need, he decided. "When I asked you to come on this trip, I pretended I was asking you just for the fun of it. The reason I asked you was partly because I wanted to be with you. But there was something else. I knew something wasn't right with Polly, I smelled it the minute she called. I wanted you here because something was wrong and I knew I'd need your help. I knew I'd need *you*."

Connie's hand, the one Pete still had hold of, turned until it laced with his. "So tell me how to help."

Pete exhaled. "Okay. Back to what I was saying before. We have to consider Polly as a . . . we have to consider Polly. Now you were in Polly's cabin when I got there last night. I take it you had already told her about the alibi you faked for her?"

Connie nodded.

"And what did she say?"

"Nothing."

"Nothing?"

Connie shrugged. "I didn't exactly phrase it like a question. I'd committed myself, you know? And I really hadn't done it for Polly. As I said before. So I was a little afraid she'd tell me to forget it, that she was alone in her cabin and she was going to tell you so. As a matter of fact, I kind of thought that's what she did say, when you spoke to her afterward."

"She didn't. Not that night, and not afterward. What she did say was that Jackson had threatened her, that he was never going to leave her alone, that she believed he never would have, and things only turned out okay because he was dead."

"Oh," said Connie.

"And there's more. Did you see her face yesterday morning when Jackson appeared? She *hated* him by then. She really hated him. Did you see it?"

Connie nodded again.

"Then he gets killed, and she's been laughing ever since."

"No, she hasn't. She's been crying, too. She's all mixed up. Every time she tries to concentrate on some good thing about him, the bad horns in. But I know what you mean. She was puzzling over everything about Jackson last night, except who killed him. Either she already knows, or she doesn't want to know."

"And Larry Morant. His cabin is right behind Emmett's, below the wheelhouse. He says when Jackson was killed he heard a woman's voice."

"So what are you going to do?"

"Nothing's really changed. I still have the same job—to collect the facts, and I just hope I collect enough of them to figure out who killed him."

"Are you sure you want to know?"

"Yes, I'm sure."

"Why?"

"Because I want to get to the end before anyone else does. At least I'll have that to give to Polly. She gets to know it from me before the—"

"So you really do think she did it."

"*No.* I don't know. I don't think so. But even if she didn't, the odds are pretty good that when the truth comes out, it's going to be hard for Polly. Maybe I can give her a chance to brace herself, to kind of get a handle on herself before she walks off the boat in Southport with a million flashbulbs in her face."

Connie gazed up at Pete in silence for a second. "So that brings me back to my question. What can I do?"

"I'll tell you one thing you could do. Janine Moss and Heather Seasons. Something's up, and I don't know what." Pete told Connie about the session in the cruise attendants' cabin. "Janine seemed . . . not right about Heather's story. Maybe if you talked to her alone . . ."

"I'll talk to Janine. What else?"

Pete thought. "What you said before about the thefts. You said you thought maybe the first items were stolen to dilute attention when the murder weapon went missing. It makes sense."

"So tell me if this makes sense." Connie slid back so she could lean against the wall, knees still hugged to chest, and told him her thoughts on why the camera had resurfaced. "But why run the risk of being seen leaving it on my door? Why not toss it over the side?"

Pete mulled that over. "Because the thief's not a thief. If the thief is the murderer, and if your theory about why he stole the camera and the money and the watch is right, he isn't stealing with the intent of denying people their possessions. He's stealing for camouflage. So when he no longer needs the stolen goods, when he's taken the harpoon and used it on his intended victim, he doesn't want to continue to deny these innocent folks of their rightful belongings. He's a killer, not a crook. He can't, in clear conscience, throw them over the side—he wants to return the stuff to their rightful owners instead."

Connie snorted.

"Okay, you think of something."

"Okay," said Connie. "Let's start where our friend the police chief would start. Means, motive, opportunity. We're assuming Polly had motive, and lacking an alibi, that gives her opportunity. But what about means? How could Polly have gotten the harpoon?

And does that mean that she planned the other thefts, laid this murder out that long ago? I don't think so."

"Why not? Objectively speaking."

Connie snorted again.

"I mean it. Everyone had a chance to steal that harpoon off the wall while Emmett slept."

"Even Polly?"

"It was common knowledge that the harpoon was there. Polly must have known it."

"But was it common knowledge that Emmett was going to pass out cold and leave his door open?"

"Stephanie. You're thinking it's Stephanie?"

"Not necessarily," said Connie. "But let's consider Stephanie. It's only her word that the harpoon was on the wall when she left, right?"

"Right. But it was there just before Emmett passed out, he vouches for that. If Stephanie took it—"

"What's her motive?"

Pete thought. "She was furious with Jackson after that crack in the lounge about the navy. But she was also angry at Brady, and she lit into me pretty well, too. So I'd pretty much decided she wasn't too crazy about men, and that was the end of it. But now I don't know. Remember when Brady got up to announce her talk in the dining room?"

Connie nodded.

"Brady knew the big thing was Stephanie's book. He admitted to me that she felt he could be more help in plugging it. So when he got up to announce her speech, he didn't even mention the book. He said she was going to talk in the lounge, and that was it. The book would have been a natural part of her résumé as an expert on the subject. The logical thing would have been to mention the book, not to leave it out, don't you think?"

Connie thought. Then she nodded.

"He downplayed the whole thing. 'Whalespeak,' he called it. And it was Brady who told me Stephanie frequented the wheelhouse roof. He also stressed to me that Stephanie had a motive—her general dislike of Jackson, naturally intensified after that remark in the lounge. I gave Stephanie a chance to lay into him in return, but she went for me, instead."

"So what?"

"So maybe Brady's got it in for Stephanie, and is trying to set her up."

"Meaning *he* killed Jackson?"

"I don't know," said Pete. "But why couldn't Brady have gone back to Emmett's cabin that night, let himself in, seen Emmett out cold and the harpoon hanging there—"

"So he hadn't planned it. That means he didn't steal the money and the camera and the—"

"Or maybe Brady had planned to break in, and the fact that the door was open was an extraneous piece of luck."

"With Emmett asleep right under the harpoon?"

"Brady's taken millions of these trips. Sure, Emmett conked out that night, but for all we know, Emmett is an extremely heavy sleeper. For all we know he's famous for how heavy he sleeps, and the whole crew knows about it. Maybe Brady knew Emmett slept like the dead. Maybe Brady knew Emmett always left his door open. Maybe all along Brady'd figured he could walk right in and nab the harpoon."

"Motive?" asked Connie.

"The grant," said Pete. "If not setting up Stephanie, the grant. Jackson planned to go home and talk to his friend Gary Fowler, the director of the agency that would say yes or no to the grant."

"So the grant's a motive. Or plain old hatred."

"Ah," said Pete. "If you're going to count plain old hatred, the field widens."

"You've talked to the rest of the crew? Of course Emmett's out, since he was with you, but what about the rest of them?"

"I haven't talked to Drew Baker, the chef, or Gilby Peebles, or Aura Caine, but I spoke to Janine, Heather, Larry, Ned, and Sam."

"Let's leave Janine and Heather alone till we sort out what's what with their stories. So start with Larry. Any motive?"

Pete thought. "As far as I can tell, Larry's about the only person that Jackson *didn't* antagonize. As Sam said, Jackson brought other people down in order to build himself up. Maybe Larry seemed down enough already, and Jackson could feel superior without going to any extra work. Besides, Larry's so introverted I'm not even sure he knows who Jackson is."

"Weak on motive," said Connie. "But opportunity?"

"For the murder, yes, I guess so. His cabin is handy enough. He says he heard noise on the roof while he was still in his cabin, but who's to say? He was on duty in the wheelhouse when the harpoon got stolen, but they have an automatic pilot that locks them on course."

"So what about Ned?"

"No alibi. Same old means. He was handy enough, too. But motive?" Pete thought. "Do you think Ned's gay?" he asked Connie.

"Ned? I don't know. Who cares?"

"Ned, maybe. If he's gay and didn't want anyone to know. Jackson was spreading rumors. I'm sure he did it tastefully, too."

Connie groaned. "So what about Sam? Any motive for Sam as murderer?"

Pete took some time before he answered her. "I like Sam," he began. "Even though he dumped my sister. He told me his reasons, and they struck me as sound. Unfortunately, I think Sam is having a little trouble trusting his own good sense right now. He feels guilty about Polly. He feels he created the vacuum that sucked Jackson in."

"Guilt is a powerful thing," said Connie.

"Yes," said Pete. "It is." And he knew what he was feeling guilty about. Polly. But why? Because he was sitting here suspecting her of murder? Or because he hadn't liked Jackson or Matthew or Damond or Donald or whoever the hell they all were? Or because he was hiding from her now, when no matter what she'd done, she probably needed him the most?

"Hey," said Connie. "Why don't you just ask her?"

"Ask her what?"

"Ask Polly if she killed Jackson. Isn't that our lesson of the day, here? Truth at all cost?"

"And if she says yes?"

"So wait till she says it. *If* she says it. Then we'll figure something out."

We. That was the only part of the plan that sounded good, the *we* part.

Pete looked at his watch. "I guess we've missed dinner."

Connie slid off the bunk. "So go talk to Polly. I'll

talk to Janine Moss first, and then the chef, and when I get through with the questions I'll try to scrounge up some food. Then I'll meet you back here, all right?"

Things weren't exactly *all right,* thought Pete, but they were getting better.

Chapter
22

*. . . & dont you think it is very cruel in
[him] to leave me here . . .*

As Connie left to find Janine Moss, she mulled over
her best approach. It wasn't much of a mull—Connie
had learned long ago that she had one approach,
direct.

Connie found Janine Moss alone at the crew table
in the empty dining room, writing in a notebook.
When Connie sat down across from her, Janine
snapped the book shut.

"Sorry," said Connie. "This'll take two minutes.
I'm part of the Factotum crew, I don't know if you
know that. Pete wanted me to talk to you."

Janine didn't exactly look surprised. And was it
Connie's imagination, or did she glance behind her to
the door of the crew cabin, at the other end of the
room?

172

"He realized afterward he should have spoken to you and Heather separately," Connie went on. "And he would have come back himself, but he's with his sister now."

Janine's face softened. "Is she all right?"

Connie shrugged. "Sort of. You know."

Janine nodded, as if she *did* know.

"Anyway, Pete got the feeling you might be able to clear up a few things on who was doing what where and when."

"What?"

"Where everyone was. You know."

"When?"

It was going to be slow going, Connie could see that. "Last night. When Jackson was killed. You were in the dining room? Heather was in the galley?"

This time she was sure Janine peeked around at the crew cabin door.

"Pete was confused, between the two of you, if—"

"*I* didn't confuse him," said Janine. "*I* was in the dining room, just like I told him. The whole time."

"So who wasn't?"

"Wasn't what?"

"In the dining room. Or the galley. Just like they told him."

Janine flipped open her notebook, closed it again, and fiddled around with the spiral for a while. "I believe Drew was in the galley the whole time. The door to the galley is right there." Janine pointed. "He was in there when I got here at six, and he was still in there at twenty of seven. I know because I went in there to check the time. It was twenty of seven, and he was in there."

"And Heather, too?"

173

Janine squirreled around with the notebook some more. "Who are you going to tell this to, anyway? The police?"

"I'm going to tell Pete."

That seemed to be enough for Janine. "I wanted to tell him this," she said. "But I couldn't do it in front of Heather. She was too busy making a boob out of herself. 'Ooh, do you like my hair? Ooh, I like older men, ooh, aren't you the cutest thing in pants I've seen in two minutes!'"

Connie looked at Janine in surprise. This was a slightly different version of the interview than the one Connie had gotten from Pete. But after she thought about it, she decided she wasn't so surprised after all. For some reason Pete never had figured out that he had a certain something where the opposite sex was concerned.

"She does this to everybody," said Janine. "I've been working with her for five months and she's now gone through the whole crew. It only took her seven tries before it paid off."

"Seven tries?" So maybe Pete didn't have so much of a certain something after all.

Janine slammed the notebook down between them and spread out the fingers on her left hand, counting with her right. "Emmett. Of course he was so polite she hardly noticed when he shot her down. Sam. "Nose in the air Sam," she called him when he didn't bite. Ned just looked right through her, of course, but old Heather would never let a little thing like—" Janine broke off, raised a fourth finger, and went on. "Then she tried Larry. Charity, she called it. Poor Larry just about had a seizure, and then he ran so fast *nobody* could catch him." Janine paused before she raised her thumb. "Okay. I'm not sure about Drew. But whatever's going on, it doesn't seem to matter either way to him. That would just about kill Heather." Janine paused. "She even took a shot at . . . *him.*"

"Him?"

"You know. Jackson. She could tell he was looking around. But he bypassed her for the other one. Boy, was she ripped. So out she goes again, and—" Janine spread both her hands wide. "Bull's-eye."

"Who?"

Janine looked at Connie as if she were deaf, dumb, and blind, and blushed from her scalp to her collarbone. "Gilby, of course."

Gilby. Of course. Bull's-eye. Straight through Janine Moss's heart. Which was why, of course, Janine was sitting here talking to Connie so obligingly about where Heather Seasons was or wasn't.

"So Heather wasn't in the galley the whole time, is that what you're saying?"

"Heather told Pete she was waiting for Gilby to get back from having a cigarette, so she could go have one. She didn't."

"Didn't what?"

"Wait. Gilby left. I don't know just when, sometime between six and six-thirty, maybe closer to six-thirty, because I remember thinking they'd only just about both fit in a break before everyone arrived for dinner at seven. But Heather didn't wait for Gilby to get back. He wasn't gone two minutes before she took off after him."

So what? wondered Connie. So Janine couldn't alibi Heather, but Gilby could.

Or could he?

"So what you're saying is that Heather and Gilby

went out on deck together to have a cigarette, some-time between six and six-thirty."

"I have no idea what or where Gilby and Heather did or didn't do," said Janine primly. "First Gilby left, and then Heather left right after him. That's what I'm saying. I didn't see either of them again until Heather sauntered back in at ten of seven. I know exactly when it was because I was checking the time then, too. I was real ticked off. There was work to do, you know? She was just lucky none of the passengers arrived before then. Then Gilby came screaming in right after that to tell us Jackson had been murdered, and that's the whole story."

"Was Drew in the galley when you checked at ten of seven?"

Janine nodded. "Yeah, that's right. He was there at twenty of, and he was there at ten of."

"And no Heather. Or Gilby."

Janine fidgeted with her notebook. "No. And I just figure Pete ought to know this, you know? He's been nice. I don't see why he should be suckered in by Heather the same as everybody else."

And, thought Connie, Janine wouldn't mind sticking it to Heather a little, either.

Ain't love grand?

"Knock, knock," said Pete, rapping gently on Polly's door. It was the kind of approach to a door that someone unsure of his welcome would make, and Pete, realizing this, found himself rapping again, harder. "Hey, Pol. Open up."

Polly opened the door.

"Can we talk a minute?"

That seemed to make Polly nervous. She stood warily aside.

176

Pete went in and sat down. That seemed to make Polly nervous, too. She leaned against the chest of drawers, hugging her elbows.

"So?"

"So what?"

Polly rolled her eyes. "So what do you want?"

All of a sudden whatever remaining patience Pete had had with his sister snapped. "I want to know why you let Connie lie. She told me she made up that alibi. Why'd you go along with it? Why didn't you tell me it wasn't true?"

"And call her a liar? It was her lie, let *her* tell you."

"She did."

"So I gather."

Pete stood up, pulled the notebook out of his pants pocket, and sat back down. "Okay, then. Officially and for the record. Where were you when Jackson was killed?"

"Aha. Are you sure you want to know?"

Pete put down his notebook and rubbed his eyes. This wasn't going the way he'd hoped. *Just ask her,* Connie had said. Well, Pete would like to see *Connie* sitting here asking her. Connie seemed to think the truth was the lesson of the day, but Pete was beginning to think that maybe his own honesty was the whole problem to begin with. He could see now, in retrospect, that there was no way he could have forced his own opinion of Jackson on Polly. She had to figure him out for herself. Maybe Polly would have been trapped in a bad marriage, but that was, after all, her problem, and her choice. It wasn't up to Pete, nor was it possible for Pete to save his sister from the consequences of her own actions, whether those actions led to a bad marriage, or to . . . to what? Murder?

Pete put his notebook back in his pocket and stood

up. "Okay, Polly," he said. "Somehow or other, between the two of us, we've done a pretty good job of marching backward into our childhood. This is where that ends. You're all grown-up. I'm sorry if I keep forgetting that. I'm sorry if you do, too. What's done is done. We can do our best to rectify our mistakes, and believe me, we're all going to pay the price for them, but here's where you and I start to do things differently. You're my sister and I love you. Whatever happened to Jackson, there's nobody sorrier about it than I am. If there's anything I can do for you, I would like to do it. If there's something you want to tell me, here I am. It's up to you."

Pete waited.

Polly's face seemed to have frozen halfway through Pete's speech. She said nothing.

"Okay," said Pete. "You know where to find me."

He left.

Chapter
23

. . . have made very slow progress . . .

Janine Moss left. Connie headed for the galley. The chef, Drew Baker, was stirring something on top of the stove. The first thing Connie noticed about the man was that he had shoulders the size of an ox and arms the size of hams. The first thing she noticed about the stove was that it had been adapted for life at sea—the grill and burners wore fences.

"Is this the take-out window?" Connie asked. "What'll it cost me for emergency provisions for two?"

Drew Baker looked up from his pot, the one on the stove, and scratched his other pot, the one straining against his T-shirt. His hair was long and his eyes were bleary. He looked Connie up and down. *And* side to side. "What do you want?"

"Anything I can get. For two. A loaf of bread, a jug of wine—" Connie hesitated. "And the answers to two questions."

Another look and another scratch. "Like what?"

"Where were you last night when Jackson Beers was killed?"

Drew kept right on looking. Connie figured his logical next question would be "who the hell are you," but either Drew already knew, or he didn't much care. At any rate, he was apparently a person who appreciated the direct approach. He pointed to the floor beneath a pair of filthy sneakers. "Here."

"Alone?" If Janine were to be believed, Connie knew Drew was there, alone, at twenty of seven and at ten of seven. Connie didn't think ten minutes of unaccounted for time was much of a problem, but she figured it wouldn't hurt to ask.

Drew shrugged. "Pretty much." He dropped his spoon, wiped his hands on his apron, and scrambled around in a cupboard. "Two of you, you say?"

Connie nodded.

Drew emerged from the cupboard with a paper bag and a loaf of French bread. He shoved the bread in the bag, walked over to a refrigerator that looked like a huge closet, and pulled out a bottle of chilled white wine and a stick of celery. He shoved the celery into his mouth, and to Connie's surprise and delight he shoved the bottle of wine into the bag. "Bread. Wine. Two answers. Anything else?"

Connie thought. "Cheese?"

Drew's arm disappeared inside the refrigerator and returned with a creamy yellow triangle. Then he found a breadboard, two wineglasses, a corkscrew, a bread knife *and* a cheese knife, and added them to the bag.

"You said 'pretty much,'" said Connie. "Can you narrow that down any? Was there anyone in here with you between, say, six-thirty and seven?"

Drew shrugged. "Sometimes."

"Like when, exactly?"

"Who knows."

"That's not much of an answer. Does that mean I get to ask one more question?"

Drew might have grinned, but around the celery it was hard to tell. What the hell, thought Connie. "So what's with you and Heather Seasons?"

Drew chewed his celery slowly, swallowed, belched, and gave Connie the once-over again. "Nothing worth missing dinner over."

"I see," said Connie.

"Nothing worth lying over, either."

"She asked you to lie over it?"

Drew didn't answer.

"Then she wasn't with you, here in the galley, when Jackson was killed?"

"She tell you she was?"

"No, she didn't."

"She tell anybody she was?"

"Not to my knowledge, no."

"So?"

"But she did ask you to lie."

Again, Drew elected not to answer.

Connie picked up the bag of goodies. "Thanks, I appreciate this," she said. "I'm sorry we missed dinner."

"Why, wasn't it worth it?"

Connie thought about that. "Yes. I guess it was."

Drew gave Connie another one of those looks. "Figured it was," he said.

It was still spitting rain as Pete came out of Polly's cabin, but nothing was blowing. He took a quick hike to the bow to see if he could see anything, but all he saw was black sky and black water. As he turned around he saw a soft glow coming from the wheelhouse, and climbed the ladder in hopes of finding Emmett.

He found Larry, instead.

Larry Morant was bent double over a disassembled radio, snipping away at the few remaining wires. The other radio, Pete saw, had gained some wire in the process. It looked like a good plan—from two broken radios, one that worked. Pete cheered up.

"Hi, Larry," he said.

Larry gulped, swallowed, and gurgled. "Low."

Pete figured that was Larry-ese for hello. "Any luck?"

Larry shrugged.

That would have been it for conversation if Pete had left it there, but he was in a mood today to meet all challenges head-on. He started with the worst.

"You know that woman's voice you heard up top last night?"

Larry leaned farther over the radio, extracted a nice piece of intact wire, and jerked his head up and down in a birdlike move that Pete interpreted as yes.

"Want to help me narrow down the list?"

Larry's shoulders twitched.

Another yes?

"Age?"

Larry peered at Pete briefly. The question seemed to baffle him.

"The age of the woman. Could you tell by the voice if we're talking, say, early twenties as opposed to late fifties?"

Larry's shoulders convulsed mildly in a shrug.

"Did the voice sound familiar?" Pete pressed. "Did it have that distinctive Southport twang?"

"Nose Port," said Larry.

What the hell was that? *Not* Southport?

"Connecticut. How about Connecticut?" Jenny Sears was from Connecticut.

Larry shrugged again.

"Listen," said Pete. "Okay. Was it Janine Moss?"

Larry furrowed his brow and thought. "Dontinkso."

"Heather Seasons."

Larry thought, furrowed, shrugged.

"Aura Caine?"

More silent musings, another shrug. "Was it Polly, dammit?" Pete shouted.

Larry's gelatinous body jumped upward out of his chair.

"Polly?" At least it was a clearly discernible word. Apparently Larry wasn't used to brothers suspecting their sisters of murder. He did his best to ease Pete's mind, with a handful of swallowed and regurgitated syllables, that the voice he had heard had not been Polly's. Pete must have continued to look doubtful. Out came a second batch of mismatched consonants and vowels, from which Pete gathered that Larry was now half inclined to think the voice had been a man's.

It wasn't exactly the party Connie had envisioned it might be. They sat on the bunk with the cheese and bread and wine, but hardly ate or drank at all. Every time Connie tried to eat, she thought of something to say instead. Everytime Pete started to pour the wine, something Connie had just said distracted him. First it was her report on the conversations with Janine and Drew.

"So I'll have to nab Gilby," said Pete. "The last hope for Heather's alibi. But I don't see what motive Heather, or Janine, or Gilby, for that matter, could have for killing Jackson, other than that of being harassed to death."

"Janine said Heather was ripped that Jackson turned her down and then chased after Madeline."

"So she killed him?"

Connie had to admit it would be an overreaction. "But he really was miserable to them in the dining room. Maybe one of them ran into him up top and he said something crass and that was the final straw. They zapped him."

"And they happened to be carrying a harpoon that—"

"All right, all right." Connie held out her wineglass. Pete raised the bottle to it, and then drew back.

"But wait a minute. What if Heather *had* connected with Jackson? Before Madeline? What if they had some understanding, or at least Heather thought they did. Then Madeline comes along and—"

"Heather steals the harpoon, kills Jackson, and tries to get Drew to alibi her. He won't, so she tries to trap Janine into it."

"I admit it's shaky," said Pete. "Very shaky." He tipped the wine bottle over Connie's glass.

Connie refrained from commenting further until the wine actually met the glass. "But that same motive would work for Gilby, too. If he and Heather were involved, and if he saw Heather with Jackson—"

"Then he steals the harpoon and kills him. But it has to be more premeditated than that or else it leaves a camera, a watch, and some missing money unaccounted for. And I don't see any motive at all for Janine."

Connie didn't either. "So how'd it go with Polly?"

"Not bad if you like to listen to patronizing, pontificating—"

"Come on. What did you say?"

"Rectify your mistakes. We all have to pay for them. What's done is done. I don't think there was a single tired cliché I missed."

"Oh, well," said Connie. "There's no use crying over spilled milk now."

Pete glared at her. "I left her there. I wanted her to tell me if she killed Jackson."

"Or if she didn't?"

"*Yes,* dammit, or if she didn't." Pete stood up and paced the two feet of cabin floor. "I was out of my mind to take this job."

"So quit."

"I tried to find Emmett and do just that. I found Larry instead. He says the voice wasn't Polly's."

"So, good."

"Then he decided it was a man's."

"Even better."

Pete looked up from contemplating his sneakers. "About Ned. I've been thinking. What if Ned's *not* gay? We've been thinking that Jackson breaking the news about Ned's sexual preference isn't a motive unless Ned is gay and doesn't want it known. But

185

suppose he isn't gay at all and doesn't much care for the implication?"

"So killing Jackson proves he's straight?"

"Of course not. But we're talking plain old anger, here. A crime of passion. Hatred. Revenge."

"A hate that simmered along nicely for three days while a watch, a camera, some money, and a harpoon got stolen."

And there they were, back where they started.

Almost.

In unison, it seemed, they ran out of steam for more talk. They ate a little cheese, drank a little wine in silence. Finally Connie noticed something about their silence that startled her.

It was comfortable.

They looked at each other. Pete pushed away the cheese and wine and other paraphernalia the chef had provided and moved toward her. "There are other things—"

Connie felt his hand against her face. It was an old, familiar sensation—the skin rough, the touch gentle. Yes, there were other things, and suddenly she was awash in a flash flood, remembering the feel of them. But was this the right time? They'd jumped into this wrong once before.

"Pete?" It was only a question, a need for affirmation.

Pete dropped his hand to her shoulder, gave it a squeeze, and stood up. "Okay."

"Pete. I don't—"

"No. You're right. Polly's expecting you?"

"Yes. No. I don't—"

Pete smiled at her. "Go ahead. Talk to her." He opened the door, and touched her shoulder again. "Good night."

"Good night," said Connie.

"Meet me at breakfast?"

"Pete—"

"It's okay. Good night."

"Good night," said Connie.

Damn.

Chapter
24

The Capt[ain] has got disgusted . . .

Polly opened the door and frowned at Connie. "What do you want?"

"Nothing. I thought I was bunking up here, that's all."

"You don't have to," said Polly, but she stepped back and opened the door wider, her actions speaking louder than her words.

Connie gave one fleeting thought to making a beeline to Pete's cabin. Then she went in.

"Look," said Polly. "I'm really bushed. I just had Pete up here. I'm not in the mood for any more talking, all right?"

Connie tried not to look relieved. "I'm pretty beat myself."

"Good," said Polly. "We'll just crash then."

They crashed.

It seemed like Polly fell asleep in a matter of seconds, but even though Connie's mouth was still, her head kept right on talking.

About Pete. About all the things she'd begun to talk to him about, barebones things she'd never articulated before. About the things he'd begun talking about, things he'd never before felt were important enough to share. There's one cliché that isn't true, thought Connie—things weren't easier said than done, at least not for them. It was so easy to do the dumb things. It was so hard to say the right ones. So which had it been downstairs? And was it too late to change it? If Polly was asleep . . .

Connie turned her head ever so softly sideways, straining her eyes to see Polly in the dark. Polly was still and quiet. Too still and quiet. Connie could hear none of the snuffly breathing sounds she associated with sleeping Bartholomews. Polly was probably lying there just the way Connie was, trying to look asleep, afraid to make a sound. And what was keeping Polly awake? Grief? Guilt? Fear?

No. *No.* They'd been through this already. How was Polly supposed to get the harpoon out of Emmett's room, not to mention steal the camera, the watch, and the money, too? Connie almost started to laugh. Good old Pete. Only Pete could conjure up a kindhearted killer who would return all his unnecessary supplies to their rightful owners. But back to the harpoon. Just suppose they gave Polly the benefit of the doubt on the other items, couldn't she still have gotten that harpoon? Polly knew Emmett from Southport. Did she know him well enough to know that he slept like the dead? *We all love Polly,* Emmett said. Hm. Maybe Emmett and Polly knew each other better than anyone thought! No. What was Connie doing, turning this boat into a floating Peyton Place? Connie knew Polly, and if Polly was engaged to Jackson, she wasn't sleeping with Emmett.

But maybe she'd slept with Emmett before she met Jackson. Maybe Polly more than anyone else knew how deeply Emmett slept. If he even slept deeply. That was Pete's whole idea, wasn't it? Maybe here was a flaw in the theory. Who *said* Emmett slept like the dead? If it was the brandy and the brandy only that had knocked him out that night, the whole premise about Polly wouldn't work.

Now Connie was really wide awake. *So shut up,* Connie told the voices in her head. *Go to sleep.*

The voices ignored her.

Connie looked at Polly's travel alarm clock, glowing greenly from the other side of the bed. It was one in the morning. She tossed back her side of the covers and crept out of bed. She pulled her shorts on under her T-shirt, checked the door to make sure she left it unlocked, and slid out of the cabin.

As she moved past Libby Smith's door, something glinted in the faint light. Connie stopped. A gold watch hung from Libby's doorknob, come home to roost the same way Connie's camera had. So what should she do, just leave it there all night? What if someone else came prowling around and pilfered it? Again? Connie slipped the watch off the doorknob and put it in her pocket. In the morning she'd return it to Libby herself. She moved on.

It was eerie out on deck. The air felt dead and still and an invisible misty rain hit Connie's face like cobwebs. There was no one up. Connie went to the bow and peered over the rail. The water was even blacker than the night. Connie turned around, looked up at the wheelhouse, and saw Larry Morant's round shoulders bending over the radio. What had he heard that night on the roof? A man? A woman? Was he going to change his story every day? Connie considered climbing up to the wheelhouse, but decided against it. She wasn't up to struggling through an interrogation of Larry. She turned back toward Polly's cabin, and found herself in front of the door to the captain's cabin instead.

Was Emmett in there, she wondered? Probably. Since he wasn't in the wheelhouse, where else would he be at one in the morning? He was probably fast asleep, just like the rest of the people on the ship. Fast asleep, sure, but *how* fast asleep? Say, for example, if someone jiggled the doorknob just a little . . .

If Connie had thought for a minute, she probably wouldn't have done what she did next, but she didn't think. She reached out, grabbed Emmett's doorknob, and gave it a small shake.

The door opened.

"Whoa!" said Emmett from his bunk.

Connie froze.

"Is this how you get even, by scaring me to death? Get in here. Shut the door."

Connie didn't move. There was a rustling of sheets. The next thing Connie knew she was being pulled into the room, and the door was shut behind her.

Actually, she was being pulled into the bunk.

"I'd given up on you," said Emmett. "I decided you were going to stay mad forever. What time is it? It must be—" and then he must have hit something that didn't strike him as exactly familiar. Resistance, maybe? He groped for the light, and they blazed into each other's view.

For a split second Connie had the advantage over Emmett—she was dressed. She used this slight edge to regain her footing, while Emmett grabbed the sheet.

"You?" He seemed a little out of breath. Either that or he was at a loss for further conversation.

Connie had to admit it was awkward.

"What are you doing here?"

"Nothing. I was just walking by. You're the one who yanked me in."

"You *opened* my *door.*"

"I didn't mean to. I just wanted to rattle the knob a little, that's all."

"What in the—" began Emmett, but he couldn't seem to figure out the rest.

"Look," said Connie. "I was just roaming around, all right? I couldn't sleep. I saw your door, and I got to wondering how somebody could waltz in and steal that harpoon with you right in the bunk underneath. I figured you must be a heavy sleeper. I thought you'd be asleep now. It's—"

"It just so happens I'm a very *light* sleeper. And I *was* asleep, until I heard you open my door."

Connie had already come to the conclusion that Emmett was not what you would call a heavy sleeper. She was also coming to the conclusion that there was something Captain Blighish about the man. Not everybody could pull off a Captain Bligh imitation while clutching a balled up sheet in front of his naked body, and Connie figured it was only a matter of a second or two before he really woke up and let her have it. She decided to go on the attack.

"So who were you expecting, anyway?"

Suddenly Captain Bligh was gone. All that was left was a naked, flustered man in a sheet. "I wasn't expecting anyone. Now would you please—"

"Okay," said Connie. "I'm sorry I woke you up."

She left.

But she was right.

Emmett *had* been expecting someone.

And she was right about something else, too.

This *was* a floating Peyton Place.

Chapter
25

Day light it commenced to rain in torents . . .

It was the rain that finally did it. It had misted all the previous evening, nothing that kept anyone from getting around on deck if they absolutely felt like it, but by morning it was a different kind of rain. Sheets of it slammed into the deck and bounced back up in fountains, making a gray wall of invisibility around *The Pequot*. It forced the passengers to either hole up in their cabins or group together for hours on end in the lounge, and it forced the crew to scramble soaked and uncomfortable between their stations.

One by one, they snapped.

Pete met Connie and Polly in the hall, just arriving for breakfast. Polly looked ashy and brittle, but Connie's smile perked Pete up. It was no small thing, he decided, to be missed.

Polly said little and didn't stay long. A bite of muffin, a glass of juice, and she was gone. Pete decided not to follow her. First of all, there was no sense saying anything else to Polly until he'd found out what she'd said to Connie the night before, and second of all, he was starving. He took a huge bite of a muffin, and that's when Connie decided to fill him in on the activities in Emmett's cabin.

Pete and the muffin wrestled each other for air. "You *what?*"

Connie chortled into her coffee. "You should have seen him, naked as a jaybird, diving for the sheet. He was crazy. He—"

"*Emmett* was crazy." Pete stopped himself from saying anything further by jamming the rest of his muffin in his mouth, but Connie seemed to be able to read around his muffin all right. She stopped chortling.

"Go ahead," she said stiffly. "Finish your thought."

"I would," said Pete, "but I can't decide which cliché to use."

"How about he who laughs last—"

"How about looking before you leap?"

Connie's fork clattered onto the table. "What's your problem here, Pete? What is it you think Emmett was going to do? Or is it me you're worried about? Is that it? What *I* was going to do? I see a naked man and *bang*—"

"I just think," said Pete slowly and distinctly, "that it was not a very smart thing to do."

"Agreed," said Connie. "It wasn't. But it was kind of funny. All right? And it did gain us some valuable information."

"Like what?"

"Like it would be pretty damned hard to sneak up on Emmett and steal his harpoon unless he was out cold. Of course I should have given him a couple of brandies first, then—"

"Brandy, yes. That would make things easier."

Connie gazed at him with clear green eyes that didn't blink. She placed both hands flat on the table and breathed deep. "Okay. I think I see the problem here. I didn't think I needed to say this, but I guess I do. For the record, all right? What happened before. The affair with Glen. It's not going to happen again." Suddenly she slammed her flattened palm into the table. "For God's sake, Pete, don't you know that by now?"

Pete was suddenly chagrined, and equally as suddenly, focused. "Yes," he said. "I do know that. I'm sorry if it sounded like I didn't."

Connie leaned back and exhaled. "I'll tell you," she said. "If this talking business doesn't get any easier, I'm not going to live a long life. So what else do we have to talk about? We've established through questionable, albeit amusing, methods on my part that Emmett Grey is not a heavy sleeper. We've also established that he's in some sort of a situation with someone on this boat. Is that it? Are we through with Emmett?"

"Yes," said Pete, with feeling. "Did you talk to Polly?"

"No. She didn't want to talk. She went straight to sleep. Or at least she pretended she did. But I found Libby's watch." Connie fished the watch out of her pocket. "You were right. A thief with a conscience. He'd hung it on her doorknob. I didn't think it was the best idea to leave it there, but I also didn't think one in the morning was the right time to knock on her door and give it back. I thought she'd be at breakfast, but I don't see her. I'll stop by with it on my way back. Got anything else for me to do?"

"Gilby," said Pete. "Somebody should talk to Gilby. Since you talked to Janine, maybe you should do it, so you can compare notes."

"Okay, I'll tackle Gilby. What are you going to do?"

"Actually," said Pete, after a minute's thought, "I have to talk to Emmett."

Connie snorted.

"I want to find out how accessible those flares in the lifeboats are. Someone got rid of those flares, as well as the ones in the wheelhouse. Emmett seems convinced that the radio and the engine were amateur jobs, and I know anyone could walk into the wheelhouse and spot the flares there, but the lifeboats might be a different story."

"Good. And while you're at it, ask him who he thought I was last night."

Pete managed a wan smile.

When Pete hit the open deck he telescoped his neck into his shirt as far as it would go, and made a dash through the rain for the ladder. As he got within earshot of the captain's cabin, a strange sound met his ears.

Emmett Grey, yelling.

"These are *emergency conditions*. Do you read me? For the duration of this cruise you will remain present and accounted for. Visible. Is that clear?"

The answer, whatever it was, from whoever it was, was inaudible.

"You are on probation!" Emmett shot back. "You were informed that you were on probation from the start of this cruise. As far as my report is concerned, as of this minute, you have violated probation. As soon as we dock, if we dock, your employment with this cruise line will be terminated unless as of now you begin to perform not only your original duties, but the duties the present state of emergency demands."

Again, an answer that Pete couldn't hear, and a sound something like a book hitting a table.

"Fine. Then consider yourself terminated as of now."

The cabin door opened and Aura Caine, ex-cruise director, appeared.

Pete had halted a safe distance from the door, but Aura shouldered past him as if he weren't there Emmett appeared in the cabin door and saw Pet. "What."

"Did I just hear you fire the cruise director?"

"In a manner of speaking, yes," said Emmett. "Now what do you want? I'm still in a firing mood, and if you haven't been informed of your teammate's investigative midnight—"

"I've been informed," said Pete quickly. "So do you get to hire and fire everyone around here?"

"If I want someone fired, they're fired. In regard to hiring, you may or may not recall that I hired you to investigate the thefts, first, and to—"

"Connie's camera and Libby Smith's watch were returned. They were hung on their doorknobs in the night."

"What?"

"I don't know about Tweetie's money, but other than that, it looks like everything's been returned. I have a theory as to why the things are being brought back. Do you want to hear it?"

Emmett grunted.

Pete explained about his conscience-stricken thief who was also a murderer.

Emmett looked skeptical.

"I'll ask Tweetie about her money. I'm kind of sorry about Aura Caine, I have to talk to her next and it looks like she won't be in such a hot mood. Now how about the lifeboats?"

"The lifeboats are fine. There's nothing wrong with the lifeboats."

Pete was plenty glad to hear it, but that wasn't what he wanted to know. "I mean how accessible are those flares? I know Sam talked about their location at the safety lecture but it didn't look to me like anyone was listening. Could anybody pop up there and find them in a hurry?"

"Come on," said Emmett. He led Pete out the door.

They took another metal ladder to the aft of the one Jackson and his killer must have taken. Emmett pointed to the plaque that clearly indicated the way to the lifeboats.

In a matter of a few seconds they were at the boats. "Two boats," said Emmett. "Each one holds thirty. See? Here are the red boxes for the flares, clearly marked, highly visible."

Emmett led him to the outside wall of the wheel-house, and showed him an empty cradle-type attachment, also clearly marked, where the EPIRB should have been.

"How does that work?"

"It rests in this cradle upside down. When it's inverted, either manually, or when it hits water and floats out of its cradle with the weighted side down, it emits a radio signal to indicate our position."

Pete may not have been solving any crimes, but at

least he was learning a lot. They went inside the wheelhouse. Pete looked at the "auto" switch he'd noticed the day Jackson was killed, and decided to learn some more.

"This is an automatic pilot, right? What exactly does that do?"

"We can preset a course, and the autopilot keeps us on it. Iron Mike, it's called."

"So you don't need a man up here at all?"

"Of course we need a man up here," said Emmett, offended. "A man has to be on the bridge at all times. This piece of electronics does *not*—"

"Okay," said Pete. He decided to go back to learning about EPIRB. "How many of you know how to work the EPIRB?"

"Every member of this crew is trained in the use of the EPIRB."

"Including the scientists?"

Emmett hesitated. "I imagine the scientists are familiar with it."

"When would you be apt to activate it?"

"If we abandon ship, if the ship is going down."

"Or if the engine and radios go out?"

"Not necessarily," said Emmett. "An EPIRB emission would launch a full-scale air and sea rescue effort. I would hesitate to activate it unless I knew we had no other recourse, or if there were an additional imminent danger, such as—"

"Such as a murderer on board?"

"Yes," said Emmett wearily. "Such as a murderer on board."

Chapter
26

Neglecting to close the window during a gale of wind I was surprise, one day in looking upon my state room floor to see articles floating in every direction.

The cruise director's cabin was on the opposite side of the hall from Heather and Janine's cabin, on the deck below. Pete was drenched through by the time he got there. He rapped on the door.

"It's open!" called Aura.

Through the door she didn't sound in too terrible a mood, but once Pete got inside, he saw the cabin was in disarray. Books littered the top of the bureau. Papers were strewn over the floor. Aura Caine stood in front of the open closet door and pulled out a navy blue suit that she added to a pile of similar suits dripping off her bunk and onto the floor.

"Well?" she said when she saw Pete. "You?"

"Just me," said Pete. "Here with the usual questions."

"I'm sorry to disappoint you." She gave Pete one of those smiles that was supposed to look perfectly pleasant but was secretly lethal. "My employment was terminated as of today. I no longer work here, and I therefore don't feel it necessary or appropriate to answer questions." She turned back to her closet.

"It's not just crew who get questions," said Pete. "I have to fire them at the passengers, too."

Poor choice of word, *fire*. Aura Caine stopped rifling through coat hangers and stared at Pete. Had it only just sunk in that she was a mere passenger now?

"Two questions," Pete barged on. "The same two questions I've asked everybody. Where were you Thursday night, from five until seven?"

Aura Caine returned to her clothes. "I see," she said. *"Those* questions. Of course. From five until seven on Thursday night I was in the lounge."

"In the lounge?" Pete couldn't remember any of the passengers he had interviewed mentioning that the cruise director had been with them in the lounge.

"The whole time? From five until seven? You didn't return here to change?"

Aura Caine pointed at the pile of nautical suits. "From one cute little blue suit to another? No."

"When you heard what happened, what did you do?"

Aura Caine turned toward Pete. "Do? Nothing. The man meant nothing to me, why should I do anything? I didn't cry, if that's what you're asking, but on the other hand, I didn't throw a party the way some people did."

"How did you hear about it?"

"The corridors were ringing with commotion. That disgusting man from Bridgewater, the one who spits when he talks, he raced in and told us all about it."

That part, at least, meshed with the story the passengers in the lounge had told.

"Did you go up on deck?"

"Of course not. I went to my room. Eventually the captain sent Sam down to get me. Sam said the captain felt my presence was needed in the dining room. For what, I asked him? Then Sam told me about the hoses and the radio. I explained to Sam that that was the captain's problem, not mine."

Pete was starting to figure out why she had been fired. What he couldn't figure out was how she'd gotten the job in the first place. "When you opened your door to Sam, did you see anyone else?"

Aura waved a hand airily. "Oh, there were a few people scurrying at the end of the hall. That young man, Gilby. The annoying couple who look like birds."

She seemed to be through with the closet. She opened a drawer, pulled out a handful of papers, and threw them on the pile on the floor. Pete recognized the brochures of *The Pequot*. As they rained onto the rug Aura seemed to pick up steam. A collection of guidebooks followed the pamphlets, then some official-looking papers labeled "Safety Regulations," then some blank forms, and her name tag.

Pete backed up. "What are you doing?"

"Packing."

"Where are you going?"

Aura Caine smiled pleasantly again.

Then she kicked the pile of papers across the floor.

* * *

Connie tapped on Libby Smith's door. When Libby opened it, Connie already had the watch out in plain sight.

Libby snatched it.

"Oh," she said. "Oh." Her eyes filled with tears.

"Somebody hung it on your doorknob in the night," said Connie. "They did the same with my camera. A repentant thief, I'd say."

Connie doubted if Libby heard her. She sat on the bed big enough for two and cradled her watch in her hands.

Gilby Peebles had a peaches and cream complexion that didn't go with a day's growth of beard or the rings under his eyes. Connie cornered him on his way to the dining room, and herded him into an empty corner of the lounge.

She introduced herself and took her usual approach to the problem. She had received two versions of his whereabouts at the time of Jackson's murder, Connie told him. She figured there was only one person who could tell her which of them was true.

Apparently Gilby Peebles didn't think Heather was worth lying over, either.

"Yes, Heather left right after me," he said.

"To have a cigarette?"

"Yes."

"At what time?"

"It was quarter past six." He seemed pretty precise as to the time, for a casual cigarette topside.

"Then what happened?"

Gilby coughed a little to clear his throat, but said nothing.

"What's the big deal here?" asked Connie. "What's

the difference if Heather was with Janine in the dining room, or with you on deck?"

Gilby coughed again.

"Unless Heather wasn't with you on deck."

"No, Heather was with me."

"On deck?"

"Well," said Gilby, and suddenly Connie got it. This boat was *worse* than Peyton Place.

"You and Heather were in a cabin somewhere, is that it?"

Gilby nodded.

"Your cabin? Her cabin?"

"My cabin," said Gilby. "For a cigarette. The captain isn't real crazy about the crew smoking. Heather wanted to get out of sight."

Right, thought Connie. "So you went into your cabin at quarter past six. And what time did you leave?"

Gilby continued to struggle with something in his throat. "Heather left around six-thirty. I know because I looked at the clock to see if we were going to be late for dinner or not. It was six-thirty when Heather left. We were talking."

Maybe they were, but somehow Connie felt Janine had Heather figured right. Heather probably didn't go into Gilby's cabin looking to talk. Either way, Heather was in Gilby's cabin for fifteen minutes, minus a minute or two travel time. "And when did you leave, Gilby?"

"It was ten of seven. After Heather left I kind of sat there, thinking. Then I heard something. I didn't pay much attention at first, I had some stuff on my mind. Then there were all these voices. All this commotion. I looked at the clock and it was ten of seven, and I went out. That's when I saw everyone hanging around on deck, and Jackson Beers with the—" Gilby stopped, apparently feeling that he'd said enough.

Actually, he had. Gilby had just left Heather Seasons with a twenty-minute gap in her alibi, the exact twenty minutes in which Jackson Beers had been killed. And Heather had lied about it. But why would Heather Seasons want to kill Jackson, because he'd spurned her affections, as Janine Moss had said? The night before, in Pete's cabin, that motive had sounded pretty shaky.

Now, after an extra day in Peyton Place, it was starting to sound all right.

Pete went in search of Tweetie next. He finally found her, standing in the corridor between their two rooms.

"Hi," said Pete. "What's up?"

Tweetie scuffed one sneaker against the other. "I got my money back."

"You did? How?"

Tweetie pointed at her door. "Under the door. Somebody slid it under the door."

So Tweetie's twenty was back. If that didn't prove Pete's theory, what did? No one could be worried about being caught with a twenty-dollar bill. "So that's that, then. Now everything's back. The camera and the watch and your money. Even the harpoon."

Tweetie made a gulping sound that made Pete remember about her gag reflex. Madeline was right. Tweetie was really upset about this. He was going to have to remember not to crack grizzly jokes around eight-year-olds. He decided to try to cheer her up.

"So," he said, "I bet I know what you're thinking. I bet you're thinking this trip is like being on an old whaling ship, chasing whales around the world. Kids went, too, you know."

"Kids?"

"Sure. Sea captains brought their wives and their kids and sometimes even their dogs. They took off for years, sailing around the globe."

"For *years?*"

"Years."

"No school?" It was the perkiest Tweetie had looked in two days, and Pete kind of hated to burst her bubble.

"There's always school," said Pete. "Usually their mothers taught them."

"Did they spear the whales, too?"

"Who, the kids? I don't think so. The crew did all that. The kids just ran around and—"

"I bet they got lonely," said Tweetie.

"Not too much. You'd be surprised how many ships you could run into, smack out in the middle of the ocean someplace. They had special chairs on ropes that they could swing from boat to boat when they wanted to visit."

"Wow," said Tweetie.

Madeline Cunningham appeared in the corridor, with Connie right behind her. "There you are, Tweetie. I don't know where you get to half the time. I'm putting your sweater in your room." Madeline unlocked Tweetie's door. There was a half-second pause, then, "Tweetie Cunningham, you get in this room this *instant*. The biggest, wettest, soggiest pile of clothes I have ever seen in my *life* is on this floor. Honestly, if I'd known you could mess up an entire ship, I'd have never let you off land."

Madeline yanked Tweetie into the room.

Tweetie burst out crying.

Madeline slammed the door.

Pete and Connie looked at each other.

"It's the rain," said Pete.

Chapter
27

. . . so far the prospects looks very unfavorable for us to make a decent passage home.

Connie went into her cabin to dry off. Pete stood in the hall wondering where to go next. He should go see Polly, he thought. But if he went to see Polly, what would he find? A grieving sister alone in her cabin, or a scheming murderer contemplating how best to pull the wool over her brother's eyes? Neither image rang true in all details, but both images rang true in one —Polly was alone in her cabin.

Pete trudged up the stairs.

He was surprised to hear voices coming from behind Polly's door. He hesitated, then knocked.

"Come in. It's open."

Pete wasn't too crazy to hear that, not with a murderer still on the loose. He pushed open the door, frowning, and saw Libby Smith and his sister sitting on either end of the wide bunk.

They were smiling.

And crying.

Pete mumbled something inane and backed up out the door.

What next? What else was he supposed to do?

Suddenly he didn't care.

He decided to do something he wanted to do instead.

Connie looked out the porthole in her cabin. It was still pouring. Through the haze of rain she watched the horizon rise and fall and rise again. It was kind of like looking through a fogged-up shower curtain with a hangover.

"I'm getting a little sick of this rain," she said.

"I'm getting a little sick of this boat," said Pete.

"I'm getting a little sick," said Connie. "This isn't my best thing, being down below cooped up in this cabin."

"Lie down flat. Close your eyes. I heard Ned tell someone that."

Connie obediently stretched out on her bunk and closed her eyes. It seemed a little better.

"Now think of something else."

"Like what?"

She could almost hear Pete thinking, sorting, discarding the personal for the general.

"Heather Seasons," he said. "Do I flat-out ask Heather where she was during those missing twenty minutes? Maybe she fit in a couple more guys."

"She's all out of guys. She's been through the whole crew. Besides, if she had another alibi for that time, why'd she lie to you in front of Janine? And she tried to get Drew to cover for her, first. I bet after Drew cut her loose she set up Janine, thinking Janine was too nice to call her bluff. I know Janine's type, though— she'll do anything for anyone, and smile and smile, and then all of a sudden one day, *boom!* She turns on you."

"Or on Jackson?" But as soon as Pete said it he discounted it. "No. Nothing seems just right. We're not solving anything with any of this. I don't even now who stole the loot. Tweetie did get back her venty, though."

Connie bounced upright. "She did? How?"

"Somebody slid it under her cabin door." Pete ghed. "That was pretty ugly out there between the Cunninghams."

"Everyone's losing it. Where's the cruise director? I don't think I've laid eyes on her twice this whole trip. It's times like these that she's supposed to be collecting everyone for charades in the lounge, or something."

"Then you'll see a few murders. And besides, Aura Caine's been fired."

Connie popped up again. "What?"

"You're right, she has been making herself scarce. Apparently she was on probation from the start of the cruise, and when all this happened she wasn't pulling her weight. She and the captain beefed it out and he fired her."

"Hm," said Connie.

" 'Hm' what?"

"So Aura was on probation. I heard Jackson berating the crew one day, and at the head of the list was Aura. He said he was going to write to the company and complain. If she was on probation, that would have meant her job, wouldn't it? Don't people kill over things like that?"

"Maybe," said Pete, but it was the kind of maybe that comes from someone who still secretly refuses to admit anyone would kill over anything.

"So where was she between five and seven?"

"The lounge, she says. I double-checked with the passengers who were in there, but only one of them remembers seeing her, going behind the bar for something, and then going back out."

"Another thing," said Connie. "If Heather doesn't have an alibi from Gilby, then Gilby doesn't have one, either."

"And if Janine saw Drew in the galley at twenty-seven and ten of seven, that's when Drew saw Janine, too. So where were they at six-forty-two? What's this Drew like, anyway?"

Connie thought. "Of course what I should say is I have no idea, since I've only talked to him that once, but I got some strong . . . sensations."

"Of what?"

"I'm not sure. Mixed. At first I thought he was checking me out, handing over cheese and bread and wine and waiting to see what I offered him back."

"Oh?" said Pete casually. "You mean like sex?"

"I thought so at first, but then I changed my mind. Don't get me wrong, there was a definite . . . innuendo. I'm sure he'd take what came his way. It's just that I can't see him breaking into a sweat to get it, you know? I think he was just having fun, giving me all that stuff. It's not his food, right? What does he care? He just orders it and cooks it. In that same vein, he acts like he doesn't care what happened to Jackson, or who hangs for it. An ethical void."

Pete thought. "You say Janine saw him at twenty of seven in the galley, and again at ten of seven. Jackson was killed at six-forty-two. Emmett knows, because he looked at the time as he left the cabin. That's two minutes to get from the galley to the roof and spear Jackson, eight minutes to get back down again."

"Come on. A two-minute murder?"

"Why not? Suppose he'd planned it ahead. Suppose he was just waiting for a good time. He'd stashed the harpoon somewhere so he'd be ready when an opportunity presented itself. Say around six-forty that night he saw Jackson from the dining room, walking up toward the deck. He'd know that at six-forty everyone would be in their cabins changing. So he followed him, stabbed him, raced back down—"

"Janine would have seen him."

"Maybe, maybe not. Janine was fuming and clock-watching."

Connie peered at Pete. His Drew theory was nuts, but she decided not to tell him. "So what else have you got?"

Pete pulled out his notebook. "I've been looking over what's come up so far, and Heather Seasons isn't the only one with a conflicting tale to tell. Libby Smith said she saw Jenny Sears leave Brady's cabin at three on Thursday, but Jenny Sears said she didn't see Brady till seven."

"So here we go again."

"Not Libby," said Pete.

"I can't see a single reason why Libby would kill Jackson," agreed Connie. "Unless it's something to do with her dead husband. That's the only thing she cares about. She's still booking a cabin for two." She told Pete about returning the watch.

"Jackson was going to start a jet ski dealership in

Southport," said Pete. "And you know this memorial park Libby is planning for her husband? It's on a pond. Jet skiers love ponds."

"So she killed him over *jet* skis?"

"Why not? It makes as much sense as some of the other things we've tossed around. And I don't know why she would talk to me all that time, telling me all those things about her personal life, unless she were trying to keep me from finding out something else. Maybe there's something about Jackson and her husband. She's up there right now, talking to Polly. They were laughing." Pete hesitated. "Crying, too."

"That sounds about right. She cried when I gave her back her watch."

Pete said nothing.

"At least we don't have to wrack our brains for Jenny Sears's motives. She hated Jackson. She thought he was a blot upon the universe."

"And she hated that harpoon. There is a certain poetic justice to it. But if she was lying about when she saw Brady, Brady backed her up. He said nothing about seeing Jenny until seven."

"But haven't we forgotten one of the most likely suspects of all? What about Madeline? She admitted she was right there just before Jackson got killed. She had reason to kill him. He toyed with her affections and then reengaged himself to Polly. Maybe she knew someone had seen her near the ladder, so she admitted she was there, but not that she went up."

"I suppose she could have taken the harpoon as easily as anyone."

"And stolen my camera. She's right across the hall. But would she take Tweetie's twenty?"

"Sure, if she were trying to create the impression of random thefts. And she cleverly said she didn't know

214

Tweetie had received a twenty from her father at all. Maybe that's the place to start. Not with alibis for the murder, but with alibis for the thefts."

Connie shook her head. "Won't work. Not with my camera, anyway. I never looked for it until that morning. It could have been missing for days. And I still don't buy this 'anybody could have taken the harpoon.' I still think the harpoon's the key."

Pete said nothing. Connie figured he was probably thinking about Emmett again.

"Here," said Pete. "Give me your watch. I'm going to check out this two-minute dash from the galley to the bridge."

So now he was back to Drew. Or Janine? Why wasn't Pete mentioning Janine? Connie handed over her watch.

Pete left. Connie watched the door for a while, but there was no sound of sneakered feet. Then she looked at the door some more. Then she got down on her hands and knees and looked at it again. Then she reached for her knapsack, and stretched out on her stomach on the floor.

Pete started for the galley, but got waylaid. As he passed the Seaview Lounge the door blasted open. The Gigolo bolted through it with a bottle in his hand and one of the Fading Flowers behind him. Neither of them noticed Pete.

"So this is how you act once the chips are down?" snapped The Flower.

"What do you want, blood?" said the Gigolo. "We're stuck. Trapped. Going nowhere. We could be out here for another week, and I, for one, can't take another minute of this sober."

They saw Pete. The Faded Flower pinched her

mouth and returned to the Lounge. The Gigolo waved his bottle at Pete. "I'm not going back in there. Not sober I'm not. How many stories of My Trip To Glacier Park am I—"

"Who's in there, anyway?"

"All of them. Every cranked up one of them. Half of them are getting rheumatic and the other half are getting PMS. Let that be a warning to you. Keep out."

Pete kept out. He crossed the length of the empty dining room until he was inches from the door to the galley. He looked at the watch and marked the time. Then he ran.

The first time he ran straight from the galley up the stairs across the dripping deck, up the ladder at the back of the wheelhouse and onto the roof. He checked his watch. Sixty-two seconds. Fifty-eight seconds left to stab Jackson, and eight minutes to saunter back down to the galley by some less conspicuous route. It was possible. But where would Drew have gotten the harpoon? From his cabin? The crew cabins were below and aft of the wheelhouse. Pete went down to the galley and tried again.

Across the dining room. Up the stairs. Over the deck. It was raining even harder this time. Pause at the crew cabins. Up the ladder behind the wheelhouse, and into Emmett Grey. He waved Pete into the wheelhouse. "What the hell are you doing?"

"Time trials."

"From where to where?"

Pete looked at Larry Morant. He was still working on the radio. Pete remained silent. He couldn't see the point in getting the word spread around that he suspected the chef, not that Larry was capable of getting the word around about anything.

"Well, take it easy out there," said Emmett. "It's wet."

Right.

Pete went below and started again.

Across the dining room. Up the stairs. Across the deck. Yes, Emmett, it was wet. To the cabin. Fiddle with the door. Reach, snatch, turn, run. Up to the top of the wheelhouse. Pete checked the watch again. Eight-five seconds. Thirty-eight seconds to stab Jackson. It was still possible. But was it probable? What had Connie said. *An ethical void?*

On his return trip Pete popped his head inside the wheelhouse. "One more question," he said. "While we sit here without power and without a radio, aren't we drifting?"

"Sure," said Emmett.

"Which way?" asked Pete.

Emmett and Larry exchanged a look.

Larry hooked a thumb over his shoulder. "Out."

Chapter
28

*For the past two days have experience
a heavy gale . . . and . . . many a roll
across the cabin.*

Connie had just struggled up onto one knee when *The
Pequot* gave a hard lurch that sent her sprawling across
the floor of her cabin. She hauled herself up just as the
boat corrected itself, and careened into the sink. *Lie
down, my ass,* she thought. If she tossed herself onto
her bunk, she'd get tossed back out in a hurry. The
hell with it. Connie clutched the edge of the bunk,
scrambled into long jeans, thick socks, sneakers, and
her slicker, and swallowing hard to keep her stomach
down south, headed topside.

She could hear passengers arguing in the lounge.
The Pequot lurched again and someone shrieked. She
plowed on, a hand on each stair rail. Once out on deck
she clung to the bow rail and moved hand-over-hand
until she hit center.

It was wild out there. Where had this wind come from? It shrieked around her, sounding sometimes like human voices, sometimes like wild animals. In three minutes her jeans, sneakers, and socks were soaked through, but her stomach felt better. So she died of pneumonia. She didn't care. She hooted into the wind.

"Connie!" someone shouted, but she didn't recognize the voice. Her slicker was tied tight over her ears. She twisted around, and saw Pete's mouth close to her ear.

"Up there!" He waved vaguely behind him. Where were they going?

Up the ladder, and into the wheelhouse, with Larry Morant and Emmett Grey.

The minute the door closed behind them most of the noise disappeared. Connie untied her hood, sat down on the bench, and held on.

"How's the stomach?" asked Emmett. There were no traces of Captain Bligh.

"Shaky. It's bad down below."

"You'll do better up here."

"You've got people screaming in the lounge."

Emmett's face fell. "Where is Sam? I told him—"

"Engine room," said Larry somewhat clearly, but then he added "dinlikalist," whatever the hell that meant.

Emmett, anyway, seemed to know. "Okay," he said. "I better go down." Emmett dashed out the wheelhouse door and into the storm.

Pete sat down beside Connie. He covered her hand with his. Nobody spoke. It must have been some sort of code. Either that, or it was self-defense against the unintelligible sounds of Larry. Connie watched the horizon and found that when seen as a panorama instead of as a rising and falling line across a small round hole, it didn't seem to dip and sway as much. Neither did her stomach. From up here the sway of *The Pequot* seemed less like an out-of-control cork and more like a metronome. The rain slashed the glass in front of her and the deck below her and the sea beyond her, but Connie, inside the wheelhouse, began to steam dry. It was a good thing, too—she was just about out of dry clothes.

Time ticked away. There was no sign of Emmett. Larry worked in silence on the radio. Pete watched him, fascinated. Connie preferred to watch the spot where the sea met the sky.

It changed before her eyes. The dark gray plate overhead began to lift, the peaks on the waves seemed to shrivel, and it grew quiet. The storm was backing away.

Connie grabbed Pete's hand. "Look!"

A square black rock, covered with yellow barnacles, popped up out of the sea twenty yards away. "*Look*, Pete! Hey, Larry!"

It was a whale, and beside it was a smaller one.

"Right whale," said Larry, clear as a bell, "and a calf."

Connie grabbed Larry's shoulder. "A right whale? And a calf? The rare ones? What's that all over them barnacles?"

"Nah barkles. Whale ice," said Larry.

"Whale *ice?*"

Larry stumbled over his tongue and made a sucking sound.

Connie removed her hand from his shoulder.

"Lice. Whale lice," said Larry.

"*Yuck.*"

"Grabs." Larry dashed a quick look at Connie. "Lilgrabs."

"What?" Connie looked helplessly at Pete.

"Crustaceans," said Pete.

"Oh!" said Connie. "Little *crabs?*"

Larry beamed.

Connie beamed back.

Larry turned bright red and dropped his screwdriver.

"They're so close," said Connie. "Aren't they afraid of a big boat like this?"

"Rightsarnt," said Larry.

Connie watched, transfixed. They seemed to be swimming in slow motion. Suddenly the larger of the two whales raised a flipper in the air. "Hey," said Connie. "I hope the others aren't missing this. Emmett's down in the lounge giving a pep talk to a bunch of cranky passengers. If they knew these guys were swimming around out there—"

"Maybe we should tell them," said Pete.

Connie took a long, lingering look, then she tied her hood up and left the wheelhouse with Pete.

Outside the Seaview Lounge they paused, listening. There were no more shrieking sounds, anyway. "Do you suppose he's still alive?" asked Connie. She pushed open the door.

Most of the passengers were pressed up against the Plexiglas windows, mesmerized. Some passengers were more than mesmerized. They were asleep.

"The old whalers loved to find right whales," Emmett was saying from his position behind the conscious group. "Not only were they friendly and slow, but after they were killed, they'd float. These particular whales are *extremely* rare." He looked behind him, saw Pete and Connie, and grinned.

Saved by the whales.

"You'll note the right whale has no dorsal fin," said Emmett.

Connie looked at the dozing passengers. How could they sleep through this? Then she looked behind her at the bar. Yes, the level in the Dramamine bottle was distinctly lower.

"There they go," said Emmett. "See the V-shape to the blow?"

Connie saw the blow. Then she saw nothing but one tail, horizontal to the sea, a waterfall sheeting from it.

They were gone.

The crowd sighed in unison. At least the ones who were awake did.

Connie looked around. "We should have found—" she stopped. "Hey," she said. "I have something to tell you."

Pete looked at her curiously. Connie motioned him to follow her out of the lounge.

When they reached her cabin, Connie shut the door carefully behind Pete and pulled him into the room, away from the door. "I know who stole my camera," she said softly.

"What?"

"And Libby Smith's watch."

"Who?"

"But not the money. There was no money."

"What?"

"And it has nothing to do with the harpoon."

Pete frowned. "What in the—"

"Tweetie," said Connie.

Chapter
29

*After such as excitement it seemed
very lonely . . .*

At first Pete fell back into the age-old defensive posture that Connie had taken leave of her senses.

"Tweetie," he repeated, with all the skepticism he could muster.

"Tweetie. Here." Connie fished around in her knapsack and removed a fairly crisp twenty-dollar bill. "Try and slide that under the door. You can't. There's a rubber lip, or something. When you were doing your hundred-yard dash, I got to thinking about old Tweetie, and looking at the door, and I noticed that there was no light shining through underneath. I tried to slide this through and I couldn't."

"So from this you conclude—"

"From this I conclude that nobody slid any twenty

under Tweetie's door. From *that* I conclude that Tweetie probably never had any money stolen in the first place. You said her mother knew nothing about her father giving her the money, right?"

"Right," said Pete cautiously. "But Tweetie not having any money is a far cry from—"

"So then I got to thinking. Why would Tweetie lie?"

Pete could think of no reason for Tweetie to lie.

"Because of you," said Connie.

Pete stared at her. *"Me?"*

"What's the first thing everyone on this ship has said to you the minute they find out who you are? Something about crime, right? Something about you being a sleuth, and solving crimes. Where's Tweetie every chance she can get? Underfoot, with her ears wide open. Under *your* feet. See what I mean?"

"No, I don't."

"Come on! She's nuts about you. You told me how she showed up at Factotum every day, giving you one dumb job after another, hanging around for—"

"Wait a minute. It was a couple of balloons, a beach ball, a bike tire, a—"

"Then as soon as you told her you were going away for a week she coerced her mother into taking her on the cruise with you."

"Now that's where you're way off," said Pete. "Nobody is going to take an eight-year-old kid on a week-long cruise just because she—"

"Her mother never suspected Tweetie's real motives. Her mother was too het up about her own problems. All she knew was that Tweetie wanted to see whales. Her husband happened to be away—"

"He's always away."

"So there. See? The surrogate father thing. Every piece fits. And once Tweetie got on board, she hung around you as much as she could, but you weren't as attentive to her here as you were back home. You were preoccupied with Polly."

"I was preoccupied with you. You were—"

"Sick. And you kept running down here to check on me. And when I wasn't sick I was hanging around you, cutting Tweetie out. From the time we went spitting in the wake she's been glaring at me, but I couldn't figure out why until later. I don't, as a rule, run into eight-year-old competition."

Pete felt himself grow red. He found this whole conjecture, this whole conversation, ridiculous.

"So anyway, old Tweetie's started plotting ways to get you to pay attention to her. Then she hit on it. Crime. She fabricated a twenty-dollar bill and reported it stolen. She figured you'd buzz around her trying to get the money back. You didn't. So what did she do? She took Libby Smith's watch. You didn't do too much about that, either, did you? So she took my camera. And you still didn't track her down. Some sleuth."

"Then what?" asked Pete irritably. "She took the harpoon?"

"Of course not. That's the one thing she couldn't have taken very easily. Assuming she got as far as the captain's cabin she would have taken something small, like a compass, not something big, like the harpoon." Connie paused. "Assuming, of course, Emmett has a compass."

"The kind you're talking about? The kind that comes in a Cracker Jack box? No."

"Don't get snippy! I'm not just making this up."

Unfortunately, Pete was beginning to think maybe she wasn't. "So go on. What then? Tweetie didn't take the harpoon. So who did?"

Connie looked momentarily crushed. "I don't know. But don't you see what happened after the harpoon got stolen? After Jackson got killed? This legendary kindhearted thief of yours went into action. The camera, the watch, the so-called stolen money, all got returned to their rightful owners. I'm not as nice as you are, Pete. I never could picture a thief returning things after he no longer needed them just to be nice. But an eight-year-old in over her head was another story. She stole some stuff. It was all sort of a joke. Then something else got stolen, something somebody actually used to murder someone. See? Tweetie panicked. She was sure we'd think what we did think, that whoever took all those other things took the harpoon, too, and killed Jackson. And suddenly this little ploy to get your attention turned into something scary. She didn't want to get caught with the goods, so she gave them back, one by one. And that scene in the corridor with her mother. To Tweetie it probably sounded like Madeline was accusing her of sabotaging the ship, too. That's why she burst out crying. She thought we were closing in."

"She's *eight*."

"I know. I know. But you have to admit she's got this half-adult brain. Maybe she didn't figure it out to the last detail the way I've described. Maybe she just got scared. Maybe she wanted to undo whatever she could that was adding to her stress and strain and guilt."

Guilt. It didn't seem fair that an eight-year-old should have it, too. Pete sighed and stood up.

"Where are you going?"

"To talk to Tweetie."

"So you believe me?"

"No, I don't."

"Do you want me to come?"

"Yes, but you'd better not." He opened the door.

"Pete?"

He turned.

"Don't elope with her or anything, will you?"

Connie lay on her bunk staring at the ceiling. If she was right about Tweetie, if Tweetie stole the camera and the watch, it was now down to the harpoon. And Connie was pretty sure she was right about Tweetie. So who stole the harpoon? Whoever killed Jackson. Who killed Jackson? Whoever stole the harpoon.

Connie went over it again. Emmett asleep with the door unlocked. Odd behavior, considering the rash of thefts, *Tweetie's* thefts. But no, Emmett had explained the open door by saying that he fell asleep before Stephanie left, and Stephanie left without locking the door. But what about the night Connie had bumbled into his cabin? The door had been unlocked that night, too. Why? Because Emmett had been expecting someone. So who's to say Emmett wasn't expecting someone every night, and his door was always unlocked? Who would know that? The person he was expecting. And whom was he expecting? Someone who knew his door was going to be unlocked. What had Emmett said when Connie barged in? *Is this how you get even, by scaring me to death?* He'd pulled Connie into his bunk as if it were a routine occurrence. Then he'd said something else, something about having given up on her, afraid she was going to stay mad forever. So Emmett was expecting someone who was angry with him. Who was angry with the captain? The fired cruise director, Aura Caine? The fanatic Jenny Sears? One seemed too old, the other too crazy, but who knew what might happen after months and months at sea? The crew of *The Pequot* spent one night on shore a week. It didn't leave much time for shoreside relationships. What it did leave was plenty of room for things to develop with someone at sea. Someone on *The Pequot.*

At least, thought Connie, if it explained nothing else, it explained the floating Peyton Place.

Now that Pete thought about it, it did seem that back on Nashtoba, and after she'd come on board, Tweetie had been consistently underfoot. Until lately, of course. Until the murder. Then she'd almost avoided him. And now?

It took him twenty minutes to find her, curled up in one of the ship's blankets, all alone on a plastic bench on the stern.

Pete sat down beside her. "Hey, it's not bad back here, now. No diesel fumes."

Tweetie looked up at him, once, quickly.

"I've been looking for you. I'd like to ask your opinion about something if I might."

Another look. "About what?"

"About these thefts."

Tweetie began to bang the heel of one sneaker into the leg of the bench.

"People have all these theories. I have one, too. I think I know who took the harpoon. The only trouble is, first I have to make sure that this person wasn't the same person who took the camera and the watch."

Tweetie stopped kicking the bench.

"It was a bad idea, a very bad idea, to take the camera and the watch. But whoever took the harpoon might have killed somebody, and that's worse. And then, of course, there's the twenty dollars. I'll tell you something, when I was eight, my father never gave *me*

228

any twenty dollars. As a matter of fact, when I was eight my father—"

Pete stopped. Tweetie's eyes were screwed shut and her mouth was wide open. A half a second passed that seemed to Pete like half a century, and then Tweetie started bawling.

Pete reached out with one arm and awkwardly patted the blanketed bundle. He tried to think of the right thing to say. "It's okay, Tweetie," he said instead. Finally the damp shape beside him was no longer convulsed with sobs. It started to tremble and sniffle instead. Word by soggy word, the truth came out.

Not the harpoon. No killing. None of the things she seemed to think her mother had accused her of, like breaking the boat and the radios. Tweetie had had no twenty-dollar bill at all, but yes, she'd taken Connie's camera, and Libby Smith's watch. Why those particular items? Like Goldilocks and The Three Bears, Tweetie had simply tried a few doors until she'd found one that was open and no one inside.

After fifteen minutes or so Tweetie wiped her runny nose on Pete's shirt and looked up at him through drowned eyelashes. "Are you going to tell Mom?"

That was a good question. Pete thought about it and came up with what he felt almost sure was the right answer. "We'll both tell her."

Tweetie didn't seem to think his answer was so hot. She slid to her feet. Pete stood up and held out his hand. Tweetie slipped hers into it, and they headed below to face the music together. With each step Pete could feel Tweetie's hand getting clammier.

Pete held on tighter.

There was a tap on the door. Connie jumped up and opened it. Pete came in, looking ragged.

"What happened? How'd it go?"

Pete slumped onto the bunk. "Tweetie confessed. I turned her in to her mother. The sentence is being served."

Connie winced. "What did she get?"

"Confined to quarters. Who knows when she'll get out. When Madeline's through being furious, I guess. But when she does get out, she has to apologize to you and Libby Smith. And Emmett."

Connie sighed. "The things we do for love."

"She's afraid the captain's going to lock her in the hold."

"What *will* he do, Pete? When the killer is found, I mean. Is there a hold?"

"Oh, he'll probably just lock him in his cabin. Take away his belt and razor, the usual routine. Or *her* belt and—" Pete looked up at Connie, his eyes bleak. "Have you heard from Polly?"

"No."

Neither of them spoke.

"So now it's down to the harpoon," said Pete finally.

Sometimes they did think alike.

"I've been thinking about that," said Connie. "And I think if we go with the obvious, things get simpler. The night I stumbled into Emmett's cabin, he'd left his door open because he was expecting someone, someone who was angry with him, someone he thought might or might not come. Maybe he expected that same person the night the harpoon was stolen. Maybe he expected that same person every night. That person would have known that Emmett's door was open, right?"

"Right," said Pete cautiously.

"So who was angry at Emmett? Aura Caine because

he'd just fired her. Jenny Sears, because she hated his harpoon. Who else?"

Pete thought. "You said Heather Seasons was annoyed that she couldn't interest him. But Jenny Sears would be a good place to start. I'd like to know if she's lying about being in Brady's room. And I think I'll have another talk with Emmett."

"So why don't I talk to Jenny and see what I can find out?"

"Okay. I want to stop in on Polly, too." But Pete made no move to get up from Connie's bunk. His eye sockets looked stretched and hollow, as if he were dehydrated, or had just run out of steam.

Connie sat down beside him. "Are we having fun, yet?"

"No."

The force behind the single word startled her.

"I wanted something from this trip, you know? I didn't want to go, I admit that, but once I made up my mind to it, once you said you'd come, there were other things—"

"I know," said Connie. "Me, too."

"I figured if we were away from the island, if we left our history behind, if it was just us some of the time—"

"And Jackson and Polly."

"And this murderer."

"There's been no time," said Connie. "At least not the right kind. Everything intrudes."

"When we get home," Pete began, but then he stopped. "You never much liked it, did you? The island, I mean."

"I don't know," said Connie. "I guess I just didn't like my own company. I hated feeling trapped, alone. It was easier to blame Nashtoba for that. And you

231

were so much a part of the place and I wasn't even a part of you."

"And now?"

And now. Connie pictured stark pines against bleak sky, dirt roads full of ruts, sand in the bed, howling wet wind, poison ivy.

"Home," she said.

Chapter
30

. . . been employed in various duties . . .

Pete dragged himself away from Connie's door carrying a double load of resentment and frustration. He wanted this to be over with. He wanted to be off this boat. He wanted to be away from everyone.

Almost everyone.

It was just as well that he ran into Emmett Grey before he got to Polly. He followed him to the wheelhouse. "I want to talk to you."

Larry Morant was there, still at work on the radio, and for some reason just the sight of him annoyed Pete.

"I have about two minutes before I have to meet with the restless natives in the lounge," said Emmett. "What do you want?"

"Alone," said Pete. "I want to talk to you alone." The back of Larry Morant's neck turned red. Emmett gave Pete another curious look and turned to his first mate.

"Larry? Do you mind? Check on Sam, will you?"

Larry collected himself awkwardly and shambled out.

"So?" said Emmett.

"So who have you been expecting in your cabin at night?" asked Pete.

"Excuse me?"

"Who is she?" asked Pete, again. "Someone who is not pleased with you, I gather."

Emmett had the good grace not to deny the basic premise, at least. "I don't see how this has any bearing on this murder."

"You've been leaving your door open, waiting for this person. This person knows you're leaving your door open. Someone walked through that open door and pilfered the harpoon. I'd say that has some bearing."

"Well, it doesn't."

"Okay," said Pete. "It's your investigation. I'm just trying to find out who killed Jackson so you can get him under lock and key before he does it again." He turned away.

"For God's sake," said Emmett. "I'm telling you she has nothing to do with it."

"Okay," said Pete. "That's that. You're the one who hired me, you make the rules. Of course the police won't see it that way, but it's no skin off my nose. I don't suppose Aura Caine's too pleased with you these days?"

Pete had to figure the look of incredulity mixed with distaste on Emmett's face was real.

So not Aura Caine. So he could only hope Connie was getting more out of Jenny Sears.

Connie hated to admit it, but she was a little afraid of Jenny Sears. It didn't help things any that when she finally found her she was standing in the corner of the Seaview Lounge, rain-soaked and white-faced, heaping a torrent of abuse on Brady Pearson.

"Right whales. *Right* whales? A mother-calf *pair?"*

"I apologize," said Brady. "Again. I only saw them myself shortly before they dove. You were in the lounge before, I didn't notice you'd gone."

"You didn't *notice.* You didn't notice I'd gone."

Connie had to admit that Jenny Sears had a point. Not noticing she had left the lounge was kind of like not noticing Morticia Addams had left your hot tub. As a matter of fact, now that Jenny Sears was in the lounge, every pair of eyes was trained in her direction.

There had been plenty of background chatter from the collection of passengers in the lounge, and some of it had sounded heated enough in its own right, but all of a sudden the noise level dropped. Brady noticed it, too. He dropped his own voice, and Connie missed most of what sounded like a major decline in Brady's patience. Pretending to be engrossed in a framed print of a nineteenth-century whaling ship, Connie moved closer.

"If you insist on continuing this fruitless conversation, we'll do it someplace else."

"Like where, your cabin? I see."

"I assure you, you don't."

There was a half second of silence. "And what's that supposed to mean?"

"It means," hissed Brady, "that nothing could interest me less."

There was a longer moment of silence, following the resounding smack of flesh meeting flesh. Connie looked over in time to see a lily-white hand withdrawing from a very red face. She hated violence. She decided it might not be the best time to talk to Jenny Sears. Besides, Emmett had just entered the lounge and was immediately accosted by at least twenty angry passengers. She didn't much like cannibalism, either.

She waited a judicious minute or two after Brady left the lounge, and followed him.

It wasn't the best time to talk to Brady Pearson, either. He whipped open his cabin door with his jaws grinding and his eyes black.

"Excuse me," said Connie. "Do you have a minute?"

"No."

Connie decided to pretend she hadn't heard. She pushed past Brady and shut the door. "Thanks," she said. "It'll only take a minute. Orders from the captain. It's a matter of a discrepancy in several reports. I have Pete's notes here, and a question has come up about the afternoon Jackson was murdered. Around three, I think it was." She snuck a sideways glance. "Oh, right. Here it is. Jenny Sears. There were reports she was seen entering your room around three, but somewhere here *you* say—"

"I don't see how it could possibly matter whether Jenny Sears came by my room at three or not."

"I don't think it does matter if Jenny Sears came by your room. Or entered your room. What matters is, who lied?"

"Why? We're not talking about six-thirty, we're talking about three o'clock. I fail to see what—"

"Maybe I should say not *who* lied, but why? That's

the thing, the lying, see? Who would go to the trouble of—"

"*I* lied!" shouted Brady. "All right? I lied. Jenny Sears was here until four or so. Now will you go?"

"Then Jenny Sears lied, too. Why? Why did you both lie?"

Brady pushed a hand through some already disarranged hair. "I assure you I'm in one of those rare moods where I could consider physically ejecting you."

"I don't blame you," said Connie. "But it'll be quicker and less painful for us both if you just answer the question."

Brady blinked. "I have never enjoyed the company of women like you. You make me realize how little sense there is in attempting to be delicate. All right. *All right.* I lied because I was mortified to admit that I spent an hour of my valuable time in a sordid sexual encounter with a half-wit."

It was something Jackson Beers might have said. "And is that why Jenny lied? She was mortified, too?"

Brady looked like he really might try to pick her up and heave her out the door. "No, she was not. As a matter of fact, I've been at some pains to try to discourage any recurrence of the event, and the aftermath, as you no doubt witnessed in the lounge, has been unpleasant."

"Then why would Jenny lie?"

"Because I encouraged her to. Because I implied that this type of activity between employees and passengers was against company rules. Because I told her it could mean termination of my research privileges aboard *The Pequot* if the word got out."

"Would it?"

"I have no idea. The point is moot. The minute this

boat touches land I'm terminating any further association myself."

"Because of Jenny Sears?"

Brady Pearson walked to the door and ripped it open. "Because of Jenny Sears. Because of that buffoon who was murdered. Because of this footlocker they call a cabin. Because of the food. Because of the rain. Because of *you.*"

Connie thought of pointing out that it had stopped raining ages ago, but she didn't think it would have made much difference.

Besides, by the time she reached the top of the stairs, it had started to rain again.

In buckets.

When Pete rapped on Polly's door and got no answer he was half-relieved and half-anxious. He rapped again, louder. "Hey! Pol. Open up."

"I will if you get out of my way," said Polly behind him.

Pete jumped.

"I was looking for you," said Polly, "If you can believe it." She pushed the key into the lock, opened the door, and led Pete in.

"What for?"

"You know, I suppose it's true that I would need a reason. How's that for a sad state of affairs? How'd we get this way, huh?" Polly shut the door behind them and flopped onto the bed. "Anyway, I've got a reason. I'm coming clean."

One of Pete's knees wobbled under him. He walked over to the dresser and leaned against it.

"It's funny, it wasn't until Libby Smith talked to me that I snapped to. I think I've been in some sort of a daze, or something. Shock? Is it shock? Libby likes

238

you, you know. She says you remind her of her husband. She also said she thought this whole thing was pretty rough for you, too. That's when it dawned on me. I thought about it all afternoon, about what I'd done, about what I was doing."

"Wait."

Pete remembered doing this same thing as a kid, after he'd already figured out there was no Santa Claus, stopping his parents when they tried to tell him there wasn't. "Before you say anything to me I think it's only fair that you know what they know, all right? I talked to Larry Morant. He says he was in his cabin the whole time, he heard the whole thing. He says he heard a voice, but he swears it wasn't you. He isn't sure who it was, but he knows it wasn't you."

"Pete—"

"Do you understand what I'm saying to you, Polly? This is all they have. They have some theories about Emmett's harpoon, but unless you're sleeping with the captain they still don't involve you. Emmett hired me to find some facts. I've found some. Not enough. Nobody said I had to solve this crime. They don't have anything, Polly. I want you to think very—"

"What do you mean, unless I'm sleeping with Emmett? I'm not sleeping with Emmett!"

"I know," said Pete, relieved. Another one down. "But that's beside the point. Anyone could have taken that harpoon, either the person who knew the door would be open, or someone that person told about the door, or maybe—"

"I didn't do it," said Polly.

Chapter
31

Rugged weather . . .

I didn't kill him," said Polly again. "That's what I was coming to tell you. I would have told you right away but I could tell by your face that you thought I did. The minute Emmett said he was dead, the minute you looked up, you looked right at me and it was all over your face. You thought I killed him. It felt sort of . . . good."

Pete stared at Polly. *The first thing I'm going to do when I get home,* he thought, *is to find a really good psychotherapist for my sister.* "You felt sort of good," he said. "You let me have eighteen different kinds of anxiety attacks over this because for one little minute you felt sort of good. Why in hell—"

"Because you think I'm such a jerk!" Polly shouted

"Because you hate every guy I ever went to the movies with! And you think I'm such a wimp I can't even menengage myself to a—"

"Wait a minute—"

"No. You have to admit that much, Pete. You were disgusted with me. Because I put up with him. Because I was so afraid of him. And then in that one second when I saw you thought I killed him . . . it was like you wanted me to, Pete. You wanted me to have done it! You were proud of me, then! And what about Connie? Why would she make up an alibi for me unless you'd told her I did it?"

"Polly, for—"

"Yes. Oh, yes. And then I tested it out. I tested you to see if you still believed it later, when you asked me where I was. You still believed it then, and you believed it today, too. You were going to lie to the cops for me, weren't you? You thought I did pretty great by killing him, didn't you?"

Pete stared at Polly. Things weren't getting any more real around here, that was for sure. "The only thing I thought," he said carefully, *"when,* for a fleeting second I *considered* it, was that you'd made the biggest mistake of your life. But I also thought we could talk about it."

"Yeah. That's your version of talking, isn't it? You point out my mistakes and I listen. *We* don't talk, Pete. I ask you what's going on with you and Connie and you shut me off like it's none of my business. What I think doesn't count, does it?"

"Wait one minute, here." Things were getting off-track. Way off track. "So you didn't kill him. So—"

"No. And I've been feeling like a real jerk for not telling you that and I'm sorry. I mean that. It wasn't fair. I wasn't thinking straight. I needed to feel that I'd done something right in somebody's eyes, just for a day or two. If you never forgive me you'll be right, I guess. But guess what else? Guess what else I figured out lying around up here all day? By the time I came on this boat . . . no, by the time I called you. Way back then. I think inside my subconscious someplace I knew that marrying Jackson was going to be a big mistake, and that's why I asked you on this trip. I wanted you to talk me out of it."

Pete stared at Polly.

"One part of me kept trying to convince you he was okay, while another part of me was begging you to talk me out of it. And it worked. You convinced me. You and Connie. And Jackson, of course. But then I had another problem. How to get rid of him. I couldn't do it. I was so afraid of him. I couldn't have—" Polly stopped.

"Killed him," said Pete.

"Killed him," repeated Polly. "But I hated him by then. I really hated him. And I think he knew what I was doing before I did. From the minute we got on this boat he turned into something . . . something mean. It wasn't this bad before. But we've been over all that. Anyway, I was coming to find you to tell you that I didn't do it, and I'm sorry for how I've been acting, and . . . and I know you were trying to help me all the time. I know that."

It took Pete a while to recover from his sister's speech, but when he did, he still didn't know what to say. Was it really true that he was incapable of two-way conversation with his sister? He didn't think so, but he was no longer so sure.

"I don't think you're a jerk," he said. "I can't stand

242

to hear you say that. And I do care what you think. If I don't tell you what's going on with Connie and me it's because I don't know what to say. I don't know what to do. I know you like Connie. I know you want us to—" Pete stopped. "But it's true I don't much like your boyfriends."

"And for once I agree with you." Polly grinned shakily, but soon her face collapsed into thoughtfulness again. "You want to hear something funny, though? Now that somebody's killed Jackson, I've stopped hating him. Does that seem weird to you?"

"I'll tell you what it seems like," said Pete. "It seems like you figured out an awful lot in a short space of time."

"Except who killed him," said Polly. "And you want to know another funny thing? Until now, I haven't cared."

"And now you do?"

Polly nodded.

"So what do you think? Who did it? Why?"

"I don't know who did it. I know plenty of people on this boat hated him, but I think hate's sort of overrated, don't you? If I were going to kill, it would have to be over something stronger than hate, I think."

"Like what? Greed? Ambition? Guilt?"

"I'd say love," said Polly. "Love is much stronger than hate. But do you think anyone on this boat *loved* Jackson?"

That brief lull in the wind and the rain must have been the eye of the storm. Both were back full force, and Connie grabbed for the walls as she careened her way to her room. What had ever possessed her to think she was finally getting some sea legs? She stumbled into her cabin and reached for Rita's box of Dramamine. There were two left. She swallowed one and collapsed onto her bunk. She wasn't sure how many minutes she'd been lying there when there was a knock on her door.

"It's me."

Pete.

Connie struggled to her feet and opened the door.

"Come on," he said. "I'm buying you a drink." He took her by the arm and led her into the hallway.

"Why? What?"

"Polly didn't do it," he said. "But we knew that, of course."

"Of course," said Connie.

Pete grinned at her. It had been a while since he'd done that. She followed him into the lounge.

It was after six-thirty. There was no one in the lounge, and the bar closed at six-thirty sharp, but Pete didn't care. He snuck behind the bar, found the beer cooler, and opened two Molson's. Apparently *The Pequot* didn't stock Connie's brand, Ballantine. She took the Molson, and clinked her glass into Pete's.

"So she didn't do it."

"Nope. But she thought I thought she did, and she didn't want to disillusion me. And on top of that, she's decided she asked me along just to talk her out of marrying him. Can you believe it?"

Connie thought about that one as she attended to her beer. "Yes, I can believe it. It makes sense, Pete. You've never once liked anyone she's gone out with, and she must have known that Jackson wasn't going to fare any better than the rest. So why put herself through a week of torture, right before the wedding, unless she secretly wanted out of the whole thing? Yes, I think that makes perfect sense."

"So what got her so gone on the creep in the first place?"

"A mix of things. She was on the rebound from Sam, and Jackson was charming and attentive, at least at first. She also wanted to be married. Plenty of couples team up for less reason than that, I guess. Which reminds me." She told him about Jenny Sears and Brady Pearson.

"So if Jenny Sears were chasing around after Brady, it seems unlikely she'd be rendezvousing with the captain as well," said Pete. "But you never know around this place. I asked Emmett about Aura Caine and he looked so shocked he couldn't have been faking."

Pete rambled on and on about something or other, but Connie had trouble listening. Her eyelids started to droop.

"Hey," said Pete.

"Sorry," she said. "This beer was a mistake. I took a Dramamine and I can't keep my eyes open."

"You took a Dramamine? Didn't I tell you you're not supposed to drink when you take that stuff?"

"Yes, you did. But I figured one beer wouldn't matter much. I wasn't—"

All of a sudden Pete straightened up as if he'd been electrocuted. He slid off his barstool and headed for the door. "I told Polly I'd meet her in her room before dinner. Would you do it? I'll be there soon."

"Why? Where are you going?"

"I'll meet you in Polly's room."

"Wait," said Connie. She had half a mind to follow him, but once again her eyelids drooped.

"Hey," said Pete. "Get Polly, all right? And some coffee. I need you awake."

Connie pushed her beer away, but it was too late. It was empty.

Chapter
32

*Getting discouraged of ever having wind
to reach port.*

Pete could hear her rummaging around in her cabin. First there was the sound of staccato footsteps, then a hastily opened and closed drawer, then the sound of running water and then a crash, followed by a yelp of pain.

Pete knocked. "Are you all right?"

"Yes. Who is it?"

"Peter Bartholomew. Is everything okay?"

"No. Yes. Go away."

"I need to speak with you for a minute."

Pete's statement was greeted first with silence, then with suspicion. "Why? What do you want?"

Pete didn't answer.

Stephanie Schrock flung open the door.

Pete looked at the bloody fingertip she cradled with her other hand. "What happened?"

"This damned ship is rolling around like a bowling ball, that's what happened. I slewed into the sink with a glass in my hand. Now what do you want?"

"Do you have any Band-Aids? If not I can—"

Stephanie Schrock walked away from him and pulled open another drawer. "Yes, I have Band-Aids." She pulled out a box of them, and awkwardly tried to open it with her remaining fingers.

Pete took the box from her and selected a Band-Aid. "You should wash it first."

Stephanie glared at him.

"Okay, let it get infected if you want."

She went to the sink and washed.

"Here. Sit down."

She sat down. Pete wrapped the Band-Aid around her finger, and motioned to her to keep it up. She propped her elbow on her knee and glared at Pete again. "So what do you want?"

"I've been talking to Emmett." Pete hesitated. "The captain."

"I know who Emmett is, thank you. So what?"

"It occurred to me—" Pete stopped. He had to make this sound impersonal somehow, unrelated to Stephanie Schrock, while at the same time grilling her about certain extremely personal, and possibly damning, behavior. But how? He decided to be honest and open. Besides it being the only method he was skilled at, he figured it would be the last method Stephanie Schrock would expect him to use. "Look. Someone inadvertently entered the captain's cabin the other night and it seemed clear that Emmett was expecting someone else. I wanted to know who it was, because I thought it might shed some light on some of the things I'm investigating. Emmett was very gallant, though. He wouldn't say."

Stephanie Schrock got up and fussed with a drawer.

"In the course of the exchange in the cabin it became clear that the person the captain was expecting was angry with him. He wasn't convinced this person would come, but he left his door open in the hopes that she would. Do you follow me?"

"Not in the least. Now if you'll—"

"You were angry with him. How did you put it?" Pete pulled out his notebook and flipped through it. " 'I'm not used to being passed out on,' isn't that what you said? Granted, you were angry with other people, and maybe Emmett took the brunt of a—"

Stephanie whirled around. "Emmett Grey took the brunt of nothing. *I'm* the one who took it. *Me.* Nobody's that tired. Nobody keels over in the middle of one of my sentences! Not that I see what any of this has to do with you. Now would you please exit the—"

"Look," said Pete. "I'm trying to do a job, that's all. It doesn't matter to me who was in Emmett's cabin or not, except for one reason. Somebody came through Emmett's open door and stole that harpoon, and I'm just trying to find out how many people might have known his door would be open. Was it left open for you?"

Stephanie turned her back to Pete without answering.

"Okay," said Pete. "That's that. I'll add only one more thing. Someone on this boat murdered Jackson Beers with Emmett's harpoon, and we don't know who did it. The boat's not going anywhere. The strain is getting to everyone, and in Emmett's opinion, things could get dangerous if the uncertainties aren't cleared up. I know he's worried sick. He wants whoever did this locked up. Now."

Pete didn't expect this amateur speech to have any effect at all—he was surprised when Stephanie turned around and he saw that she was crying. She didn't cry the way Connie did—other than some rigidity around the mouth her face was not contorted, and she made no sound. Only the tracks of a few hastily wiped tears gave her away.

"Emmett Grey used to leave his door open for me, yes."

"Thank you," said Pete. "I don't . . . It's only because—"

"Skip it. He left his door open for me. Now is that it?"

"How long has he been leaving the door open?"

"If you're trying to find out how long I've been sleeping with him just say so," she snapped. "The answer's not long. Since the end of the last trip. We teamed up on shore and talked about how we'd handle things once we were back on the ship."

"So the arrangement with the open door only began at the start of this trip?"

Stephanie nodded.

"He left the door open for you every night?"

"The ones when it wasn't his shift. It was roomier than this place, and besides, the captain couldn't be seen prowling around among the lowlifes. If I felt like it, and no one else was lurking around, I went up. It seemed the safest way."

"Did anyone else know about the two of you?"

Stephanie thought. "Sam Lederman did. He caught Emmett kissing me, out by the lifeboats. Emmett *said* he didn't see Sam coming, but I happen to think otherwise. Men and dogs. They have to mark their territory, you know?"

Pete coughed. "That's it? Just Sam?"

"I suspect if Sam knew, Ned knew, too. Those two are tight."

"Anyone else? Let's go down the list. Aura Caine?"

"I doubt it. If she'd known, she'd have blackmailed the hide off Emmett. She couldn't stand him. He kept making her work. He also kept threatening to fire her. He finally did it, too." For a half second Stephanie smiled. "But the others? I don't know. I didn't tell them. Ask Emmett."

"How about Brady Pearson?"

Stephanie took a moment before she answered that one. "I was particularly concerned that Brady Pearson not know. I told Emmett that. I didn't want to stay after Brady left that night, I didn't want anything at all suspicious in front of Brady. But Emmett managed to detain me, anyway. He'd gotten Larry to cover that shift so he could do his bit of diplomacy with me and Brady, but when the diplomatic gesture went out the window early on, he saw no need to go back and relieve Larry. Emmett hated to waste an opportunity. So I stayed. At considerable risk to my own professional reputation. And for what?"

Pete decided to abandon his own line of questioning and continued with the opening she'd provided. "So Brady left and you stayed. You had no more brandy, but Emmett did."

The word *brandy* did it. In a flash Stephanie was back in a state of siege. "Brandy. Oh, yes, we're supposed to pretend it was that fancy brandy. It wasn't the brandy. I've seen him drink a lot more than that. He was bored, that's all! Okay, I admit it, I stayed that night because I wanted to stay. I wanted to talk to him. I was upset. I had a few things to get off my chest. But it was clearly asking too much to expect him to listen. There I was, in the middle of a conversation about my career, about my life, about my soul, and Emmett Grey can't even keep his eyes open."

Can't even keep his eyes open. Yes, that was it. Of course.

"It's always *his* needs, *his* plans, *his* schedule! He has the night off? I hop to. I have a few problems? Tough! And all this gallantry of keeping his mouth shut about us. As if it isn't all going to come out the minute the police get into it, anyway! You can tell Emmett Grey for me that I don't care what he says to anyone. The only thing Emmett Grey cares about is Emmett Grey, and you can tell him I said that, too!"

Yeah, she was mad at Emmett, all right. She stood in front of the dresser in a knot of pain, but much of it, Pete now suspected, was self-inflicted.

"I appreciate your candor," he said. "And I think I owe you some in return. Unfortunately, I'm not sure enough to give it. But could I make a suggestion based on what I think I might know about one thing, and what I'm pretty sure I know about Emmett?"

"What?"

"Give him the benefit of the doubt. At least until tomorrow."

Stephanie Schrock's eyes became brittle. " 'Stand By Your Man.' Is that it?"

"Only until tommorrow. And after that, only if he's worth it." Pete grinned.

Stephanie didn't grin back.

* * *

This time Pete found Emmett in his cabin. The minute the captain closed the door behind him, Pete said, "I talked to Stephanie."

Emmett's face froze.

"It's all right. Sort of. At least she knows you said nothing to me, but she admitted she was the one you've been waiting for."

"In vain. I've been waiting in vain, did she tell you that?"

"She's pretty steamed."

"I know that," snapped Emmett. "Because I conked out. The crime of the century, right?"

"I think," said Pete cautiously, "that maybe your timing wasn't so hot. She had some problems she wanted to discuss."

Emmett rubbed his forehead. "I know. I know. Brady's really gotten to her. She's thinking of quitting and it would be a shame. That's why I was trying to help. This job is everything to her. She thinks she's getting nowhere, but really, she's accomplished a lot. And I think Brady knows just how much, too, that's what scares him. But I figured if I sat down with the two of them and cleared the air on who's out for what—unfortunately, the air never cleared. Brady left, and Stephanie starting talking, and then what did I do? The big pillar of support?"

"You passed out. And that's what I've come to talk to you about."

They squatted behind the bar and in front of Emmett's liquor cabinet. "Okay," said Pete. "Let's do this one more time. You shipped on with two sealed bottles of Napoleon brandy in your private liquor cabinet. You say you and Sam tried a glass out of one bottle prior to the night when you and Brady and Stephanie had some in your cabin. Altogether the three of you had four drinks that night. There was plenty left in the bottle, though. You're sure about that?"

"I'm sure. I saw it in the tray on the floor the next morning. I took it back to this cabinet and locked it up."

"Then you gave me the keys to the cabinet after Jackson was killed, so I could give some of the good stuff to Polly."

"Right," said Emmett. "And then you say—"

"That when I opened this cabinet there was one bottle of brandy, still sealed."

"So where was the other one?"

Pete sighed. "Let's take this step by step. On the night in question, what did you do? We were all on deck watching the whales. You decided it would be a good time to try to patch things up with Stephanie and Brady. Which did you do first, invite them for the drink, or get the brandy?"

Emmett rubbed his head. "Let me think. When I left the deck I went to the wheelhouse to talk to Larry. It was time for my shift. Sam was there. I asked Larry if he could hold the fort while I tried to bribe my scientists with booze."

"Then you left to get Stephanie and Brady?"

"I took the wheel to give Larry a chance to use the head and get a cup of coffee. Sam stuck around for a minute or two. I remember he was pretty worked up about—" Emmett stopped.

"About Polly," finished Pete.

Emmett said nothing.

"About Polly?"

"Yes, about Polly. He'd gone down to her cabin,

thinking she'd be alone. He felt he should talk to her, and he wanted to back up her decision about the broken engagement. He was afraid after Polly got home and found herself alone again she might back down. He knocked on the door and Jackson answered. Old Jackson made it pretty clear things were already back on. Sam was furious. He called what Polly was doing a suicide. I tried to settle him down a bit. I told him—" Emmett stopped again and rubbed his face with his hands. "I told him to butt out," said Emmett. "I told him that in situations like this it was useless to play Good Samaritan. Then I left. Larry was back by then."

Both men were silent. After a minute Pete picked up the thread again. "After you left the wheelhouse, what did you do?"

"I went to find Stephanie and Brady."

"Before you got the brandy?"

"Before. I was far from sure they'd come."

"And Stephanie says you told her the specific reason for the invitation was to try some special brandy. Did you tell Brady about the brandy, too?"

"I don't know that I specifically mentioned the brandy. Wait, yes, I did mention it. I told him I'd like him to have a glass of my private stock of Napoleon brandy in honor of our first whale sighting. He'd been antsy as hell because there hadn't been any whales. Both scientists agreed to come. I told them to meet me in my cabin in fifteen minutes, and then I went down to the bar and loaded a tray with the glasses and the brandy."

"The already opened bottle of brandy."

"Yes."

"Okay. And then you went straight to your cabin?"

Emmett nodded. "And in fifteen or twenty minutes

Brady and Stephanie came. The rest you know. We talked, had a drink, Brady left, I convinced Stephanie to stay—"

"And you had another drink."

"I had two, total, the whole night."

"And you remember Stephanie talking about—"

"About Brady, and the boat, and the job. I do remember something about that." He looked so miserable that Pete moved on.

"And in the morning you saw the partly empty bottle, brought it down here and locked it up in the bar. What did you do with the key?"

Emmett pulled the key out of his pocket. "I keep this one with me." Then he reached under the lip of the bar, and detached a key from a small, hidden clip. "I keep this one here."

Pete's heart sank. Back on Nashtoba the police chief was always yelling at the populace for leaving their houses unlocked and their keys in their cars. This boat was almost as bad. "So who knew the key was there?"

"All the crew," said Emmett. "They all do bar duty off and on."

"And the scientists?"

It took Emmett a while to answer. "Stephanie. I told Stephanie about the key one night so she could bring something up."

"But not Brady Pearson?"

Emmett shook his head. "But anyone at the bar could have seen one of us reach under there for the key, then turn around and open the cabinet."

Pete moved around to the other side of the bar.

Emmett reached for the key and then turned to the cabinet.

Yes, it was pretty obvious.

"So what's the big deal?" asked Emmett. "I admit it's odd the bottle is missing, but so what?"

"I think the bottle went missing because there was something besides Napoleon brandy in it," said Pete.

Emmett looked skeptical. "Like what?"

Pete reached over and picked up the bar's bottle of Dramamine with its clearly labeled list of warnings. "This."

Back in the wheelhouse, they talked for a long time.

"This can't be left alone much longer," said Emmett. "Everyone's about to blow."

"Realistically, how long do you think we'll be out here?"

Emmett shrugged. "We're due in Southport tomorrow morning. It depends how long it takes them to figure out we're not coming."

"No luck with the hoses?"

"Sam said to forget it. Ned's tried one useless piece of tube after another. And Larry's wired and rewired that radio twenty different ways without a crackle."

Pete looked at the radio.

Emmett was right.

Twenty different ways, and not a crackle.

Chapter
33

. . . was invited . . . to dine.

Connie woke to the sound of familiar voices.

"Where have you been?" That was Polly.

"Delving into secrets. Being the sleuth you've al ways hoped I would be." That was Pete.

Connie looked around to get her bearings. That's right, she was in Polly's cabin, where she and Polly had been waiting for Pete. And waiting.

"I'm starving," said Connie. "You've made us miss food."

"No, I haven't," said Pete. "The captain's invited us to share a late meal with the crew. He's specifically hoping to see you there, Polly."

Connie yawned and struggled to her feet. "I'm so sorry I took that Dramamine."

"I'm not," said Pete.

Connie peered at him. What the hell was that supposed to mean? Pete just gazed steadily back. If he was trying to tell her something, she was too foggy to figure out what.

Pete turned to his sister. "I know this is tough on you, Polly. It's bound to get tougher, too. Would you like something up here, or would you like to come down?"

Polly shot Pete a shaky smile. "I can't hide forever. I'll come down. Come on. Let's go get dinner. If things are going to get tougher, at least we can fortify ourselves with food."

When the Bartholomews entered the dining room, Emmett rose to greet them. He smiled at Connie and squeezed Polly's shoulder, but his real state of mind was evidenced in the look that he flashed Pete. Emmett was tired.

And worried.

Come to think of it, thought Connie, so was Pete.

Connie looked around. It was long past dinner hour, and the dining room was empty except for the crew. The entire crew, even the chef, Drew, sat at two long tables they had pushed together, and the tables were covered with bowls, glasses, and platters, family style. Aura Caine, Connie noticed, has situated herself at the far end from Emmett. Gilby, however, had somehow managed to plop himself down right between the two other cruise attendants, Heather and Janine. When the new arrivals approached the table everyone stopped talking, and all the men, except for Larry, who seemed frozen, and Drew, who kept eating, stood up. Since all eyes were on Polly, it was clearly meant as a token of respect for her, rather than an example of nearly extinct table manners. As Polly and Connie and Pete pulled out chairs and sat down, Emmett Grey spoke.

"We're happy you were able to join us tonight, Polly. We want you to know you're among friends."

"Thank you," said Polly. "I know. Thank you all. I appreciate the invitation. I'm sorry for what's happened. I . . ." she faltered.

"I appreciate the invitation, too," said Connie. "I'm starved."

They laughed. Bowls were passed. Janine Moss hopped up and brought them drinks. Sam Lederman asked Polly how she was faring with the rough weather; as if everyone had been watching and waiting for just such a conversational raft to cling to, they all jumped in with a lively discussion of The Weather.

"This is the roughest trip I've ever been on," said Janine.

"Oh, this is nothing compared to last September," said Gilby.

Heather Seasons chimed in. "Are you talking about the weather, or—"

"Not only is this the roughest trip I've ever been on, it's the *last* trip I'll ever be on," said Connie.

"It was the last trip Jackson'll ever be on," said Heather. "The lucky stiff. At least he's not stuck here. I swear, when I find out who sabotaged us I'll kill him." Then she looked at Polly. "Or *her.*"

There was a scrape of a chair. A fork clattered to the floor. Polly stood up. "I have to go," she said. "Thank you for the meal. I—"

Connie and Pete started pushing back their chairs, too, but Polly turned on them before either of them had reached their feet. "No. Please stay. I'm exhausted, that's all. Good night. I'll see you both in the

260

morning. Thank you, Emmett, for including me in your meal. Good night."

Polly left.

As soon as the door closed behind her, Drew Baker spoke. "Hey, let's get real. Everybody's thinking about it. Everybody's going crazy trying to figure out who killed him. So why *not* her? He was a creep, right? She was stuck with him, right?"

Sam Lederman half rose in his chair. Drew Baker pointed a knife at him and something told Connie he wasn't just making a conversational point. Ned Tate pulled Sam back into his seat, and everyone except Larry looked embarrassed. Larry looked like he was going to faint.

Nobody looked at Pete.

"Well, what's the big deal?" Heather hollered. "You can't tell me I'm the only one who's thinking it! And who's been put in charge? Her brother!"

"Knock it off, Heather," said Sam.

"And what's it to you if I don't? What happened with you two, anyway? Did she try to kill you, too, Sam? Or was the problem something else?"

"We all know you're an ass, Heather. Don't overdo it."

"Speak for yourself," said Drew. "I think she's got a point. Her fiancé gets zapped, her brother gets hired to cover her tracks."

Emmett's voice cut through the mud. "All right. That's enough."

"Who says?" snapped Heather. "You're the one who hired him. Why him? You said it yourself. He's no cop. Is there someone you're trying to protect?"

"I hired him," said Emmett, "because he was with me when Jackson Beers was killed, so I knew he couldn't have done it. And not only does he have an alibi, he has investigative experience as well. As it happens, his sister has an alibi, too. Now as you seem to be through eating, Heather, perhaps you'd like to clear."

"Wait a minute," said Gilby. "That's not fair. Heather's right. Okay, so he has an alibi, and his sister has an alibi. So that's the first we've heard of it, you know? I think we have a right to know what else you know. I think we have a right to know what *he* knows." Gilby nodded toward Pete.

Oh God, thought Connie.

"As a matter of fact, Emmett," said Brady, "I'm inclined to agree with Gilby. Everyone at this table has been under considerable strain of late, and some of it has been caused by a state of uncertainty over this kangaroo investigation of yours. If any information has come to light, I say we hear it now. This is not, after all, an official investigation."

"Neither is it a democracy," said Emmett. "And as long as we're aboard ship—"

"Death to all tyrants!" shouted Drew.

"Will you cut the crap?" said Ned.

"Oh, go back to your boyfriend and leave us alone," said Heather.

Silence fell.

Nobody looked at Ned.

Ned laughed tightly.

Emmett stood up, moved around the table, and spoke quietly to Pete. Pete followed Emmett into the galley.

"I'll tell you what," said Janine. "Let's clear the air right now. We'll go around the table, me first." She put her hand over her heart. "I, Janine Moss, confess that I loathed Jackson Beers, and that I intentionally spilled clam chowder on his shirt. I did not, however, spear him. Now who's next?"

"I did it," said Stephanie. "All right? Now will you all shut up and eat?"

Aura Caine stood up. "This is all very amusing, my dears, but I, for one, have had it. Finis. My heartfelt thank-yous for including me in this lovely little family feast even though I am no longer flesh and blood, but I believe I'll leave you to devour each other without me. Good-bye."

Stephanie Schrock stood up, too. "I've lost my appetite, thanks to all of you. Good night."

"And I, too, have had enough," said Brady, pushing back his chair, but he didn't get as far as the others.

After what seemed a year and a half, Pete and Emmett emerged from the galley.

"You'll stay, please, Brady," said Emmett. "You, too, Aura. Stephanie? Please sit."

Emmett's voice, the captain's voice, froze them all in their tracks. Brady first, then Stephanie, and finally Aura, sat. Emmett was right—this was no democracy. He crossed the dining room in total silence and locked the doors. When he returned to the table, he stood at its head.

"I've come to the conclusion," said Emmett, "that the longer this drags on, the greater the chance for another catastrophe. All right. Gilby? Brady? You feel you have a right to know what we know? I've decided that you're absolutely correct. Pete? Would you be so kind as to inform the gathered parties exactly what you've been able to learn about our murderer, please?"

What was this, something out of a *Thin Man* movie?

Across the table, Pete and Connie's eyes met.

Yes, that's exactly what it was.

Emmett sat down.

Pete stood up and cleared his throat. "To begin with, there was a theft."

Connie groaned.

Chapter 34

Commenced to scrape bone.

He left Tweetie out of it, and started with the harpoon. It read like a dime-store novel. "On the night of September fourth, the captain's harpoon was stolen from his unlocked cabin as he slept."

Connie eyed the table. There were no more pouts or smirks. Everyone's eyes were on Pete.

"The first thing I was able to determine about this theft was that it occurred between midnight and six A.M., since up until that time there were witnesses who vouched for the presence of the harpoon on the wall. Now—"

"What witnesses?" asked Gilby.

Pete's eyes roamed the table and came to rest on Stephanie. "The captain, himself, and the two guests he had invited for a late night drink. Stephanie Schrock and Brady Pearson. The captain fell asleep before the last of his guests had left, and when he woke, at six the next morning, the harpoon was gone.''

Nicely put, thought Connie.

Brady Pearson looked at Stephanie. Several others looked at Brady *and* Stephanie. Most of them looked at the captain. Connie could see eyes widening all around.

"I realized it would be futile to try to establish many alibis for the night of the theft, since most sensible people would be sleeping from midnight till six," Pete went on. "But there were several things that struck me as odd about this evening drink in the captain's cabin. The first, obviously, was that the captain fell asleep, after only two glasses of brandy, with guests still in the room. The second was that both guests and the captain himself expressed a distaste for either the brandy itself, or the aftereffects of the brandy. What exactly did you tell me, Brady? That you weren't much of a drinker, but that brandy in particular didn't agree with you, I believe?" Pete pulled out his notebook. "Oh. And you said that one of the reasons you left when you did, after the one drink, was that you were 'extremely tired.' Isn't that right, Brady?"

Everyone looked at Brady again.

Brady nodded.

"And, Stephanie." Pete flipped a page. "You told me that Emmett's expensive French brandy was 'no big deal.' You didn't choose to finish the one drink. The next day Emmett Grey was obviously suffering from a hangover, after what he felt was an insufficient amount of alcohol to either cause him to pass out or to give him such a head. There were a few other factors that led me to conclude that Emmett had not fallen asleep, or passed out, without help. One of the factors was the content of the discussion taking place at the time that he nodded off. It didn't strike me as the kind of discussion that would have been sleep-inducing, at least not to someone like the captain."

Connie saw Pete and Stephanie exchange a look. What the hell was going on around here?

"Even so, most of this 'evidence' would fall under the category of out-and-out conjecture. The missing brandy bottle, however, does not."

Will he go for the dramatic pause?

Yes, he did, the sap.

"So I talked to the captain. In the morning he had discovered the bottle on his floor, with some brandy still in it, and had locked it up in the same place he had gotten it from the night before—his private liquor cabinet. Later that same day, Jackson Beers was murdered."

Pete paused again. Around the table a few feet shuffled and one chair creaked. Larry Morant retrieved his fork from the floor.

"Not long after the murder, the captain offered me the key to the liquor cabinet for the purpose of medicinally treating my sister for shock. When I opened the cabinet, there was no nearly empty brandy bottle to be found. The only brandy in the private stock cabinet was one with the seal still unbroken. I have since concluded that the bottle had been disposed of by the murderer, in order to destroy the evidence."

"Evidence of what?" snapped Heather. "Evidence of *what?*"

"Evidence that the captain had been drugged."

And pause for gasp of shock?

Pete paused, all right, but nobody gasped. Everyone but Heather had gotten there long ago.

"Oh, get real," said Heather. "Emmett was drunk."

Gilby, at least, ignored her. "What was he drugged with?"

"Dramamine," said Pete. "From the bottle in the bar. The bottle with the clearly labeled warnings about the effect on the central nervous system if consumed with alcohol. Brady had only one drink, and left 'extremely tired.' Stephanie drank very little of hers because she didn't like it. Emmett, on the other hand, had two good slugs of brandy heavily laced with Dramamine, and passed out. By the way, Stephanie, what did you do with your unfinished glass?"

It took Stephanie a minute to come out of her trance and stop staring at Emmett. "The glass of brandy? I put it back in the box tray, with the bottle."

"The box tray. The tray specially designed for use on shipboard, to hold bottle and glasses upright despite the ship's roll? That tray?"

"Yes. That tray."

Pete turned to Emmett. "Was the glass there in the morning?"

"The glass was there, but there was nothing in it."

"You're sure?"

"I didn't drink it," said Stephanie hotly. "I didn't—"

"No," said Pete. "But whoever took the harpoon, emptied it out. And whoever took the harpoon, took the bottle from the liquor cabinet the next morning, and disposed of that, too."

"Why not that night? Why not dispose of the bottle that night?"

"Because Emmett Grey would be looking for it in

the morning. The odds of him remembering if Stephanie had finished her drink or not were slim. As a matter of fact, he thought she had finished it. But he'd surely notice if the bottle itself were gone. So the bottle was left till morning, Emmett locked it up, and then it was removed from the liquor cabinet later that day."

What a weird crew, thought Connie, looking around. Here Pete was, blabbing away about a murderer, one of their own, no doubt. And what were they feeling? Stephanie Schrock's forehead was buckled in confusion over some obviously minor point of her own, Heather looked bored, Janine acted like she was watching a made-for-TV-movie, Gilby looked full of nothing more than the importance of his own questions, Aura Caine's face was full of disdain, Larry stared straight ahead as if his ears were full of cotton, and Drew Baker looked like he was having a ball. Only Sam, Ned, and Brady looked the least bit shaken, but it was Brady Pearson who finally coughed and spoke.

"So the captain was drugged in order to . . . in order to—"

"To assure an undisturbed entry into the captain's cabin in order to steal his harpoon."

"So who—" began Brady, but his voice trailed off.

Yes, thought Connie? Who? Who could have done this? The cruise director, whose job was in jeopardy, who had been threatened with letters of complaint by Beers? The cruise attendant Jackson had spurned? Or maybe the cruise attendant who strove so hard to please, and was finally pushed to the breaking point by Jackson's demands. Or the other cruise attendant, Gilby, also pushed, possibly jealous? And which of the scientists would be more likely to kill Jackson, the one with the grant or the one with the book? And then there was the gay or not gay deckhand, Ned. And what about Sam? Had Sam tried to save Polly from a fate worse than death—a life with Jackson?

Who was left? Connie doubted if Larry could walk and chew gum, let alone steal and stab. She suspected Drew Baker had only thrown his weight in with Heather in an effort to entertain himself by stirring up confrontation, but who knew what else it might have amused Drew to do?

Connie could almost feel the tautness behind the eyeballs as everyone strained not to look at anyone else.

"The brandy was only a factor because it enabled the murderer to steal the harpoon," Pete went on. "So that brings us to the next question. Why the harpoon?"

"Our weapons arsenal's a bit low right now," said Drew.

"Is it?" asked Pete. "What about your galley, Drew? Any sharp knives? But if the murderer used a sharp knife, it would point straight to the galley, wouldn't it? It would implicate the chef, wouldn't it?"

For a fleeting second Drew almost looked taken aback. Then he grinned, and leered at Connie. *"She's been in the galley a time or two."*

Connie almost choked.

Pete, older and wiser by now, refused to rise to the bait. "True. And then there was that thing I saw you using the other day, Ned, when you were working on the line. What was that?"

Ned, looking more and more rattled, reached into his back pocket and pulled out an eight-inch-long steel spike.

"What is that?"

"A marlin spike."

270

"And what would you use that for?"

"Splicing line."

Pete surveyed the table. "How many of you carry ne of those around?"

"Me," said Ned quickly. "Just me."

Sam shot him a look. Connie was hard-pressed to ecide whose face was whiter.

"So if the murderer had used your marlin spike, at would certainly have implicated you. But what bout the harpoon? Thanks to the dedicated whale- ollower Jenny Sears, just about everyone on board new that there was an antique, wrought-iron whaling arpoon mounted on the wall in the captain's cabin. he captain was, of course, in the wheelhouse with e, *underneath* Jackson Beers when he was killed, nd just about the only person on board with a ast-iron alibi. The captain, therefore, was unim- licable."

Unimplicable?

Pete caught Connie's eye and winced.

"So what if someone wanted to kill Jackson Beers, ut didn't want any of his or her friends blamed for he crime? In that case, the harpoon was the perfect hoice."

"It sounds pretty flimsy to me," said Stephanie.

"It sounds to me," said Gilby, "as if you think omeone at this table is responsible for this crime."

"Why not?" asked Pete. "Which one of you has an libi? You were alone in the galley, Drew. Gilby and Ieather left Janine alone in the dining room, and they :ft each other alone for the crucial time in question. Irady, Stephanie, and Larry have indicated they were ach alone in their respective cabins. Aura, you say ou were in the lounge with the passengers, but only ne person recalls seeing you, and only briefly. Ned, you say you were alone on the stern deck splicing line, and Sam was in the engine room, also alone. Unless anyone wants to correct me?"

Connie noticed that Pete looked at Heather. Her unaccounted-for twenty minutes was still bugging him.

Heather didn't speak.

Neither did anyone else.

"So that eliminates alibis." Pete shot a look at Connie, and then swung around to face Emmett, who was leaning against the wall behind the deckhands. "By the way, Emmett, I should have corrected you earlier. Polly did not have an alibi. Now on to motive. Why would someone kill Jackson? Because Jackson pushed too far? Because someone was going to be harmed in some way by something Jackson did or was planning to do? Because of hate, or fury, or fear, or a desire for power or money or success? Polly thought of another one—love—but she couldn't think of anyone who loved Jackson. So where do each of you fit in the motive category? I think there are enough of them, and enough of you, to make a few matches here and there."

Connie watched Pete look around the table. By now it didn't seem safe to look up at all—everyone's eyes were cast down except Stephanie, who watched Emmett, and Larry, whose gaze still seemed frozen somewhere in midair.

"And what else? We know each of you had the opportunity to kill Emmett, but there are other factors that point to the people at this table." Pete held up his hands and began to tick things off on his fingers one by one. "The murderer had to know where Emmett kept the brandy. He had to know about the harpoon, he had to know about the area above the

heelhouse and that it was frequented by Jackson. So
ur anyone could have observed or overheard enough
o provide him with those facts. But the murderer also
ad to know that in order to isolate *The Pequot* from
he world, not only did the boat have to stop, but two
adios, a phone, the emergency flares, and the emer-
ency position-indicating radio beacon had to be
ecommissioned. I admit that for a while I took each
ncident individually and did not necessarily feel that
ny one act in particular pointed to the crew. The
abotage to the radio and the engine hoses was
omewhat obvious, and anyone who listened to the
afety lecture knew about the flares. The EPIRB is
nounted in plain sight on the outside wall of the
heelhouse, clearly labeled. Taken item by item, I
ould see any number of people doing any of these
hings. But if taken as a whole, aren't we stretching
hings a bit to imagine all this was done by someone
ther than one of you?"

No one answered Pete.

"And there was one other thing the murderer had to
now—that Emmett Grey was going to be drinking
randy with the scientists Monday night."

"They knew," said Heather. "Brady and Ste-
hanie."

And now they were finally down to it. The pointing
ngers.

"But Brady and Stephanie were drugged, too," said
am.

"Not enough," said Gilby. "The captain was the
nly one who passed out."

"Right," said Drew. "Quite the coincidence,
ouldn't you say? Neither Stephanie nor Brady liked
apoleon brandy?"

273

"Why don't you go back to the galley and soak your head?" Stephanie snapped.

"Temporarily and for the sake of argument," said Pete, "I'd like to remove Brady and Stephanie from the discussion. If we do that, we see some other things. It didn't matter if Brady and Stephanie fell asleep or not. If they did, the way still would have been clear for the theft of the harpoon. If they didn't, they would leave. Even if the captain didn't drink enough to put him out, he would have eventually gone to sleep, and he would have slept more heavily than usual. The thief, the murderer, if you will, knew the door would be open, and—"

"Why?" asked Gilby. "Why did he know the door would be open?"

Pete's eyes roamed the table but they only came to rest when they met Connie's. "I think we'll just leave it that he suspected the door would be open."

"Still," said Heather. "Why are you leaving Brady and Stephanie out? You said whoever did it had to know Emmett was getting the brandy, and those two knew. Brady and Stephanie knew."

"I'd like to know why you're so hot to pin this on me," said Stephanie.

"Or me," said Brady.

"I fail to see—" said Aura.

"Oh, for God's sake," said Janine. "Do you know who killed him or don't you? If you know, why don't you just say so. If you don't, why don't you—"

"Shut up," said Drew.

Pete ignored him. "There were others besides the two scientists who knew about the plan for the brandy."

This time the silence was complete, uninterrupted by feet or chairs or voices. Even Pete seemed reluctant to speak. He cast his first nervous glance at Emmett, but Emmett was unrelenting. He jerked his head. *Get on with it.*

Pete cast one more miserable glance at Connie, and went on.

"When Emmett arrived in the wheelhouse to ask Larry to relieve him, Sam Lederman was there. Emmett explained what he had in mind regarding the brandy. Isn't that right, Sam? You heard Emmett tell Larry he was going to invite the scientists to his cabin for some of the Napoleon brandy?"

"I don't remember," said Sam. "I don't remember what he said."

"Do you remember, Larry?"

Larry said one clear word. "Yes."

"And do you remember what Sam said? About Polly?"

Larry turned red and gulped down a half-sound or two.

Thank God Pete decided not to extract a verbatim testimony. "Sam was upset about Polly, wasn't he? Sam had just come from Polly's cabin, assuming that she was unengaged, and would be alone. But Jackson was there. He told Sam the engagement was back on, and Sam was furious, wasn't he? What did he call Polly's reengagement to Jackson Beers, do you remember? Sam, who had at one time been seriously involved with Polly himself. He called it an act of suicide, isn't that right?"

And here goes Perry Mason, thought Connie. And then a second later she thought, *Sam???*

"Sam Lederman stood in the wheelhouse next to you and ranted and raved about the fate worse than death that awaited Polly. It wasn't the first time you'd heard him carry on about this, was it, Larry? For some time now Sam Lederman had been beside himself about events regarding my sister that he perceived to be partly his fault. It was now clear to Sam that Polly felt unable to free herself from this man. What could Sam do about it? What *would* Sam do about it? He was in the wheelhouse when the captain informed you of his plans for his personal stock of Napoleon brandy. You left to get a cup of coffee before extending your wheelhouse shift, but when you returned, Sam was still there, in no better mood than before, despite the captain's efforts to calm him down. Then Sam left. He had time, didn't he? The captain had to go first to Stephanie Schrock's cabin, and then to Brady Pearson's. Sam had time to go down to the bar and—"

"He didn't do it," said Larry, as clearly as if he'd just finished Public Speaking Number Ten. "Sam didn't do it."

"No?" asked Pete. "Then if Sam didn't, who did? When the captain left Stephanie's cabin he went straight to Brady's. When he left Brady's he went straight to the bar. Neither Brady nor Stephanie had time to get to the bar and doctor the brandy before Emmett collected the bottle. If Sam Lederman didn't do it, Larry, who does that leave?"

"Me," he said.

Chapter
35

Squared away for the straits.

I don't get it," said Polly. "I just don't get it."

"Neither did I until I figured out about the brandy," said Pete. "After I figured that out, and talked to Emmett, it meant it was down to Sam or Larry, the only ones who knew beforehand that Emmett would be drinking that brandy that night. And then I thought about the radio. It seemed to be going backward, not forward. Larry must have been spending hours up there, undoing what he'd already done."

"But why?"

"He's nuts about you," said Connie. "Since you first landed on Southport, it seems. He was able to live vicariously through his friend Sam while you two were dating, but once Jackson came on the scene, that was different. Sam didn't help things by pumping him full of all the details, either. When Sam told him about the reengagement and painted your future in such hopeless terms, Larry decided he had to do something to save you."

"So he killed Jackson?"

"So he stole the harpoon with the intent to kill Jackson," said Pete. "He had to wait another day for the right circumstances, that's all—Jackson alone, no witnesses around, and Emmett, whose harpoon he planned to use, with a cast-iron alibi. After I clued in to the state of the radio, Larry seemed to be the logical suspect, but I still didn't believe it. I couldn't come up with a motive. Then I thought about it. You started it, Connie, with all your theories about Tweetie, all that stuff about the things we do for love. And you, Polly. You said you thought love was a much stronger motive than hate. You said you couldn't think of anyone who loved Jackson. But it wasn't a question of who loved Jackson, it was a question of who loved *you.* And then there was that thing about the voices. Larry concocted this whole thing about hearing voices just before Jackson was killed. At first he probably said it was a woman to deflect suspicion from himself, but then when I questioned whether it might have been you, he saw his mistake and panicked. It wasn't going to do you any good to be free of Jackson if you were going to go to jail for his murder. So all of a sudden he became sure it wasn't you. He couldn't say for certain it wasn't anybody else, but he was positive it wasn't you, even reversing his position, now thinking it was a man. At dinner tonight I watched Larry the whole time. He turned beet red the minute you came in and went dead white when Drew and Heather accused you. The minute you stood up to leave, he dropped his fork. I think we would have noticed it all sooner if Larry weren't so—"

"Invisible," said Polly. "He could be in the room for an hour before you noticed he was there. Honestly! I can't think of a single time when I said a single word to—" Polly broke off.

"That's just it," said Pete. "That's why he escaped notice every step of the way. He was in the background at every scene of importance, but nobody noticed. The night he stole the harpoon—"

"I still don't see why he used the harpoon," said Connie. "Couldn't he have found something less conspicuous?"

"But that was just it. If he used any of the more obvious tools, one of the crew might have been suspect. Once he realized that other thefts were going on, he decided to steal something that would fit in with the other stolen items, something of value, like the antique harpoon. That night he drugged Emmett. He knew all about Stephanie and the captain. This wasn't the first time Larry had been asked to fill in. He knew Emmett left his door open. He flipped the boat over to automatic pilot. I saw Emmett do the same thing the day Jackson was killed. A man is *supposed* to be on the bridge at all times. But that doesn't mean a man can't sneak out for a minute or two without anyone the wiser, if the ship is automatically held on course. Then Larry crept into Emmett's room, took the harpoon, and hid it in the one place no one would go, unless we were sinking."

"The lifeboats," said Connie.

"The lifeboats," said Pete. "And then he waited. The moment came. Jackson on the roof, alone, not ten feet from where the harpoon was hidden."

"But why did you confront Larry in front of everyone that way?"

"I know. I felt the same way, at first. But when Emmett hauled me into the galley and laid out his plan, I saw his point. There really wasn't much hard evidence to tie Larry to the crime, and Emmett was afraid that whatever evidence there was would have been either destroyed or contaminated by the time the authorities got to it. Besides, Emmett wanted this over with. He didn't want false accusations hanging over everyone's heads for the rest of the trip, or, for that matter, for cruise after cruise, if they never solved the crime. And I didn't want this hanging over your head, Polly. Emmett seemed to think a confession was the only way, but as long as it was only Larry's neck at risk, why should he admit to anything? If his friend Sam were in danger, though—"

"I still think it was rotten," said Polly.

"Lest we forget," said Pete wearily, "Larry Morant murdered someone. And left us to drift out to sea."

"And that's another thing," said Connie. "Why such an amateur job of sabotage? Surely the first mate could have stopped the ship or jammed the radios with a little more finesse than that."

"Of course he could," said Pete. "But again, if he used a technique that exhibited much skill, it would point straight to a member of the crew, if not himself, then one of his friends."

"But why the sabotage at all?" asked Polly. "He must have known he'd get caught sooner or later. What good did it do to stall us for a few days?"

"Emmett asked him that, first thing, when we took him back to his cabin. Larry wouldn't say, but again, I think it was because of you. You were here. A captive audience. Free. The minute *The Pequot* hit port, you'd go your way, Larry'd go his, if not to jail, then back to sea. The longer we wallowed out here the more time it gave Larry."

"The more time for *what?*"

"To be near you. Ideally, I suppose, to finally talk to you, to tell you how he felt."

"In a million years—" began Polly, but then she stopped. She walked to the window and looked out to sea.

Pete looked at Connie. "A few minutes ago Larry managed to miraculously unearth some extra hoses. We'll soon be under way. He gave Emmett a few hints about the radio, and they'll go to work on that, too."

"And Larry?" asked Connie.

"In his cabin under lock and key. Emmett's still talking to him." Pete yawned. It had been a long day.

The yawn must have been louder than he thought. Polly turned. "It's late. Enough's enough. Let's all go to bed, huh?"

Nobody had to ask him twice. Pete stood up and yanked open the door. He heard a few quick steps behind him, felt a hand on his shoulder, a kiss on his cheek. "Thanks, Pete. I . . . it helps to know. I think."

"Yeah," said Pete. "I think."

He closed the door behind him. From the other side of it he could hear their voices, dropped low.

Connie would stay with her. Polly would be all right.

He was in front of his own door with his key in his hand before she caught up with him.

"I thought you were staying with Polly."

"She doesn't want me," said Connie. "Do you? Or should we call it a night? You're talked out, aren't you? Yes, I can see that. I'll—"

"No, no," said Pete. "I'm not tired." And he wasn't. Not anymore. He pushed open the door.

Connie squeezed through.

They stood face-to-face in the middle of the tiny cabin, but for some reason neither of them seemed anxious to say the first word. It seemed to Pete that it had been a long time since he'd been alone with her, since he'd been able to talk to her, to look at her. "I must warn you," he said. "I'm in the mood for a change of subject. No Polly or Larry or harpoons or—"

"I love you," said Connie. "Other than my own mental health, there's nothing more important to me than you. Polly told me to tell you that. The last part, anyway. I came up with the first part on my own."

Pete stood there quietly for a minute, absorbing her, taking her in. *She's everything I want,* he thought. *She always was.* And she loved him. And she was here, in his room.

"Well?" she asked. "How's that for a change of subject? Will it do?"

"Oh," said Pete, reaching for her, "it'll do."

Chapter
36

A large body of whale. Lowered the boats. captured one which made 50 [barrels].

It was morning. The hoses were repaired. The storm had broken. Emmett Grey steered *The Pequot* over the gently undulating sea toward Tanner Head, the nearest port.

Tweetie had been let loose. She was on deck with her mother, looking for whales. "So when's Dad coming home, anyway?" she asked.

"Not for a while yet," said Madeline. "But I think when we get home, we'll call him."

"In *Japan?*"

"Sure. What the heck. You can tell him all about—"

"The murder?"

Madeline shuddered. "I suppose we'll have to mention it, yes."

"Will we tell him about . . . all of it?"

Madeline looked down at her daughter. "I think right now we'll just tell him the important parts," she said. "Later, when he's home, we can fill in the rest."

Stephanie Schrock crossed the deck, pausing by force of habit to scan the glistening surface of the sea for spouts, fins, or tails. She saw nothing. She continued on her way, climbing the ladder to the wheelhouse. "Good morning, gentlemen," she said.

"Good morning," said Emmett.

"Good morning," said Ned.

"Still working on the radio, Ned?"

Ned nodded. "We want to make contact with the Coast Guard before we dock."

Nobody said anything else.

"Gee," said Ned after a minute. "I've got the wrong kind of pliers here. Maybe I'd better—"

"Yes," said Stephanie. "Maybe you had."

"Take your time," said Emmett. "We're still a ways out."

Ned swung through the door.

Emmett gazed after him. "I wonder how Jackson knew he was gay," he said.

"Why not?" asked Stephanie. "*We* all knew, didn't we?"

Heather Seasons came out on deck, sucking on a cigarette. Now that it was all over, everyone was goofing off. Even Gilby and Janine were out on deck, hanging over the port rail. *Talking.* Heather moved away. What did she care? They were too good to live. They deserved each other. It was a beautiful day and she was feeling good. Of course it had been nip and tuck for a while about those crucial twenty minutes without an alibi, but in the end she'd managed to leave the poor guy out of it. And speak of the devil, here he was. Heather almost laughed out loud. He sauntered up and stopped beside her, looking straight ahead, talking in a whisper from the side of his mouth. "Thank you," said The Man, happy again. "For everything."

When Polly finally got up the energy to face the noonday sunshine, most of the passengers were already on deck. She could almost see the bees of gossip flitting from person to person before she actually heard the buzz.

"Larry Morant."

"Harry Morant?"

"*Larry.* Larry Morant. The first mate."

"*Him?* Why?"

"The girl. The one engaged to Beers. He was—"

"Shhh! Here she comes."

Polly wavered, and would have turned, but a sturdy arm hooked hers at the elbow.

"Hello, dear. I have a nice spot over here in the sun. Doesn't it feel nice, that sun? I've been wallowing in it since ten. Kind of healing, I always thought." Libby Smith pointed to a pair of plastic lounge chairs, tactfully separated from the rest.

Polly sank gratefully into the farthest one. She closed her eyes. Yes, there was something healing about the sun.

Suddenly Polly opened her eyes and looked around. "Have you seen Pete? or Connie?"

"Not a glimpse," said Libby.

Polly looked at her watch. Twenty past twelve.

"Hey!" screamed Tweetie. "There! Over there!"

A balloon-shaped mist burst into the air. Below it, a long, black torpedo popped through the surface of the sea.

"Wow! Oh, *wow!*"

"Look, Tweetie," said Libby. "There's another, over there."

"And behind it! Look!" Polly was on her feet, too. So was everyone else. They crowded against the rail. Polly watched the huge creatures as one by one they arched their backs, raised their tails, and dove.

Were they playing, Polly wondered?

"Humpbacks are buoyant," said Stephanie Schrock from behind Polly somewhere. "It makes them fun to watch. They need to kick their tails to dive. Acrobatic, too."

They must have heard her. Suddenly fifty feet of gleaming black beast shot clean out of the water, gave a half-twist in midair, and plunged back into the sea.

"Where *are* those two?" asked Libby. "They'll be just sick to have missed this."

"Hey," said Connie. "I've been thinking."

"Mmm," said Pete.

"Get your mouth out of my ear and listen to me. First there's Polly and Sam. Then there's Polly and Jackson. Then there's Jackson and Madeline, and Brady and Jenny, and Emmett and Stephanie, and Gilby and Janine and Heather, and Drew and Heather, and God knows who else and Heather, and then all that mess with Larry. And Tweetie and you, of course."

Pete drew back and glared at her. "Your point being?"

"My point being," said Connie, "that if you consider all of them, and the mess they've all made of it, you and I don't look so bad. Do you think we should get up?"

"No. What could we possibly be missing?"

"Nothing, only—" Connie craned her neck backward to look out the porthole. "It seems awfully light. Hey, Pete!"

Pete tried to turn with her, cracked his elbow against the wall, and yelped.

"What?"

"I think I see it."

He leaned around her and looked. The sun caught a wave and bounced back at him, making him blink. "What?"

But before she could answer his vision cleared, and he saw for himself.

Land.

Chapter
37

Again the island . . . meets our view . . .
many thousands of miles have separated us,
many a storm have we endured, but at last
we are brought safely back again.

The sun was September hot, which meant it wasn't.
The sky was September blue, which meant it was. The
men on the porch in front of Beston's Store had just
finished arguing over whether there was or was not a
September bite to the air, and now that they had
sufficiently disposed of the weather as a topic, they
moved on to something else.

"Say again?" asked Ed.

"Get the wax out of your ears," said Bert. "I said
the Coast Guard impounded *The Pequot* up there in
Tanner Head. Pete called Rita and told her they were
going to be stuck up there forever, answering a lot of
fool questions. Rita called the chief, and the chief
drove up and brought 'em all home."

"Pete and Connie? The chief drove all the way up to Tanner Head and brought Pete and Connie back home?"

"Least he's good for something. He brought Polly back, too."

"Polly? Pete's sister, Polly? Polly's here, too?"

"Christ on a raft, Ed, are you just deef or are you dumb, too? I said Polly, I mean Pete's sister, Polly. How many Pollys do you think he knows?"

"She's staying with Connie," said Evan. "Since Pete doesn't have much room. Seems on the ride back from Tanner Head, Pete and Connie and the chief, they all kind of ganged up, convinced her to stick around."

Ed gazed thoughtfully at Evan. "The chief's never met Polly before now."

"Nope," said Evan. "Not before now."

"How long's that ride from Tanner Head, anyway?"

"Six, seven hours, give or take."

"Who the hell cares how long the ride is?" snapped Bert.

"No one in particular," said Ed. "Still six or seven hours, that's long enough to get acquainted, I'd say."

"Speaking of getting acquainted," said Evan, "I saw Pete on the beach this morning."

"On the beach?" asked Ed. "You saw Pete on the beach? Was he heading for Connie's?"

"No," said Evan, "more like coming from, I'd say."